THE BEGINNING OF NEVER

THE BEGINNING OF NEVER

O. E. BORONI

Published by Waves Corporation 2015

For more information, visit
oeboroniauthor.com

Logo Image Copyright © america365
and used under license from Shuttershock, Inc.

Copy Editing: Melissa-Jane Fogarty at
www.mjediting.com
Cover Design: Alisha at
www.damonza.com

ISBN: 0692433066
ISBN-13: 978-0692433065

To my God,

for your love, encouragement, and teachings.

Thank you for being patient with me.

Acknowledgements

I want to sincerely thank all the people who have helped me survive the birthing of this novel.

My God, for helping me whenever I got stuck, and for helping me see beyond my doubts. You were there at every moment to encourage me, and teach me all I needed to know. You are my everything.

A big thank you to my parents for always supporting me; To my mom for being so selfless and caring, and to my dad for your constant encouragement. You are the best parents that anyone could possibly ask for.

To my siblings, Odalo, Edafe, and Ahuose, for your enthusiasm when you found out I was writing this book, and for your threats when you thought I was being too slow. I love you all.

Uyi, Amaka, Toya, Viano, Sasha and Layla. My amazing beta readers and friends; You've helped so wonderfully in shaping this book. Uyi, for encouraging me to finish this story, Amaka, for threatening me if I didn't, Toya, for encouraging me with your enthusiasm, Viano and Sasha, for taking the time to add an extra shine to the final manuscript, and Layla, for all your advice and support. Thank you for listening to me constantly talk about this book, and for your honest feedback. I sincerely appreciate you all.

To Nene, for being as excited as I was when I shared the idea of writing this book with you, and to Busayo for being a wonderful reading buddy.

Edozie, your presence in my life is priceless. Thank you for your wisdom and your love.

My editor, Melissa-Jane Fogarty, who contributed so powerfully in making this story the best it could possibly be. I appreciate you for your patience, and for your willingness to always offer your advice.

And thank you my dear reader, for taking a chance on me and picking up this book. I do hope that it inspires, and entertains you. May others help support your dream, just as you've helped support mine.

CONTENTS

ൟ

« CHAPTER 1 »

Today was the second Friday of the summer term, and the day that it all began. I woke up to a freezing room, and reminded myself of how much I loathed Lancaster... and my roommate... and today.

Lancaster was a small town in North West England that couldn't help its lot for rubbish weather almost as much as my roommate, Olivia Doyle, couldn't help her need to be evil. My bed was right next to the window, which was the only one in our room, and every night I'd go to bed with it locked only to wake up the next morning to find it open, inviting wafts of cold air to float enthusiastically into the room.

I still wasn't certain if she did it just to provoke me, or if she actually needed the cold air at my expense as she got ready for school each morning. Mind you, she was always fully clothed, and would sit at her desk, wrapping strands of her blonde hair around her curling wand, and singing along to whichever song was blaring out of the pink stereo by her corner. I'd considered smashing the damn thing against the wall more times than I could remember, but since I would have to replace it, I restrained myself.

Just then, a slight shiver rocked my body, so I turned to my opposite side and tugged at the duvet until it was raised high enough to completely cover my head.

Today was the 17th of April, and today three years ago, my mom had died. It was also the day before my sixteenth birthday.

So far, I'd never been able to go through the day without falling apart but today, I promised myself, was going to be different. I was going to go through it with the same detachment that I did every other day, and I was going to succeed. Today, I swore, I was going to prove that I had finally risen above the pain.

The door to our room clicked open, and ushered in the banter of the remaining two of Olivia's trio - Emma and Tess. Emma, I think was from Lancaster itself, while Tess was from Wales. Olivia said something to them as soon as they came in and they broke out in laughter, completing ignoring the fact that I was in bed, and probably still trying to sleep.

Admittedly, I should have been up and getting ready because I was running late for everything. However, it didn't bother me too much because it was a Friday. Breakfast was already on-going in the dining hall so that was automatically out of the agenda for me. But since there was no assembly or chapel today, all I had to do was get up and meet my first class by 9:00 am.

I lowered the duvet down my face so that I could glance at the black alarm clock that faced me on my desk. I never officially used it because my roommate's grating voice was all the anguish I could stand each morning, but it did help to inform me of when I was becoming too tardy- like right now. I saw that it was almost 8:15, but still, I chose to wait until ten minutes later, after Olivia and her pack had taken their leave.

Walking to the bathroom in my towel, I placed my toiletry basket in a stall before returning to the counter to brush my teeth. I straightened after the brush had gone into my mouth, and met the familiar pair of dull grey eyes that stared back at me through the gigantic mirror on the wall. The loud whoosh of active shower heads held my attention for a while but soon, my mind zoomed out to another day- in what now seemed like a life time ago- when I'd destroyed the mirror in my bathroom back home with my hair dryer. I'd clubbed it repeatedly, until every part of the shattered glass reflected how I felt inside.

It was in the early days, just after she'd died and I'd become *so* angry. I'd cursed at everyone and everything, and people pardoned me because they thought that it was my way of dealing with the pain. But back then it had been much more than pain; a part of me had been violently ripped out and more than anything, I'd felt the dark, excruciating absence.

All I'd known to do was to avoid anything that made me feel too much, and back then, people wanting to offer their condolences topped my list.

Each time someone told me how sorry they were, I felt the huge hole in my chest that constantly reminded me that I didn't have a mother anymore widen. Instantly, my air would be literally cut off, until it felt like I was struggling to breathe. So my automatic response would be to walk out on them or pick a fight, and I always got away with it because after all, I *was* the girl who was grieving.

The mirror incident however, finally brought my dad to the end of his rope. When he'd come in to see what had happened, and found me staring at the colossal cracks as if they were communicating a truth that only I could decipher, he'd walked out without a word and the next morning, served me with my penance for acting like I was losing my mind.

Since the car accident a few weeks back, I'd barely spoken a word to him and had tried to ignore him as much as I could. But that morning, I'd come in from Carlie's, my best friend who'd lived next door to us since we were five, to meet him reclined on the living room sofa. It was surprising because he was never down from his bedroom that early in the day, and a conventional thought on my tantrum the previous day was long overdue. His silence had already got me thinking, that maybe he really didn't give a damn about me.

Calmly, and just as if he was reminding me that the plastic milk jug in the refrigerator had long expired, he announced that I was going to boarding school.

"What?"

Flicking onto another channel, he said in a bored voice. "I've repeatedly warned you against spending the night at Carlie's without my permission, but you've blatantly ignored me every single time."

"I don't get it, how does that correlate to you sending me to boarding school?" I asked, certain that he was bluffing. I'd never known him to about anything else in the past, but I just couldn't believe that he actually meant what he was saying.

He ignored the question, and rose from the sofa to head into the kitchen. After a few moments of waiting for him to respond, I'd started to turn away in irritation when he'd stopped me again.

"Start getting your things ready, you're leaving in September," he said, and at that, I'd whirled around to face him.

"What do you mean I'm *leaving*?" I asked, now alarmed. "I'm starting eight grade in September."

"No, you're going to boarding school." He said, and without taking his cold watchful gaze off me, lifted a glass of water to his lips.

Tears rushed to my eyes as I finally realized that he was serious. My body began to shake. "Is this a joke?"

"No it isn't," he said. "Lenora your anger has become unmanageable."

"So you're kicking me out?"

"I'm not kicking you out; I'm giving you a change. You need it."

I tried to speak but it felt like I would choke on the anguish that had tightened my throat. I eventually did, and each word was thick with the pain that I had bottled up for so long.

"I have been *trying* to be okay. I've been quiet –"

"That's the fucking problem!" he suddenly yelled, startling me.

"Quiet anger- that's what it is right? It's been three months, and this is the first time that I've seen tears in your eyes."

I brushed away the irritating display that had now rolled down my cheeks.

"You have been cold and brutal to everybody, and not once have you shared anything that's going on inside you. I can see the poison accumulating and at the rate you're going, I doubt that you'll ever be able get it out."

Another tear fell, and slid down the side of my face as I glared at him with all the hate that I could muster. "Why won't you just let me handle this the way I want to?"

"I *have* let you," he said. "I've tried to give you time but you're still not handling it, so you have until September to become human, or I'm sending you away."

I was now terrified, but never in a million years was I going to let it show. He'd lost the privilege of my honesty towards him during all the years he'd preyed on my mother's weakness with him. So I'd glared at him with a hate that I hoped would cut him as deeply as he'd cut me, and turned around to head to my bedroom.

The choice had been tough, but I knew that I wouldn't have survived if I'd handled it the way he wanted me to. So I'd become even more hardened and kept silent all through the summer. In September, I was on a plane and on my way to Lancaster Academy.

I was in my third year now, and still, the only thing I liked about the school was how much it resembled the 'Lancaster Castle', which was the oldest standing building in the town. The academy had existed for almost a century, so sometimes, I allowed myself to get carried away and pretend that I did live in a castle.

However, things like strands of hair trapped in water puddles on the counter, and smeared toothpaste around the edges of the sink were always sufficient enough to irritate me back to reality. I rinsed my mouth, and hurried back into the stall.

∞

9:04 am saw me running down the already deserted hallway, and then opening the door to my first class of the day. It was Maths, and Mr. Barron had already arrived. He was standing behind his wooden desk going through a stack of papers, and as I walked as silently as I could into the classroom, I prayed that he would ignore me.

He didn't.

"Nice of you to join us Miss Baker," he said, and I froze mid-creep. Sighing, I wondered why he never deemed it fit to just leave me alone. Other teachers got that I wasn't completely normal and they let me be, even flat out ignored me most times, but this one never did.

"Why are you late again?" he asked, but I didn't feel like cooking up an excuse like I usually did. Once, the story had been that a spill of cranberry juice on the sleeve of my white dress shirt had forced me to return to my dorm to have a quick change. Another time, it had been a quick trip to the infirmary for an upset stomach that had plagued me all night, and so on the list went. He never believed me, of course, but today, I couldn't work up the need to lie so I just told the truth.

"I woke up late."

"And *why* did you wake up late?"

"I don't know," I replied, upset that he was making me stand there with the eyes of the entire class on me. I wanted to yell at them to turn away and mind their business.

"Let it happen again and we'll take a trip to the headmaster's office." he threatened, but he'd made so many similar promises in the past and broken them every time, that they didn't mean anything to me anymore. Relieved that he finally let me go, I headed to my desk which was the last one on the first row from the left.

The room was as regal as a school built to resemble a castle could get, with polished mahogany furniture, intricate wooden mouldings and high windows. Mr. Barron began to speak so I looked towards the front of the room and tried to pay attention, but after jerking awake twice from dozing off, I gave up trying and turned to gaze out of the window.

Although the sky was clear there was no sunshine, so a slight chill still remained in the air. Egrets were strewn across the courtyard; some were pecking away at the ground, while others just hung atop the wooden picnic tables and benches. A particular one caught my eye, and as I watched it, I felt a small stirring inside my chest.

With lovely white plumes and an impressive stance, it stood on the edge of the table with its neck outstretched, and just stared, as if it was watching something that only it could see. It was beautiful, but it's long, thin and naked legs, dented its grandeur.

I watched it and thought of how each time I'd returned home for breaks, my father had expressed his disappointment at how completely frozen I'd become. For a normally astute man, it had surprised me at how he'd seemed to completely believe that I had turned into a hardened mess, instead of the hurting girl that I knew that I was. I hid everything I felt just because I'd managed to convince myself that if I did it long enough, then maybe the memo would reach my heart, and it'd stop hurting so goddamn much all the time. It terrified me that I might always feel this way because it was exhausting, but what I truly wanted was not to heal, but to become desensitized enough not to notice that I hadn't.

Today however, I chose to rest in the hope that if I really was able to pull through without falling apart, there would be a reduced cause for concern because for once, it would be a huge step in the desired direction. So with a small smile that I allowed to curve my lips, I started to condition myself to look forward to it when Mr. Barron's bark doused my reverie like water to flames.

"Grace!" He yelled out my middle name.

I gave him an icy look that would probably have made any other teacher uncomfortable, but not him. He always made me remember that I was just an angry fifteen-year-old, all bark and no bite, instead of the oddity the other teachers had marked me out to be. And from a conversation that I'd once had with Carlie, I'd been informed that my wild mane of dark brown, slightly curly hair and light grey eyes, cast a shadow around me that seemed to amplify my already peculiar nature. So yeah, people did find themselves a little wary when I was around.

"I suppose you'd very much like to join the egrets outside, wouldn't you?" he asked, and I was almost amused. Stretching my lips into a humorless smile, I gave him my answer, and as he looked away shaking his head, I was sure that he comprehended that with no apology whatsoever, I would have loved to.

෩

The rest of the morning crawled on as I stared blankly through the remaining four periods. To my right was Danielle, a quiet French girl with dark hair and a sphinx-like smile, who was every bit as detached as I was. But unlike me, she seemed more lonely than alone, and her nervous smile when people found reasons to talk to her always gave away her relief. I on the other hand, appeared aloof whenever people spoke to me, and it always came across as impatience. Most of the time I intended it, but at other times I didn't; it had simply become my default facial expression.

In front of her was Cassandra, the 'Olivia' of my class whom to my annoyance, had spent the entire morning chatting away with Ryan, the boy in front of her whom I had classed as the *male* version of Olivia.

I sighed and shook my head. The way I classed people as versions of Olivia, I was starting to become concerned that I would need therapy later in life to get rid of my 'Olivia complex'. It was just that she was so one-dimensional … or maybe I was the one that was one-dimensional. Maybe just like the way I chose to see only her snotty side, others chose to see only my snobby side, and I was more than that. At least I hoped so; sometimes it scared me how much I liked to be away from people.

Anyway, in front of me was Adrian, and he was a light-skinned guy with curly hair. Although he was among the 'cool' ones in our year, he shamed the stereotype of dumb hunks and actually paid attention in class. It impressed me, and made me feel guilty every time I dozed off which was more times than I was proud of.

Then all the way across the room, with pink-rimmed glasses and long legs, was Kate Wilson. She got up and started to head towards me the moment the much awaited lunch bell, pierced the dulled atmosphere of the compound.

She was my … friend. In the sense that I *did* like, her but for some reason, I wasn't completely comfortable around her. With creamy skin, chestnut brown hair and hazel eyes, she was quite pretty and kind, and that, at Lancaster Academy, stood out like a chicken amidst hawks.

Today however, I knew why she was coming over, and it didn't excite me.

"Hey," she said as she approached, but I ignored her. She didn't take it personally because she was quite familiar with my standoffish ways.

"Ignore me all you want, but remember your section's due soon."

I continued to shun her, until she reached me and took a seat right on the edge of my desk. I was forced to look up then.

"Hi," I said, my greeting sounding like a threat, but she just smiled when I rolled my eyes.

"I and Anjola have been able to get examples of teens with personal experience of the drug, so we passed that on to Mitchell and Samuel," she said. "It'll probably help them in compiling their effects section. What about you?"

"I'm on it," I said, as I zipped my bag closed.

This term, even though a major reshuffling had been done, we'd again ended up in the same team in our biology class for project activities. Our first task was an in-depth research on a drug, but for the life of me I couldn't remember what it was or what part I had been assigned in the project.

"Where exactly are you?" she asked. I rose to my feet, with feigned annoyance marring my face.

"Ours is on ecstasy by the way," she said and I was tempted to smile. She knew I had forgotten. "And it's due in two weeks. I'm just saying."

"Noted," I said and was about ask her what my section was again, when a girl I knew to be her roommate, yelled her name and ran over. The classroom was almost empty from lunch hour escape, so her need to yell was baffling, and equally I realized, was my need to eat something. I suddenly felt ravenous.

"Kate, he's in the cafeteria," she said, almost out of breath, and I watched as the level-headed girl I nearly liked, turned into a babbling mess of teenage hormones.

"Oh my God," Kate squealed, and her face suddenly lost color. I was almost worried for her.

"Where?" she asked.

"He's in line for lunch but I'm not sure where he's going to have it." Kate's roommate said, and I dragged my eyes away from the strange red blotches on her face. Kate was fanning herself with her hands now, and looked like she was about to collapse. I had to ask.

"What's happening?" I said, and instantly regretted it. I wasn't supposed to care about anything today. Kate rushed to explain and was already a few feet away from me before she completed her statement and hurried off. Still, I caught all of it.

"It's this terribly cute guy in the upper sixth. He's in the cafeteria now and it's the first time I've seen him since we resumed. Later."

I stood there for a few more seconds, thinking of the many reasons I could have done without that piece of information. Grabbing my bag, I made my way out of the classroom and towards the cafeteria.

« CHAPTER 2 »

There were two gigantic stone fireplaces built at opposite ends of the cafeteria, and wooden panels covering about eight feet of its twenty foot wall. The roof was supported by massive log beams and the floor covered in gleaming wooden flooring. The entire room looked like a massive cabin, and it was elegant and cozy, but I usually avoided it.

Hundreds sat there each late morning to catch up on the latest school gossip; who was dating whom, or who had broken up with whom; who had gotten beaten up, or who had been suspended, and generally, anything that made the school seem more interesting than it really was. It was also a wonderful place to obtain new gossip subjects, mock the old ones or watch them being mocked by others. So essentially the place was a boarding school disaster, where the smell from the disdain and blabber of green-eyed monsters overpowered the scent of the food.

Steeling myself to endure the deafening roar of their chatter, which was more than I was prepared to deal with today, I walked in and stood in a line that was so long, I was assured that I would be there for a while. With a groan, I kept my head lowered until it was my turn. After ordering the chicken salad sandwich and a cup of tea doused with milk, I made my way towards the courtyard.

I had about fifteen minutes left until lunch ended, so I started opening the sandwich pack on my tray as I went through the sliding glass door that led to the courtyard. However, when I looked up to see all the picnic benches already filled, I stopped and let my mouth hang open in astonishment.

Although the sun was shining brightly today, it was still cold outside, so I had counted on the fact that very few people would be as crazy as I was to prefer braving the chill, than endure the tumult of being in the cafeteria. Apparently I was wrong, but before I could decide on where else I could head to that would allow me to eat in peace, someone bumped into me.

It all happened very fast, so before I knew what was happening, my tray had flown out of my hand and I was plunging headfirst onto the stone walkway. Thankfully, and through the graces of someone that reasoned that I did not deserve to lose a tooth for just standing in the way, a strong hand slung across my middle, and pulled me back before I could hit the ground. I was saved from the injury and embarrassment that would have accompanied the fall, but as the culprit tried to stable me, all I could see was my lunch, in slices of bread, chicken and lettuce, strewn across the lawn.

The tea cup had burst open, and now lay separated from its cover and drenching the grass with its creamy contents. My stomach tightened in annoyance, and as I gazed at my ruined lunch, I almost felt like crying.

"Let me go!" I said, my teeth clenched to restrain myself from yelling. Jerking my arms away, I whirled around to face the idiot that had just ruined my morning.

"Didn't you see me standing right there?" I lashed out, but in that second I almost forgot my anger because I was now looking at one of the most attractive people I'd ever seen. He had the most sultry eyes in a deep blue, and jet black hair that swayed away from his face to fall just below his ears. With a frown as to how someone could look so unreal, I cocked my head to regard him again.

In a deep but quiet voice, he said, "I'm sorry, but you were standing in the way." And that immediately scratched the disc that was starting to roll in my head at how attractive he was.

"Excuse me?" I said.

He repeated himself, "You were standing in the way."

I felt like killing him. "And you're an idiot who can't see."

He blinked, but I refused to shut up. "I was standing right in front of you. You could have injured me, and all you can say is that I was standing in the way?"

He was frowning now. "Why are you yelling?" he asked, and it made me feel a flash of shame. Then I became infuriated.

"Are you kidding me?" I asked, my tone now lowered since I realized that people were actually beginning to stare. "Is that how you're going to apologize?"

Shifting his weight to another leg, he lifted his arms to fold them against his chest, and said, "I'm not apologizing."

"What is that supposed mean?" I asked, surprised that he was as offended as I was. I was the one who had almost been knocked to the ground!

"It means that I am definitely *not* going to apologize to you."

I was silent for a moment. Then I asked. "What is *wrong* with you?"

He directed the question right back at me. "What's wrong with *you?*"

I didn't know what to say, and so standing apart in the walkway, we just stared each other down until a gust of cold wind blew my wild hair across my face. Angrily, I shoved it behind my ears, finally accepted the un-repentance in his eyes and chose to let it go.

Shivering from the bite of the cold, I scowled at him as I turned around to retrieve the tray. Then I walked over to the strewn pieces and had started to pick them up, when I felt him crouch down beside me. Before I realized what I was doing, I had risen to my feet and was swinging the black tray towards him. It hit the edge of his shoulder with a resounding smack, and let out a terrifying cracking sound.

I gasped, and then froze when I saw the zigzagged split towards the middle of the tray that confirmed that I had just indeed, broken the tray on his back.

My eyes slowly turned to him and I watched, my heart pounding in my chest as he closed his eyes in a bid to control his temper. He then looked away and after a few seconds, rose to his feet. I took a few steps backwards, the tray still stuck to my hands, and only then did I notice that my head barely reached his shoulders.

I took another step back, but the tray suddenly fell from my hands, and clattered noisily on the ground.

He turned to face me, but I refused to meet his eyes.

I'm so sorry, I wanted to say, but as I opened my mouth to speak, the words wouldn't come out. All that did was an empty croak that made me feel even more nervous than I already was. So, swallowing painfully, and with my eyes away from his stare, I waited for his reaction.

But he completely surprised me.

Just when I'd thought that he was going to come forward to hit me, he turned around, and walked away.

I remained in that position for a few more seconds before I could even get myself together enough to retrieve the tray, and wasted food. Not even daring to look back to see how much of an audience we had gathered, I tossed them into a nearby garbage can and quietly made my way back to my classroom.

I arrived in an almost morose state, still incredibly shaken from the attack I had just discharged. Flattening my palm against my forehead as I took my seat, I began to sincerely wonder if I was okay. Was I turning into a crazed animal? How did I break a tray on someone's back just because they had run into me? This was a complete stranger for Christ's sake and for all I knew he could be with the Headmaster at that moment, reporting that there was a mad student in his school. With a loud groan, I rested my forehead on my desk to hide my face underneath.

This was not how I had planned to survive today, I lamented, but after a few more intense minutes of disturbing remorse, I had to ask myself exactly why it continued to bother me so much. Other than the obvious – in that you just didn't physically attack another human being for no reason – varied considerations like a loose reign on my self-control, to the fact that I could very well get suspended over this or sued, began to run through my mind. Because even if he didn't report me, someone else who had seen it was bound to have become concerned enough to.

Lifting my head from my desk, I shook it to dispel my thoughts but then it hit me once again: *I hit a human being with a freaking tray!* Nothing could justify that level of lunacy, and soon, I found myself wishing I could see him again so that. I could apologize. Assuming I wouldn't be summoned by the authorities before then, but somehow, and in my mind, I knew that I'd be surprised if I was. He just didn't seem like the type.

But in all fairness he had been wrong not to apologize, I began to justify, but stopped, when I could almost hear my mother's voice in my head. *No Nora, you were the one at fault.* She would have said. *And I'm telling you that that temper of yours will get you into real trouble someday if you don't find a way to control yourself.*

My normal response to her would have been to roll my eyes, and respectfully direct the temper at her, but now that she wasn't here anymore, all I could do was smile and foolishly wish that I could hear her voice just one more time.

Admittedly, I and my mom hadn't been the best of friends, and it wasn't because we weren't alike because we were. It was just that I could never understand why she chose to remain with my dad when he made her so miserable, and it made me kind of resent her for it. But it also made me love her and want to protect her even more since the man that had promised that he would, had failed at it every single day.

I knew she was strong, but for him she made herself appear weak, and I could never understand why. Once I had asked her and all she had said was this: "I made a promise Nora, and I want to do my best to keep it."

I'd always thought that was bullshit, and I still did.

My mind was beginning to wander too far, so I jolted myself back to the present. If I even had a hope of keeping my promise to myself- that I wouldn't be overwhelmed by my memories of her today- I had to stop thinking about her. So I shifted my thoughts to the boy that I had just hit. I sighed, and sincerely hoped that the incident would be the biggest hurdle that I would have to jump today.

Just then however, I noticed that the steady buzz maintained in the room from all the chitchat had lessened to an almost quiet. When I looked up, I expected to see that our history teacher had come in, but when my eyes connected with the ones of *the* boy as he walked towards me, I knew instantly that my troubles were just beginning.

He doesn't look angry, I immediately judged, but my terror continued to rise as he neared me. All I could think of was that he'd worked up his anger, and was back to probably say or do something that would undoubtedly destroy my day.

I noticed also that the entire class seemed particularly interested in this episode, and were watching with rapt attention. This worsened the entire situation for me. So when he had almost reached me and his hand rose from his side, I reflexively leaned slightly away from the chair.

He stopped when he saw what I was doing, and frowned in confusion. When I realized that I was overreacting, *again*, I straightened and watched as he placed a brown paper takeout bag on my desk. My eyes widened in surprise but before I could ask any questions, he turned around and walked away.

"I didn't ask for this." I heard myself say, but by then he was already out the door. Curious eyes turned back to me. Completely embarrassed, I dropped my head on the table to bury my face underneath it again.

ℴℴ

Both incidents occupied my thoughts throughout the next period, until I made up my mind that the next time I saw him, I was going to sincerely apologize. That relieved some of the remorse I felt but as the afternoon progressed, and ever so slowly, another issue arose. I had begun to feel queasy as soon as he had left, but now the feeling had heightened, along with the ache in my stomach that had been building over the last hour, and had now turned into a steady pain.

I suspected the reason for it so I wasn't alarmed. I tried to ignore it for a while, but when it began to interfere with my ability to be thoroughly bored, I reached to my side for the takeout bag. With a quick glance to see that our biology teacher, Mrs. Ibbitson, was still at the opposite end of the room passing out test papers, I pried the bag open to see a plastic pack containing a chicken salad sandwich. It was the same thing I had previously bought, but now instead of a cup of tea, he had gotten me a bottle of Coca-Cola and still water. I frowned at the slight oversight, but my mouth still watered – I was starving.

"Lenora, what do you think you're doing *while* in my class?" I heard Mrs. Ibbitson ask from somewhere behind me, just as something else in the bag caught my eye. I looked up to see her heading towards me. Her thin eyebrows came together in a frown when she reached me, and her overly long and bony nose wrinkled with displeasure. She didn't give me a chance to explain why I was considering eating in her class and instead, she slapped my test paper on the table. I didn't need to look down to see the loud 'F' in bright red pasted on top of it, but I hoped that she would at least refrain from reprimanding me publicly, as all eyes were now on us.

"It's not enough that you fail your tests but now you have to eat during class too?" she said, and low-toned snickers broke out from all corners of the room. I refused to take my eyes away from hers.

"Either throw that thing out right now or leave my class with it," she ordered and then walked away to hand out more scripts. I lowered my head and considered my options for a few seconds. Then loudly scraping the iron-legged chair against the wooden floor and with the takeout bag in hand, I rose to my feet and walked out of the class.

Tears filled my eyes as I slammed the door behind me, but I immediately forced the tears back. Nothing else was going to get to me today, especially not an ancient woman with pitiful bangs and a chinless face. The stomach ache that I'd been nursing seemed to intensify as I walked down the hallway and towards my locker, but it was only as I reached it that I felt the light-headedness.

I stopped to steady my vision, which had turned blurry, then after a few seconds, resumed walking. I had just reached my locker when I realized that I couldn't remember the last time I'd eaten, especially since my period had begun about two days before. I looked down and was about to reach for the soda bottle when I lost all feeling. It seemed as if my legs had left the ground and I was being turned upside down. My grip on the bag loosened, just before my eyes connected with the ceiling.

« CHAPTER 3 »

When I regained consciousness, I could feel the brightness of the sunlight that poured in through the window on the side of my face. A sharp ache throbbed at the side of my head and although my hand felt heavy, I managed to raise it up to press my fingers against my temple. It took me quite a few more moments to get my eyes open.

Slowly, surprise registered in a part of my brain at the sight I met, but I felt too weak to show any reaction which was okay, because I probably would have overreacted – again.

The blue-eyed boy sat on a chair beside the bed, and was watching me. I didn't know how to feel at the sight of him there so I just closed my eyes, and tried to swallow the knot that had formed at the back of my throat. After a few more seconds of nagging disorientation and self-consciousness, I pushed myself off the bed to sit upright, but kept my head lowered to shield my face from the sun, and of course to recover enough to face him.

What is he doing here? I wondered, even though at that moment, that should have been the least of my problems. The pain at the side of my head seemed to worsen with every passing second, and as I weakly glanced around the room, it registered that I was in the school infirmary.

How did I get here? I thought, but only when he answered did I realize that I had said it aloud.

"You fainted in the hallway," he said, and again I squinted at the sunlight. Seeing my discomfort, he got up and gently closed one side of the tall curtain and finally, I was able to look up. I pushed my hair out of my face.

"Oh good, you're awake." I heard a soft, feminine voice say from behind me, but I didn't bother turning around. A woman dressed in white scrubs came over with a glass of water in one hand, and a smaller cup in the other. She immediately handed both of them to me.

"I'm Laura," she said with a kind smile. "He told me you might have hit your head when you fell. Do you feel pain anywhere?"

I nodded, and took the cup from her to see two white pills. "The side of my head," I said, but my voice was a low rasp so I cleared my throat and repeated myself.

"They're painkillers dear – Ibuprofen," she explained.

I immediately popped them into my mouth, and downed the glass of water to flush it down.

"Do you have any idea why you fainted?" she asked, and I automatically glanced towards the boy. Seeing him leaning against the wall beside the window with his hands folded across his chest, and his eyes focused intently on me made me feel uneasy. It also didn't help that the sight of him was competing with the beautiful, stark red maple tree in the yard below, and winning.

My self-consciousness heightened to a disturbing level as I shifted nervously on the bed, and suddenly had a problem with my hair not falling down to cover my face. I subtly tousled it so that it fell, and to cover my intent, grabbed the glass to take another sip.

"I'm not sure," I responded.

"Have you eaten today?" she asked, and I shook my head.

"When was the last time you had something to eat?"

I lifted my eyes to consider the question, and then realized that I couldn't remember. I told her so and she was quiet for a few moments.

"When was your last period?" she asked, and my eyes shot up to her, widened and astounded. Instead of understanding what my mortification was about, like any normal woman or nurse for that matter would have, and adjusting her approach to maybe asking the conspicuous boy in the room to briefly excuse us, or better still, take his leave, she continued right on and even repeated the question when she probably assumed that I hadn't heard her properly.

My head dropped then, and in a low tone, I answered, "I have it now."

"Pardon?" she asked, and my temper flared. But before I could reply in what I doubted was going to be a polite tone, the boy stepped in.

"She said she has it now," he said in a flat tone. My head remained down.

"Well, that explains a lot," the nurse finally said. "You're losing blood so it's very important that you maintain a very —"

"I get it." I interrupted and rose to my feet. She looked puzzled, but didn't pursue the issue any further.

"Come back instantly if you feel any worse, but right now, I suggest you get something to eat first. I doubt the cafeteria would still have anything appropriate but it's just a few minutes before the end of the school day, so you should have a meal waiting for you back in the dining hall."

"She has a sandwich she can have before then," the boy offered from behind me, and the corners of her mouth lifted in a pleased smile.

"Well that's brilliant. It should hold her for the walk back. Why not go with her to ensure that she gets a decent meal?" she said, and my patience snapped. They were talking about me like I wasn't even in the room.

"I can take care of myself," I said, offended, but she lowered her eyes and muttered loud enough for me to hear, "Apparently not."

I rolled my eyes.

"Well ensure you have that sandwich now, or we can order something else for you if you want."

"That won't be necessary, I'm fine," I said coldly, and with one skeptic look from above her glasses, she turned around and took her leave. Pushing my hair out of my face, I took a deep breath before I turned to face the boy.

I didn't know what to say to him, and it occurred to me that a 'thank you' would have been a good place to start. But at that moment, I didn't feel up to it.

The fact that he was still standing there caused an unusual warmth inside my chest that I might have been able to tolerate, but the head and stomach ache I still felt made me feel like I was coming down with a fever. Anyway, he had a flat look on his face that was enough to convince me that he didn't expect any gratitude, so I just stood and grabbed my tie from the small table by the bed. He, on the other hand, returned to his seat and took the brown bag from the table.

"How did you know I had fainted?" I found myself asking. He answered as he searched for something within the bag.

"I met you on my way to get my wallet," he said, and he produced a black leather wallet from the bag. "I forgot it inside."

"Oh," I said, and remembered catching a glimpse of it just before Mrs. Ibbitson had come up to me.

He brought out the sandwich pack and placed it on the table.

"You need to eat," he told me, when I just stood there staring at him, and that pulled me out of my thoughts. It seemed silly, but up until then I hadn't noticed that he looked sort of Italian. He was definitely not British. His accent was also very hard to place. I retrieved my blazer from the foot of the bed.

"I'll take it with me," I said, but he refused.

"Eat it now before you leave."

"I'm not going far," I said, feeling weaker by the second. "I just need to get my things from my locker and head to the library. I have an assignment to work on."

Just then, the bell that announced the end of the day sounded, and I started to head off. However, his gentle but firm tug on my arm pulled me back. I landed awkwardly on the bed.

"Look," he said, "I had to carry you across an entire block and up two flights of stairs to get here. I'm not looking to do it again, and given our history so far today, it would be highly advisable to put an end to our acquaintance."

I blinked. Since I'd met him earlier, that had been the longest sentence he had spoken.

I blinked again. "Uh, I'm fine," I said, slightly offended at everything he had just said. I rose to my feet. "And I can assure you, you won't ever have to lift me up again."

"You're not leaving this room until you eat," he stated, and my mouth dropped open at the bold threat. Then I became amused.

"Uh, right," I said, a malicious smile struggling for dominance across my lips. "Try and stop me."

He got up immediately I turned to leave, and in no time had planted himself so close to me that I fell back unceremoniously onto the bed. Furious, I scrambled to get up, but regretted it again because it brought me too close to his body, making me have to crane my head to meet his gaze, which by the way, glowed potently with irritation.

"What the hell do you think you're doing?" I stuttered, as I placed my hands on his chest to push him away. He brushed my hands away.

"Hey!" I yelled and tried to do it again, but he pulled my hands down, and pinned them by my sides. I didn't feel any pain, but the embarrassment at the effortless way he had stilled me was overwhelming. I was about to jerk my hands away from his, and then push him away with all my strength, when he suddenly let me go.

He took a few steps back, and gave me a hard look before reaching for his wallet.

"Fine. Do whatever you want," he said, and walked out of the clinic, leaving me standing and staring after him, completely rattled.

Strangely, I grew dizzy after that and had to sit down to stabilize myself. The light-headedness worsened still, until I was forced to just lie back in defeat and eat the sandwich, feeling more foolish with every bite.

Eventually I was done, and stabilized enough to walk without the frustrating feeling of wanting to smash my head against something. After checking in with Laura, I retrieved my bag and headed towards the library.

ဆာ

When I reached it, I sighed at how much the familiar space relaxed me. I walked past the huge mahogany desk at the reception, straight into the maze of bookcases and headed to my favourite table. It was situated in a dimly lit and almost deserted corner on the last floor, and it was a place I could stay in for hours to be alone, without any fear of unwanted interruptions. People rarely visited this section. For one, the lighting wasn't encouraging and the bookcases were filled with old encyclopedias and ancient history books. Google was now much easier than sorting through massive dust-garnished materials.

It was just a little past 2:30pm, so almost everyone would be heading back to the dining hall for lunch. I hardly ever had lunch because I preferred to wear myself out in the library reading, and then return to my dorm for a nap before dinner in the evening.

When I reached the table, I decided to rest for a while because my legs still felt pretty heavy. I was taking my movements slow for the fear of inciting another fainting spell. I was still a little shaken that I had actually collapsed in the first place, and shuddered to think of how long I'd have probably been lying down on the ground, if he hadn't found me.

He, I mused. It was funny how we'd had more than two tense encounters in the same day and yet, I still didn't know his name. I thought of what it might be, but eventually gave up because it wasn't worth tasking my weary brain over. But for what it was worth, I didn't expect it to be a 'John' or a 'Michael'.

After sitting down, I rested my head on the table. The plan had been to briefly close my eyes, but I found myself waking almost half an hour later. I really was exhausted I realized, so I decided to start on the assignment before I lazed out and procrastinated it again

I had just brought out my notepad and was about to skim it for details, when I saw the sticky note at the top corner that read, *Ask Kate for your topic.*

Just then, I remembered the conversation I'd had with Kate earlier, and how I'd scribbled the note just before I'd been kicked out of biology. The thought of having to push it again to the next day made my head spin, so I lowered my head back to the table, and thought again of all the reasons I had for not dropping out. The strongest one was still that I'd rather be here, than have to live with my dad. I didn't hate him; I just preferred to not be around him because having him around made everything harder for me.

I pulled my backpack towards me from across the table so that I could retrieve my purse. I knew exactly where what I was in search of was, and boldly ignored the voice of reason that told me that it would be a bad idea. I'd just had too much already happen today, and I missed her, so I at least deserved a look.

After I retrieved the picture from my purse, I laid it flat on the table and straightened so that I could stare down at her beautiful face. Without the picture, I already had it perfectly engraved in my mind, but this – this was priceless. Her hazel eyes stared back at me, and with a sad smile I remembered how they could literally flash with fire when she was mad.

She had yelled a lot and so did I, and more than anything it just showed our inability to keep a leash on our emotions. We cried when we were hurt and caused havoc when we were angry, and although the transparency was sometimes liberating, I wasn't entirely certain that I didn't consider it a serious flaw. So far, it had been fairly easy for me to keep it all in, but after all that had happened today, I only wished that I was able to get through the day without causing any more damage to myself, or anyone else.

My wild hair was the stark difference between us because it was so different from her slick, shoulder-length one. She'd tried for years to grow it past mid-length but when it seemed like it never would, she'd just cut it into a bob and maintained the style. I brushed my thumb along the side of her face. I missed her so much.

She'd been in tears when she'd zoomed out of the house three years ago, and I'd been beside her in the front seat. It had all started with an argument in their room, and although I couldn't decipher what it was about, I hadn't bothered to try because for as long as I could remember, it had been the norm. Also, I'd figured since the fight had been dragging on for a couple of days, that that day would be the day it finally ended.

I couldn't have been more correct.

She emerged from the room just as I came out of mine, more furious than I'd ever seen her and jogged hurriedly down the stairs.

"Mom!" I called and ran after her, but she was already in the car by the time I reached her. So I went around, and got into the front seat before she could stop me. Even though she tried to get me out, I refused, until finally, she set the gears in motion and zoomed out of the driveway.

"I'm going to Aunt Leslie's," she said and I lightly touched her hand, hoping it would provide some sort of comfort for her. She looked at me, saw something in my face, and started crying again. She'd never allowed me to see her cry, but sometimes I had heard her. Heavy drops streamed down uncontrollably, and soon they moved to racking sobs but through it, she managed to keep driving. Only when we were more than fifteen minutes into the drive had she finally stopped. I chose not to interrupt, understanding her need to express some of the pain, and then I asked her the question that had been lodged in my heart for as long as I could remember.

"Did you ever suspect it'd be like this? Before you married dad I mean." I asked, and that was the last time I looked into her eyes.

She'd turned to me, surprised … and then I'd heard the deafening blare.

I never did get the answer to that question, and I suspected that it would always nurse a particularly outstanding sore in my heart. Someday, I'd need an answer to it, but never get to hear the one that I would have wanted to hear the most.

"The truck came out of nowhere," I'd been told. "And at the speed she'd been going, it was impossible to slow down."

One statement, and it had changed my life forever. Somehow I'd survived, but I was tired of wishing that I hadn't. A tear fell from the corner of my eye, and created a blot for itself like all the others that already dotted the picture. I brushed it away, and then did the same for the rest that had pooled in my eyes. Replacing my things back into my bag, I stood to my feet and left the library. I decided to leave the picture in my locker for the weekend, because if I took it with me, it was just going to make everything worse.

"Don't you dare cry," I warned myself as I headed towards the overhead walkway that connected my block to the library, but it didn't stop the tears from coming. My throat had tightened from the pain and as each moment passed, it became more and more difficult to breathe.

The walkway was lined with impressive cast stone columns that showed the exquisite outlay of the school through their opened arcs; its colourful landscape and medieval structures. Usually, it was all able to draw appreciation from me but not today, because with every step that I took, the more I wanted to drop to the floor and just lie there, exhausted from the dejection.

Soon I got into my block, and continued to head down the hallway which led to the stairs that would take me down towards my locker. I held the photograph to my chest and decided that I was allowed to cry, until I got to my locker. But when I neared the staircase and heard the laughter from a couple of boys that hung around it, I was forced to quickly wipe the tears off my face with the sleeves of my dress shirt.

There were about four of them, and they turned to watch me as I approached. Even though it didn't particularly bother me, the last thing I'd expected from them was any trouble. But when I reached the stairs and asked the two boys that were standing in front of it to excuse me so that I could pass through, they refused.

"Why are you crying?" one of the boys that stood in front of me asked. His hair was a reddish brown and his entire face was covered in freckles. The one beside him had a long bony nose, and a disheveled mass of jet black hair.

"Excuse me," I repeated again, not in the mood for whatever prank they wanted to pull.

"Come on, talk to us," one of the other boys that were behind me said, but I didn't turn around. Suddenly, I felt his fingers slip into my hand by my side, and swiftly pull away the picture of my mother. Instantly, I whirled around.

"Give it back!" I yelled, and went after him, but he was walking backwards and away from me.

"Oh, so is this what you were hiding?" he said with a mocking smile. The sight of the picture in his hands as he held it away from himself and stared at it, made my skin crawl. I wanted to kill him. I quickened my steps as I tried to catch up, but when I almost reached him, he made a sharp 'U' turn and continued walking backwards, but now, towards his friends again.

"Let me see," another boy said, and before I could get to them, the boy that had the picture had passed it on. I wanted to run mad.

"What are you doing you bastards?" I cried, and went after the one who now had the picture. But he too passed it on before I could get to him.

"Relax," I heard them say from somewhere beyond the fury that had set my ears on fire. "Just have fun with us."

"Give it back!" I cried, and went after the Indian boy that they had now given it to, but he passed it on, and this time to the red haired boy that had been the first to stop me. I didn't even realize what I was going to do but one moment I could see him, and the next, I had rushed towards him and shoved him with all my strength.

The last thing he had expected was to be thrown down the stairs but he was lucky, because at the last moment, he was able to grab unto his friend beside him who had also immediately held unto the wooden handrail next to him, to keep from flying down the stairs. But, because the shove was so forceful, his hand had still slipped away from his friend's. The reflexive grip had broken his fall, so instead of crashing unto the stairs' landing, he'd only tumbled down and managed not to turn the entire episode into a nightmare for everyone involved.

Everyone gasped as he fell back, including me, and we all watched hoping that he would be okay. When barely a few seconds after, he groaned and started trying to rise to his feet, everyone was able to let go of the breath that they had been holding.

Then they all turned towards me. They were all looking at me like I was insane, and before I knew it, the boy that had been beside him but had been saved by his grip on the handrail, shoved me.

"What the hell is wrong with you?" he barked, and came after me even as I stumbled, and then fell to the ground from the impact of his shove. Turning around, I immediately tried to get up but before I could lift myself up from my knees, he reached me and with the side of his feet, cleared my legs off the ground. The sweep was more with the intention to keep me on the ground and humiliate me than to actually hurt me, but it didn't stop my jaw, elbows and knees from being knocked against the linoleum floor.

I turned to see that the rest of them had gathered and were watching me, with barely controlled anger on their faces. However, when the fear really gripped my heart was when the one that I had pushed down the stairs finally emerged, and started to come towards me with eyes ablaze with fury. One of his friends held his hand and tried talking him out of whatever he wanted to do but he refused, and continued walking towards me, his eyes fixated on mine.

"What's happening?" I heard someone roar, and they all simultaneously turned. I looked up to see the blue-eyed boy staring at us with shock on his face. Then he recovered and hurried past them, towards me.

"Are you okay?" he asked when he reached me. I nodded, and tried to push him away as he held my arms to pull me up, so that I could get up on my own.

"What are you still doing here?" he yelled at the boys, and immediately, they started to turn away and head down the stairs. Only the red-haired one stopped, and making sure my eyes met his glare, he raised his arm up to show me the picture of my mom that he had in his hand. With a dirty smile on his face, he lifted his second hand to the edge of the picture and ripped it, straight through the middle.

I gasped, tears filling my eyes again as I watched the pieces drift to the floor. He was still going to take a moment or two to gloat, but when the blue-eyed boy turned and made to walk towards him, he fled. Hurrying over to the ripped pieces, I bent down to retrieve them and tried to see if it would ever be possible for me to piece them back together.

"Why did you let them go?" I yelled at the blue-eyed boy, my insides twisting with pain. At that moment I felt so alone, and cold, and the huge emptiness inside of me felt like it had widened out even more.

Rising to my feet, I walked over to him and shoved him but it only moved him back a few steps. Wiping the tears off my face, I turned to pick my backpack up from the floor, and with one last glare at him, walked out of the hallway.

« CHAPTER 4 »

The incident set the pace for my entire weekend, and it was horrible. I'd returned to my room and spent the rest of the Friday in bed and bitter. Soon, Saturday rolled by and it was another nightmare because it was my birthday. And each time it came around, the feeling that I had somehow cheated my mum out of her life only to have one more year added to mine rose up, and tormented me. My cramps had also come up at varying times throughout the weekend, but it had always passed as quickly as it came and for that, I had been grateful.

To take my mind away from it all, I'd stayed in bed with a Julie Garwood novel and finished it just before dinner. Olivia constantly had friends over so I also had to put up with all the racket they made, until I started wishing I could just collapse again, and remain unconscious for a while so that I could get away from everything.

The dejection continued all weekend long but by the time Monday rolled by, I didn't feel so heavy hearted anymore. However, I was in class during third period when Mr. Barron called my name. I'd been lost in thought about the novel I'd read over the weekend so I didn't hear him the first time. But the sharp bark that followed had been more than enough to call me to attention.

He waited until I reached his table to relay the message, and I appreciated it immensely when he did it in a lower tone than he usually spoke in. The entire class was watching with ardent curiosity.

"The headmaster wants you in his office," he said, and must have seen the fear that flashed across my eyes because he asked. "Is everything alright?"

It was said in a tone that relayed genuine concern instead of intrusive curiosity, so I shrugged my shoulders instead of just ignoring the question.

"It'll be fine," he said, and I acknowledged his condolence with a nod.

The lady who had come to deliver the message smiled automatically at me before leading me to the office, which was located in the administrative tower.

The headmaster's waiting room was empty when I arrived, but when the entrance doors swung open a few minutes later, I looked up to see one of the boys that had attacked me on Friday; the dark-haired one that had pushed me to the floor. I only noticed that he was limping slightly when the other three filed in behind him.

The woman that had come to get me came in last, and then closed the door behind her. Again, she smiled at me when she saw my puzzled look, but offered no explanation. All four boys took their seats in front of me so I turned away and ignored them. I did notice that the red-haired boy that had torn up my mother's picture was bruised on the side of his face, and had a bandage across his nose. *What had happened afterwards to get them this way?* I wondered.

My answer came a few minutes later when the door opened again, and the blue-eyed boy walked in. As soon as he saw me, he stopped in his tracks. I held his stare since I had no idea what the problem was, and assumed he had something to say. Instead, his eyebrows drew together to form a small frown on his forehead, and the action convinced me that I was the last person he wanted to see today. Offended, but too confused to look away, I watched him take a seat at the extreme edge of the room, away from all of us.

Everyone was quiet, but since I couldn't control myself I continued to sneak peeks at the boy as he plugged in his earphones, effectively blocking the rest of us out.

The door that led to the headmaster's office eventually opened, and a bright woman with streaks of white running through her hair, and a pair of piercing brown eyes poked her head through.

"Mr. Deacon will see you all now," she said, and the boys rose to their feet. Their groans, low but unified enough to sound their grief, followed them as they filed in though the open door. The blue-eyed boy stood to his feet also and without a glance at me as he passed, went with them. I started to rise then but the woman shook her head.

"Just hold on dear, we'll be with you soon," she said, and shut the door behind her. I stared at it, and tried to slow my breathing but failed. I was nervous, because although the incident hadn't entirely been my fault, I had inflamed it by pushing the boy down the stairs. Rising to my feet, I stood and paced around the huge reception, ignoring the occasional glance from the receptionist. Ten minutes later the door clicked open again and I was told to come in.

Immediately I rushed forward, but stopped just at the door until the headmaster invited me to stand in front of his gigantic oak desk, a few feet away from the others. In all my years here this was the first time that I had ever been in Mr. Deacon's office, and as I took a quick glance at the huge, and unwelcoming room, I hoped with all my heart that it would be my last.

"Miss Baker," he called, and I turned my head to meet the gaze of the tall man I'd only see from afar in my three years at Lancaster Academy. He took off his glasses before he started speaking to me, and that instantly made him look less aged and intimidating.

"Miss Baker," he called again, and I focused my attention on the hardness that lined the corners of his mouth. "Mr. Roque tells me that his assault of these boys was because they attacked you after school hours on Friday. Is this true?"

I couldn't resist a glance at the blue-eyed boy, whose surname I had now found out was Roque. He was watching me, but moved his eyes away after a few seconds. I returned mine to the headmaster.

"Yes," I said.

He leaned back against his chair and asked. "Could you narrate the incident to me?"

I nodded, and went through what had happened as accurately as I could. Only when I stopped did I realize that my heart was pounding in my chest, and automatically, I turned again to gaze at the boy. He was watching me.

"Did Mr. Roque tell you anything after this?" he asked.

I shook my head. "He didn't. I haven't seen him since last Friday." I turned to the other boys. "I haven't seen any of them."

"Well based on what they've all told me, that seems to be accurate. Mr Roque here took it upon himself to, as you can see, thrash these two over here. But their houseparent intervened and put a stop to it. Quite frankly, I am gravely disappointed in all of you, and even you Miss Baker because although you were provoked, a lot more damage could have been done by pushing Clinton down the stairs."

"Mr Roque has also been considered to replace the current Pendle House prefect, since we are not certain that he would be returning this term, but this incident has definitely disqualified him."

My mouth dropped open in surprise as I turned to look at the boy, but he seemed unmoved. In fact, it looked as if the anger I had previously sensed from his gaze was cooling off and in its stead, his usual cool mask of quiet detachment was replacing it. Still, I felt horrible, like I had somehow cost him this. The slight pain around the corners of my stomach intensified, but I stifled it enough to speak.

"Excuse me, but he didn't do anything wrong. He was just trying to help me," I said, and for about a second, the room became completely silent.

Mr. Deacon was the first to speak. "I understand that," he said. "But he went too far."

"But I ..." I started to argue, but in a solid voice the boy said, "Let it go."

I ignored it.

"Who knows what else they would have done?" I proceeded to argue. "He did the right thing."

"I'm not disputing that," the headmaster said. "But he should have reported the incident immediately after, instead of taking matters into his own hands. This is a grave issue – harassment is not tolerated here and neither is bullying. These boys obviously fear him enough to have let go the minute he came around, so he should have reigned in his temper. If their houseparent hadn't intervened, one could only imagine how much more damage he could have caused."

"But Mr. Dea –"

"Nora let it go!" the boy repeated and this time I listened, and kept my mouth shut. Another cramp twisted the lower part of my abdomen and I briefly closed my eyes to stomach the pain.

"Are you alright?" the headmaster asked. I nodded and although he didn't look like he believed me, he didn't force the issue. He turned to the battered boys.

"The appropriate punishment is to suspend all of you, but for now I need you all to leave. I'll send my decision across as soon as it's made." And with that, we all filed out of the room.

The cramps worsened as I walked slowly out of the office, and headed back to my class. As I walked along, the pain heightened to such an unbearable degree that I had to stop and bend over. I refrained from groaning out loud and had to squeeze my eyes shut to battle the pain. I could barely hear anything, and as I tried to regain my composure, I thought back to what I had eaten that would have caused it to get this bad.

I figured the yoghurt I'd had in the morning for breakfast had something to do with it, because although I sometimes felt slightly discomforted during my cycles, there had only been a handful of times when it had gotten so bad.

Another spasm hit and this time I doubled over, more than grateful that the hallway was empty. Eventually crouching down so that I could stomach the pain, I slapped my hand over my mouth to stifle any unexpected cries, and tried desperately to breathe as deeply as I could. Somehow it worsened, and I was just about to lie on the floor and fold into a ball until it passed, when a pair of arms touched my shoulders.

"Are you alright?" I was asked, but I was in too much pain to respond. The arms retreated and then came around me again to try to lift me up. I slapped them away.

"Ow!" I heard the small complaint, but I was too occupied to care. The pain was reducing now and slowly, my breathing was returning to normal. Inclining my head a little to the side, I turned to see who it was and closed my eyes again when I realized it was *him*. I felt so ashamed that yet again, there was a reason to be thoroughly embarrassed in front of him.

"I'm fine," I said as I started to get up, but found myself struggling. He tried to assist me and again, I made to slap his hand away. He managed to pull it out of the way so my hand met with thin air.

"Would you stop that?" he said, and I sensed him straighten to his full height.

"I'm fine," I repeated in an almost whisper, and tried again to get up on my own. I eventually did, with my palms stretched out on the floor for support, but just as soon as my knees began to straighten, another awful cramp struck and I was back to my knees. I was thankfully saved from falling headfirst onto the floor when his hands shot out to catch me. Before I knew what was happening, I was in his arms, and being carried to the infirmary.

I vehemently wanted to protest, and was even consciously gearing myself up for it, but then I suddenly didn't care. Wrapping my hands around his neck to make my weight lighter, I clung to him, my breathing louder than I would have liked.

In no time at all, I was being lowered onto a bed and almost immediately, I heard the familiar voice of the nurse that had treated me the last time, enter the room.

"What's wrong with her?" she asked as she headed over. I began to think about how I'd have to ask him to get out so that I could explain, but to my utter surprise and embarrassment, *he* explained.

"Menstrual cramps," he said, and I felt my face turn a bright red.

"I'm fine." I said, but the nurse gave me an incensed look.

"Didn't I *just* see him carrying you in here?" she asked. Then she turned around and headed back into her office. She came out with a file a few minutes later, along with a small tray. She told me to sit up, which I did, and I collected the tray from her to down the two pills in the small plastic cup.

My back was turned to him since I was still too embarrassed by everything that had happened over the past few days. *God, I wished he would just leave.*

"Stay until lunch to rest- you should feel much better by then," she said, and then she turned to the boy, "Thanks for bringing her in again. Do you have any classes now?"

"Yeah, I do," he answered.

"Well, you can just get to it then. You can come by for lunch to check up, and maybe bring a sandwich for her."

"Okay," he said, and I heard him start walking around the bed. He was soon in my line of vision and I watched, a tumult of emotions filling me, as he walked out of the infirmary without so much as a glance back. I laid back down right after he'd left, but found myself unable to sleep. Some of it was due to the lingering pain and discomfort around my midriff, while the rest, which was actually most of it, had to do with him.

I understood that he didn't particularly care about me but for some reason, a nagging sense of responsibility pushed him to help. But still, it bothered me that all of *this*, whatever it was, would soon end. There was only so much rescuing that one could need and so far, I suspected that I'd gone through my spell of incidents for the entire year in one weekend. The fact saddened me that afterwards – and that was if he actually bothered to come back to check on me – I might never get to talk to him again. The school was surely big enough to not bump into people since he'd obviously already been here for who knew how long, and last Friday had been the first time I'd seen him.

I knew that I shouldn't have been concerned about any of this, but that was exactly what kept me up. I *was* concerned and I didn't know how *not* to be.

Lunch came, and when I realized as I woke up that the pain had dissipated, I felt incredibly relieved. Then I remembered my previous concern that the boy wouldn't stop by again, and since no one had awakened me, I realized that it had come true. I began to feel a sort of gloom that I definitely wasn't ready for, so I kept my eyes shut and tried to push it all away before I had to head back to class.

"Are you ever planning on waking up?" I suddenly heard him say. My eyes flew open with shock, but even as a rush of confused excitement filled me, I managed to remain still. I also didn't want the emotions to show when I turned, so I took a deep breath and then gently sat up.

I pushed my hair away from my face and took him in. He was seated on the chair by my bedside with a small book open on his lap.

"Hi. You came," I said, my voice sounding annoyingly breathy, like I'd actually *wanted* him to. It made me cringe inwardly, so I cleared my throat and tried to sound like a normal person. "Um, I mean, I thought, you had like … other stuff to do."

He watched me for a few seconds. "I do have other stuff to do," he said, then turned to grab a brown paper bag from the table. I briefly shut my eyes at the complete fool that I seemed to be making out of myself, but reopened them just before he turned and gave the bag to me.

"Thanks," I said, suddenly uncomfortable with accepting it. "I'll pay you back but I don't have my wallet here. How much was it?"

"Don't worry about it," he dismissed, and returned to his book. I took a peek in the bag and saw that he'd gotten me what appeared to be a baguette, bottled water and a huge chocolate chip muffin. I felt the need to insist on a reimbursement.

"Thanks, really, I appreciate it, but this is the second time in a row you're buying me food. I just can't accept that."

He looked up from the book with what seemed like amusement in his eyes. "I thought I owed you the first time?"

"*Well* yeah, you did, that's why I'll pay you for just this time around."

"Don't worry about it," he said, and again returned to his book, but I still insisted.

"I *will* worry, that's why I have to pay you back."

He raised his head again. He started to say something but seemed to change his mind at the last moment. He asked. "And if I don't accept it?"

"You don't have to. I just have to find a way to get it to you and make you know that I have." He stared again, and then returned to his book.

I let him be, and took the muffin out of the bag. Underneath it was a small chocolate bar that I guessed he'd added on a whim. To have it now would probably be a terrible idea because it would worsen my cramps, but the consideration was moving. I couldn't control my smile, so I waited until it had worn off before I raised my head to speak to him.

"You're actually a pretty decent person, but you seem like a total snob."

"Maybe I *am* a snob," he said, still not looking up from his book.

"Right, so what do you call the last few days?"

"Common courtesy." he said, and that pricked me.

"You call beating up four boys and repeatedly bringing me here *courtesy*?"

He frowned. "I didn't beat up four boys."

I rolled my eyes. "*Still*, if that's your courtesy, I wonder what your intent looks like." I said. I wanted him to agree with me so that I wouldn't feel ashamed for trying to complement him.

Instead, he said, "Actually, you're a bit of a bother." And it made me frown.

Did he just politely call me a nuisance? I thought, affronted, and started to think of what I could say in retort. I eventually decided to just drop it, and he looked up then to see why I had gone quiet. Just then it occurred to me that I still didn't know what his name was. So I asked him, but instead of answering, he just held my gaze and flat-out stared- again.

It was so uncomfortable that I had to move my eyes to the window beside his head, and then back to my muffin, like it had become the most fascinating thing in the world.

Why did he do that? I wondered. His face however, remained in my mind's eye, so I started to search through my memory because he reminded me of someone. There was a certain familiarity in the olive-toned skin, dark hair and defined jaw that I couldn't quite shake off.

I returned my gaze to him, expecting to find him still watching me because of the heat that still burned on my face, but I was disappointed. He had his face back down to his book, and had quite possibly forgotten about my existence. Sighing, I turned to my muffin and gazed at it with all the love I could muster. *At least, you'll always be here for me,* I serenaded, and then started to slowly peel off a side of the wrapper.

You'll be sweet and ever-present when I need you to be, I sniffed under my breath.

You'll never leave me, I wailed in my head, just before I raised it to my lips and took a bite. At the taste of the blackberries in it, I almost spat it out. I hated blackberries.

"Is there something wrong?" he asked, and my eyes shot up to meet his. The distaste on my face immediately disappeared, and I shook my head before managing a small smile.

"Nope," I lied. "Everything's fine."

He returned to his book while I returned the muffin to the brown bag, shaking my head. Even a muffin couldn't come through for me; life was seriously screwed up. But on the other hand, I reasoned, I *did* have a gorgeous boy right here and up close, that I'd probably never get the opportunity to ogle at again. So I took the chance to stare and to completely memorize his features, just in case I needed to use my imagination for whatever benefit it would warrant in the future.

He had all the works, but what I decided fascinated me the most were his eyelashes. Softening the slight hardness of his face, they made mine seem like the thinning hairs among the patch on the head of an aging man. But I was probably exaggerating because I did consider mine acceptable by any standard.

His eyes had a radiance to them, and coupled with the striking blue colour, they almost seemed liquid. Mine on the other hand, were just a plain, light grey.

"What's your name?" I found myself asking again, now seriously needing to know.

"Why do you want to know?" he asked, and that should have been more than enough to make me not care anymore, but I pressed on.

"Because you know mine."

"No, I don't."

That surprised me, so I pointed out. "You called me Nora earlier,"

He revised his statement. "I don't know your full name."

"It's Lenora Baker. People call me Lennie, sometimes."

"Any middle names?" he asked.

"Grace."

Then to my utmost discomfort, he again watched me for a few seconds before returning the favour. My temper had begun to rise as I waited, and I couldn't believe how much it would have upset me if he hadn't told me.

"My name's Alex," he finally said, before I could read anymore into his silence. "Full name: Alexandre Nathan Roque."

"Alex," I repeated testing the sound of it in my mouth, and to my ears. "Can I call you Nathan?"

"No."

"But earlier you called me Nora."

He seemed amused at my upset. "And?"

"Well no one calls me Nora, apart from my mom. So for that I should be able to call you Nathan."

I expected him to argue but he just remained silent, watching me again like there was something on my face that he was trying to decipher. It unsettled me, so to throw the unnerving feeling off, I went on to cement my stance.

"I'll call you Nathan," I stated firmly, and when he didn't respond I chose to ignore his silent stare and took the opportunity to ask more questions.

"Are you Italian?" I asked. He shook his head.

"I'm Portuguese," he said. "And you're American I suppose."

"I am. That obvious huh?"

He answered plainly, "It is."

I chose not to read too much into the probable basis for that conclusion.

The bell signifying the end of lunchtime rang then, and instantly, he rose to his feet. I was disappointed. I wanted him to stay a little bit longer.

"Are you okay to attend class now?" he asked, and I nodded, rising up too. He left to go talk to the nurse, and in no time, we were out and on our way. He escorted me across the block to my floor, and as the few people still remaining in the corridors took the trouble to stare at us, I started to feel uncomfortable.

We stopped at my locker so that I could drop the lunch bag, and when he stretched his lips into a soft smile as a farewell gesture, my breath caught at the back of my throat. Shyly, I returned it and he left, leaving me to wonder when I was going to see him again.

« CHAPTER 5 »

I didn't see him for the rest of the week, and it bothered me. On Monday in class, I absent mindedly stared out the window and wondered why my not seeing an almost stranger for a few days had managed to take over the entirety of my thoughts. Up until the previous weekend I'd been unaware of his existence, but now, it seemed as if I couldn't get him out of my head.

A cold breeze that somehow found its way through the edge of the closed window interrupted my reverie. Looking away from the courtyard scenery below, I took a brief glance around to re-orientate myself with the dull class, and then my eyes fell on the initials I had written out on the top corner of the opened page in my notebook.

N.A.R, it read. Picking up my pen, I wrote out his name in full, and in the very best cursive I could work up. The results were pitiful but as I stared down at the name, I found myself feeling as distressed as the letters appeared. Each time I thought of him, something warm would heat up the pit of my stomach and excitement would flutter in my chest. I didn't yet know what to make of any of it but one thing was for sure; I didn't like it.

Brushing my hair away from my face, I focused my attention on the chemistry element symbols scribbled across the board, and the flat tone of Mrs. Zimmerman's voice. None of her scribbles made much sense to me, so after a few more moments of trying to understand what she was talking about, my mind slinked back to a certain pair of blue eyes.

This was a healthy diversion I finally decided, and gave up trying to fight the thoughts off. On other days, my mind would have wandered away to times with my mom, and all the ways I'd need her in the future but would never be able to have her with me. Then I'd think about my dad, and how I hardly ever heard from him. And no, I didn't think he was a terrible person, rather, I thought he was just very self-absorbed.

His selfishness hurt our relationship, and so did my inability to look past the fact that because of how miserable he made my mom, she had literally driven herself to her death. Of course there was more than enough within the story to vindicate him, but so far, I found that resentment worked well for me. It kept me angry, and an angry me when it came to my father, kept me un-emotional, and that was the state I needed to be in to be able to function.

I didn't have any grandparents. My mom had mentioned to me that it was one of the things she'd expected would connect her so strongly to my father; the fact that they were both orphans and could lean solely on each other. It didn't quite play out as well as she'd hoped.

Generally, my default thoughts were sooty and unpleasant so having this, a little excitement at the thought of someone who I still wasn't sure what to make of, was a welcome distraction. So I allowed my thoughts to run wild, and by lunch time, had incited myself so much that I wanted nothing more than to get another glimpse of him.

My safest bet was the cafeteria, so I headed towards it. It was crowded, as usual, so I didn't take my time at all. After a quick scan, I decided that there was no sign of him and left. I felt foolish as I wandered through the hallways, my eyes alert in case I ran into him, but there was of course no such luck. So I decided to go up to the seniors' floor. It was meant for the seventeen and eighteen-year-olds, whom were only a few months away from University and the real world. I envied them and also avoided them, but this was dire.

I reached the floor but stopped at the top of the staircase to have a quick look around. It took only a few curious glares at me for me to snap back to my senses, and turn away. I was scared that one of them would call me back to ask what I wanted, so it was only when I walked into my class and exhaled in relief at a safe arrival, did I allow myself to relax.

However, my shoulders drooped in disappointment; where was he and why was he so hard to find?

෴

With my backpack slung over my shoulder, the end of the school day found me heading to the library. As usual, it was almost empty when I walked in, so I eagerly headed over to *my* corner and settled down on the carpeted floor to continue my read. It was a historical novel set in the 1800s which told the love story of a barbaric highlander, and a prim English aristocrat. It usually helped me escape for a few hours, but after about an hour, I had to literally stop reading or have my heart explode from want.

I was so jealous of the protagonist. She was in love and careless, consumed by the thrill of romance and favored by the throes of adventure. It sounded cheesy enough to choke me, but I wasn't even joking. Nothing in my own life came close to being interesting and as far back as I could remember, my budding feelings for Nathan were the closest I'd ever come to a crush.

One time though when I was in the fourth grade, I did pay especial attention to a really skinny guy just because he told me he liked my hair. But when he also told me how much he disliked novels because "they weren't grounded in reality enough and therefore, a complete waste of time", my attention to him had immediately translated to disdain.

Rising to my feet, I decided to head into other sections so I could browse for books on more sensible things that would help take my mind off all the silliness I was surrendering to. I still had my looming biology assignment, so I decided to finally do something about it and go in search of a book that I could use; the deadline was sometime this week.

I found what I wanted in minutes, but as I headed back to my table with the book and the intention to begin the assignment, I suddenly felt exhausted. So I gathered my things, and headed to the receptionist's desk. She greeted me with a smile, and accepted the book so that she could check it out.

The sight of a picture in the corner of her desk, showing two small boys – whom I supposed were hers – hugging a dog between them, occupied me while she worked. The absolute delight on their sunburned faces pulling a smile from me.

Just then, I felt someone come up beside me, so I turned and saw a tall boy with ginger colored curly hair, placing an impossibly high stack of books on the desk. When his polite smile met my widened gaze, I just had to ask.

"Are you going to read all that?"

"No," he replied, his smile widening in amusement. "It's a list our physics teacher requested ... I'm just helping him retrieve them."

"Oh, okay," I said with a nod. He had a clear sharp voice that anyone would have expected to belong to a bold person, but he seemed to be very self-conscious. His right arm kept going up to touch his left elbow as if he couldn't quite figure out how to place them, and his eyes were shifty as he spoke, like he couldn't quite focus on me for more than two seconds at a time.

His smile was also shaky, I realized, when he stole a glimpse and caught me watching him. I found it amusing, but in a good way, endearing almost, and it instantly drew me to him. He seemed like an interesting person.

"So, are you a senior then?" I asked, as I collected my book from the librarian. He nodded before handing the signed note for the order over to her.

"Yup," he answered. "I've seen you around – you're in fourth year I suppose."

I smiled, "I'm in the third actually."

"Well, you could easily have passed for fifth," he said, and I beamed at his ill attempt at flattery.

"Style" was what more or less distinguished the years, and I knew that I would have passed for someone in the second year (in fact, I was almost certain that I did). My navy blue pinafore still hung loosely from my body, my hair was constantly a wild mess and my face, ever devoid of even a hint of makeup, would have easily led anyone to believe and conclude that I had an aversion to it. My disregard for refinement was glaring, there was no argument there.

"Do you need help with that?" I asked, not genuinely with the intention to assist, but with the hopes that I could be acquainted with him enough to ask if he knew Nathan. It was petty and selfish, I knew, but I had run out of options.

At first he looked indecisive, but I wasn't sure I would accept no for an answer so I saved him the trouble, and took a few of the volumes off the stack before he could make up his mind. He of course nodded his agreement then, and we walked away together.

"So how come you're the one on library duty?" I asked.

"Because I'm the library prefect," he said. "And the geek of the class. Actually the second geek; my cousin's the first."

"Your cousin's in your class? That sounds nice."

"Yeah, it is. Well, only sometimes, and I guess the duty just fits me more than anyone else."

"You don't really seem like the book type," I teased, and he laughed, a hearty and genuine sound.

"You definitely missed the curly hair memo."

"There're no glasses," I pointed out as he used his back to push, and hold the door to his class open, so that I could walk in.

"I'm just lucky on that count," he said. "My cousin couldn't escape it though."

Walking over to the teacher's desk, I placed the books on top of it while he came over and did the same. We turned to each other.

"So ..." I started. "It was nice meeting you."

"It was nice meeting you too," he said with his hand held out for a handshake. I took it awkwardly; his eyes were still shifty. It was adorable.

"I'm Lenora by the way," I said.

"I'm James – James DuPont."

Just then, the door to the classroom opened and as I turned to see who had walked in, the smile was completely wiped off my face. Immediately, I turned away.

"Alex," he called, "did you meet Mr.Maine ?"

"No," I heard his curt reply, but I still couldn't turn around to face him.

"That's my cousin," James said, still chirpy from our chat. I was just surprised that I was even able to control my mouth from hanging open. My heart was pounding furiously and suddenly, I needed desperately to be out of there.

James called him again, probably to introduce us, and that was all the warning I needed. Like a flash, I was out and rushing towards the staircase. I didn't slow down until I was well on my way back to my house.

❧

You're such a coward, I thought to myself as I arrived at my house. I almost felt like laughing. Almost.

After so long in wishing I'd see him again, I finally did, and instead of standing my ground I'd scurried away like a rat. I couldn't even remember the excuse I'd given as I hurried off. I wondered what they'd think of me now. What he'd think. I hoped he wouldn't read too much into my rush, and figure out that it was probably because I was attracted to him. That would be too embarrassing for me, and he already seemed too cocky a person.

"Hey!" someone suddenly called, startling me. Frowning, I turned to my right to see a blonde girl with light brown eyes, standing at the door to the common room.

"What is wrong with you?" she asked, irritated when she saw my frown. It was rhetorical anyway because she went on to say what she wanted. Through the door I could see that a crowd of seniors, had gathered by the huge bay window seat at the extreme end of the room. It seemed like a meeting was going on.

"Run up to my room," she said. "It's B27. Just knock, my roommate is in. Tell her I sent you and that she should let you have the notebook you'll find under my pillow."

"Beverly!" someone yelled from the room, and she turned to respond. It was then that it hit me; this was Olivia's sister! Right then I felt like walking out, but for my safety I remained. She turned to me and frowned.

"What're you still doing here?"

I was sure she expected me to scamper off to do her bidding, but when I just calmly walked away, I heard her snort before she retreated back into the room. I considered going to get the notebook for her before I returned to my room but when I reached my floor, my backpack suddenly felt too heavy. So I allowed myself to go in so that I could drop it. The room was empty when I arrived, which I was more than grateful for. Hanging my bag on the end of my chair, I walked over to my bed and sat down to take my shoes off.

Our room had green curtains to represent the official color of our house. There used to be a dark green rug in the center of the room, but Olivia had removed it without my consent, and replaced it with a pink one of her own. I never complained because I'd learnt in my years here to choose my battles, so I couldn't have cared less even if the wooden floor was bare.

What I *would* have cared about, was if she'd had the audacity to query me about the dark blue bedding that I'd exchanged for the green and pink one that we'd been given at the start of the year.

The green and pink would have obviously complemented the room but I preferred my blue duvet, which completely rebelled against the green and pink theme. I'd had it since my first year at Lancaster and it'd come to feel too familiar to be replaced. So she kept her opinion to herself, which I was thankful for, despite the sour looks that I sometimes still caught on her face when she stared at my bed for too long.

The other houses, each named after regions of the Lancashire County were decorated just like ours but with their respective colors. Cartmel was a dark magenta, Lonsdale was a bright red, Grizedale was laminex blue, and Bowland was a deep yellow.

Lonsdale was by far the prettiest, and I always thought that I should have been in Lonsdale. However, I had been assigned to Pendle since my first day here with the promise that house choices were always fated; I was yet to see the benefit of being in mine. A small compensation however, was that it did have an interesting history being that it was named after the Pendle Hill; a region in the county where witches had been tried and executed in the 17th century.

A small knock sounded at the door and I looked up to see Kate come in. Although she lived in Cartmel, which was quite a distance away, she had already stopped by a couple of times since the year began. She had friends here that she usually came to visit but still, I appreciated her drop-ins, especially since I had only been to hers once.

She had a small box in her hand and instantly, I recognized it as the chocolate fudge cake that was rarely ever available in the dining hall. My mouth immediately watered. Just then, Olivia came in with her friends and automatically, my small smile flat lined.

To my injury, they were excited about something and that meant a lot of squealing and laughter. I was sure they never completely let loose like this in public but in here, I had to be the victim of all of it. Kate cringed from the noise as she lowered herself to sit beside me.

"I didn't see you for lunch," she said.

"Do you *ever* see me for lunch?"

She cocked her head to the side as she considered this, and then agreed. "That *is* true. Anyway, you missed a little drama." She lowered her voice and leaned a little closer to me. "Do you remember the boy I ran off to see in the cafeteria?"

I nodded.

"Well he came in a while ago to pick up a snack from the buffet. Olivia went over to say hi."

My eyebrows rose in feigned interest, but I still turned to see Olivia's friends gazing upon her with awe as she no doubt re-narrated the event to them. It was amusing, especially when I watched Kate listen attentively to them and realized that this was probably why she had stopped by today.

"Did he talk to her?" I asked, turning to see the gloomy look on Kate's face as she watched Olivia's beam with joy.

"He did, but only for a few seconds. What do you expect? He's probably too polite to refuse her," she said. "I'm making a move next time."

I raised my thumb sarcastically at her. "Go for it!"

She caught the mockery and reached over to playfully slap my elbow. Then she handed the box over to me. "I brought cake." She said, and I didn't wait for her to change her mind. Thanking her, I accepted the box and immediately opened it.

"I better get going," she said as she stood. "Later?"

I nodded, a piece of chocolate fudge cake already finding its way to my mouth.

« CHAPTER 6 »

I forgot to attend to Beverly's errand, so that evening, I skirted around at dinner, dodging every senior who had the Pendle's witch logo pasted to the front of her shirt. Thereafter, I had fallen asleep and awoken later in the night to begin my assignment, only to discover that somewhere along the line I had misplaced the textbook that I'd borrowed from the library. It had been so upsetting because I'd finally worked up the urgency to do the assignment, and I couldn't.

However, after retracing my footsteps, I realized that I had left it under the pile that I'd helped James carry the previous day. In my haste to run out of the room, I'd completely forgotten about it. I expected that in a way, I should have been happy about it because the oversight would give me a solid reason to go back to the seniors' floor and probably catch a glimpse of Nathan. But after my performance the previous day, all I could feel was dread; dread that I could run into Beverly, or that even if I did run into him, he would ignore me. I wasn't sure which would be more distressing.

So far I'd managed to keep my head low, but my carelessness over the last two days was exposing me to more seniors than I would have liked. I didn't have a choice anyway because the option of just waiting until the school day ended, with the hope that I would see James again was too risky. My assignment was due the next day.

So by lunchtime, I was prepped for the worst, but when I reached their floor to see that it was practically emptied for lunch unlike the previous day, my shoulders slumped with relief. I would be barely noticed.

In no time, I found the classroom and pushed the door open, hoping with all of my heart that James would be in there. I was immensely disappointed because instead of James or even Nathan, were two of the boys that had attacked me the previous week; the red-haired one whose name I think was Clinton, and the dark-haired one that had pushed me to the floor.

They were sitting on desks and laughing about something, and both simultaneously turned to me when I came in. Fear instantly struck my heart, and I had started to turn back around when I caught sight of the stack of books on the table.

"Hey!" one of them called, as if daring me to come forward, but he needn't have, because the moment I caught sight of my book, I was more than ready to go through anything. I moved, walking forward as quickly as I could, all the while trying my best to completely ignore them. Hurriedly, I studied the stack on the teacher's desk and was relieved when I saw mine at the bottom. I retrieved it and turned around to leave, but they had planted themselves in front of the door.

They looked ridiculous as they stood there, with arms folded across their chests and aggravating smirks on their faces.

"Leave me alone," I said, not interested in getting into any further trouble even though I wished that I could smash their heads together. The headmaster was yet to inform us of when we would be suspended, and I didn't want to make it any worse.

"I knew you'd come back for us," the red-haired one said, and I wondered how someone could be so annoying.

"Get out of my way," I demanded, surprised at how bored I sounded. It in no way mirrored the panic that I was beginning to feel. They laughed, and even though the sound sent chills down my spine, I knew they were constrained in the damage they could inflict since school was still fully in session. But still, we were in a closed room, on an almost empty hallway. I swallowed.

"In your dreams," he said, and started to move towards me. "Do you see this?" he pointed to the bruises that still darkened the side of his face. "This is all your fault. My neck still hurts, and that day, you almost broke my *fucking* arm. You're a stupid bitch, do you know that?"

It took all my willpower not to retreat, especially when he'd come close enough to me that I could smell the garlic on his breath. Wanting to gag, I contorted my face in disgust, but I didn't expect what he did next.

He swung his arm, and struck the side of my face with a resounding slap. It turned my head to the side and I gasped, dazed at the blinding pain that burned across my cheeks. Even his friend took a step forward and touched the side of his hand in caution. "Clinton," he called, but Clinton pulled his hand away and raised it to point his fore finger at me.

"That," he said, "Is for what I went through last week because of you."

Tears rushed to my eyes, the burning pain that was clawing at the side of my face making me so angry that I could scarcely breathe. I looked up, my eyes ablaze with rage and my body shaking from the fury I felt. I was going to control myself but he took another step towards me, and I lost it.

With the textbook I had in my hand, I swung my arm as hard as I could and it hit the side of his face with a loud blow. He was so shocked that at first he just stared at me with widened eyes. Then he recovered, and shoved me.

The book fell out of my hands as I flew backwards and tried to break my fall, but I was glad that he hadn't done something worse like punch me in the face. It should have been surprising to me that he didn't mind hitting a girl but I had a dad that I'd watched beat up my mother more times than I cared to remember, so it didn't move me. Bastards like these existed everywhere.

71

I landed on the floor, and just then, I heard the door to the classroom open. Trying my best to rise to my feet as quickly as I could, I glanced towards the door and almost stopped breathing when I saw Nathan standing at the threshold and watching me. I felt relieved that he was there, but as I watched his face change when he took in the sight of me on the ground, and then turned to the boys, I was suddenly very scared for them.

Closing the door behind him, he came towards me to help me to my feet. I stumbled against him, and it took me a few seconds to stabilize myself before I could meet his eyes. It was a mistake, because although he appeared calm, his eyes had turned a very dark shade of blue- like clouds had gathered across a previously bright sky. I felt his anger like heat against my skin and for a moment, I almost shrugged his arms off because they seemed to be burning right through my sleeves.

"I'm fine, don't worry about it," I quickly said, and started to turn him away so that we could walk out together. But he refused, and gently pulled my hand down from his.

"Leave," he said, but I refused.

I held his hand again and tried turning him to come with me, and he did, but he stopped as we got to the door and gently but firmly, pushed me outside. Then he banged the door in my face.

I stayed there for a few seconds, exhausted and upset.

Then I heard the first blow, accompanied by a shout and the crashing of somebody into the furniture. Terrified, I jumped and ran back into the room to see the dark haired boy already on the floor. Right then, Nathan grabbed Clinton by the collar, and my hand shot up to stifle my gasp as his fist connected with the boy's face, driving it to the side. I could have sworn I saw sparks fly.

"Nathan!" I yelled, and I ran to him, but before I could even get to him, he had delivered two more blows. Blood poured from the boy's broken nose as he fell to the floor, but Nathan refused to let him be. He lowered himself down to meet him, and drew his arm back for another blow.

With my heart in my mouth, I grabbed Nathan's arm but the force of his swing easily displaced me and I was thrown forward, barely missing the blow myself by only a few inches.

That stopped him, but it brought me face to face with the blood that had gathered on the boy's face. Tears erupted from my eyes.

"Nathan," I cried, and he immediately took hold of my arm. He rose with me and I held on for support, my quiet sobs piercing through the deadly quiet room. He turned me to him, and I buried my head against his neck. When I had gotten myself under control, he held my shoulders and pulled me slightly away to look into my eyes.

"Look at me," he said, but I couldn't. My eyes were still filled with tears. I caught another glimpse of how bloodied the boy's face had become, and the tears seemed to come down even faster.

"Look at me," he repeated, this time a little harder and I was forced to look into his frozen blue eyes.

"Go now, to your class," he said, but I started to look away to try to find my textbook. He saw what I was after and shook his head.

"Leave that for now," he said. "But wait for me in your class a few minutes after school, and I'll bring it to you."

"What happened here?" I heard a familiar voice say behind me, and we both turned to see James with eyes that had widened to the size of saucers. That was more than enough to prompt me back into action as I realized the severity of the situation if anyone else was to come in and meet the scene. Immediately, I turned and started to pull Nathan along with me but he stopped me again, and forced my eyes to meet his.

"I'll be fine," he said, but still, I hesitated. James turned me around and led me out.

෨

Nathan met me sitting down with my left hand around my midriff, and my teeth, nervously biting away at the nail of my right thumb. He didn't know it, but it was a significant improvement from tapping my foot, which I had done all throughout my classes until my French teacher had threatened to throw me out. Then I'd had to find a more quiet way to manage the whirlwind of agitation inside of me.

My thoughts had run rampage in the wait for him, imagining every possible scenario that could have taken place after I left. How much trouble had he gotten into? Had he been sent to the headmaster again? He was bound to be in deeper trouble this time around, and it'd be entirely my fault. I reasoned too late that I should have stayed to at least bear this with him. He shouldn't have to take the heat alone.

"Here's your textbook," he said.

I was startled because he was now standing just a few feet away, and I hadn't even realized when he had come in. I rose and took the book from him, but immediately he turned, and started to leave.

"Wait!" I called, but he didn't stop.

I found myself going after him, and just before he reached the door, I reached out and lightly touched his arm. He stopped then and turned around, but his stare was still so cold that reflexively, I took a step back.

"What happened?" I asked, but he didn't seem to have heard me because his eyes were now searching my face, and for what, I had absolutely no idea. I was about to repeat my question when his eyes finally settled on mine; my stomach tightened in response.

"It's fine," he said. "I handled it."

"Did the headmaster call for you?"

"No."

I was surprised. "How come?"

"Because I left him there. James helped him to the infirmary."

I was shocked. I wasn't sure what to feel, but one thing I did know was that I was disappointed.

"How could you just leave him there?" I cried. "Didn't you see how badly he was hurt?"

"Yes, I did see how badly he was hurt, and that was why I got out of there before I did any more damage," he said acidly, and then his tone increased like he was finding it very difficult to control his temper.

"He hit you, and you still just stood there. What's *wrong* with you?"

I was silent for a few seconds as I tried to understand what he was saying.

"I thought ..." I began, but he interrupted me.

"Do you know how much more they could have hurt you?"

Then he exploded. "What were you even doing in that class?" His tone was still not loud enough to be heard outside the room, but it was loud enough to frighten me. It made me defensive, so my tone went up too.

"I have an assign –" I started, but again, he didn't let me finish.

"Why couldn't you come back? Didn't you see them in there?"

"What was I supposed to do? Walk away?"

"Yes! Exactly!" he yelled again as if he couldn't understand why it hadn't occurred to me. "That was exactly what you were supposed to do, at least until there were other people present. This was the same thing you did last week; instead of trying to get help you kept on trying to take on four boys! Are you out of your mind?"

He was furious. "The hallway was empty and school had closed for the weekend. What happened to calling out for help? What happened to screaming? What happened to running away? Anything could have happened, or did you think that shoving you around was the worst thing they could have done?"

He stopped then and exhaled, while I just stared blankly at him, too stunned at his outburst. With one last glare, he thrust his hands into the pockets of his camel-colored coat and strode out of the classroom, leaving me to feel like a bucket of ice had just been poured over me.

I went after him.

"Nathan!" I called out when I saw him start to climb up the stairs at the end of the floor, but he didn't respond. I went back to grab my backpack and then hurried after him, quickening my steps so that I could catch up. I wondered why I was even bothering, but I couldn't seem to stop.

We reached the second floor and he left the block, heading out towards the skywalk that connected all the buildings. I was walking as fast as I could but couldn't catch up with him until he had exited, and then entered the tower that housed the library. I reduced my steps to an extent then, because the muscles in my feet were beginning to hurt. Walking in, I went past the librarian and onto the study floor.

I spent the next twenty minutes searching for him, but I couldn't find him. Eventually it got to the point where I started to doubt if he had even come in here at all. I went around again and again until I finally gave up, terribly upset.

The bathroom was on my way out so I stepped into the hallway to quickly use it. When I came out minutes later, I noticed an exit door to my right. I had never been through it and expected that there was probably a way that led directly to the ground floor. So I went in and took the stairs.

It did take me to the ground floor but I found that the exit that indeed led outside, was locked. Irritated, I turned so that I could return to the staircase, when I noticed that another door, a little ways down the dim corridor, was slightly ajar.

The corridor was empty, and I expected the room to be empty too but somehow, I found myself walking towards it. I pushed it open to find a dark room, with only the entrance slightly illuminated by the light from corridor. Thankfully, there was a switch to the side of the wall so I immediately flicked it on.

A bright warm light filled the room from the single bulb that hung from the ceiling, and I saw that it was an untidy storage room filled with books. There were various boxes in the middle of the room, some sealed and others opened, as well as piles of books just stacked carelessly against the walls. There was nothing of interest here, so I started to turn back when I noticed what appeared to be the side of a metal lion's head. It wasn't particularly eye-catching, but it was peculiar enough for me to want a closer look. It was behind a bookcase that seemed to have been moved to the side, so when I reached it, I had to push the case even further away so that I could get a decent look.

It was indeed a huge lion head knocker, to a small door that had been hidden behind the case. The knocker was extremely unsettling; its ferocious dentition was exposed through a gaping jaw, and as I continued to stare at it, a sliver of dread crawled down my spine. I intended to leave but found myself reaching out to run my finger along its fang-like tooth. It was surprisingly smooth, considering that it looked like it had been there since the school had been established. As expected, it came away with a thick layer of dust that showed that it had been ignored for a long time.

Cautiously, I poked at the fang, marveling at the detail that went into it only to be startled by the gentle creak that ensued. Looking carefully, I realized that the door had come slightly ajar. This, I realized, was my cue to leave, but instead, I pushed the door open despite its stiffness, and then squeezed myself behind the bookcase so that I could slip inside.

The darkness I met was overwhelming, but it wasn't enough to deter me. Encouraged by the light still visible through the slightly open door, I slowly moved forward until my eyes adjusted to the darkness enough to notice a string dangling from what I expected was a ceiling. It was too dark to be certain.

The string had a small knob attached to its tip, so I pulled on it. Thankfully, a soft light which flickered for a few moments before finally stabilizing, filled the room. A quick glance around showed me that it was another storage room, so I was able to breathe more easily.

It wasn't a very large room. It had an irregular shape and was stacked with ceiling high bookshelves. I could see cobwebs and dust that had made themselves at home in every corner of the room, and piles of books that couldn't fit into the bookcases scattered around the floor. The grime and the lack of windows made the room so stuffy that I could almost touch the dust in the air. It was agonizing to breathe, and soon I began to feel like I was going to collapse. I had had enough.

So I turned around and started to head towards the door, but suddenly, my foot caught on something hard. I tripped, and fell head on into a pile of books by the corner. I did try to break my fall, but it didn't stop the pain I felt in my ribs and elbow when I landed on the dusty floor. I thought about getting up, but for a second just decided to remain the way I was, since life wasn't tired of throwing obstacles in my way today.

I was definitely tired of trying to stay sane, and at that point, I felt like just losing it and strangling somebody or destroying something. However, I wasn't ready to be bitten or attacked by whatever could've been hiding in the shadows for the last century. So I got up, and dusted my uniform.

Turning to examine what had tripped me, I noticed a slight bulge protruding from underneath the worn out rug on the floor. I hadn't even noticed that there had been a rug on the floor, and as I bent down to examine it, I noticed that once, a very, *very* long time ago, it had probably been in a deep, exquisite red with delicate gold embroidery. Now, and like everything else in sight, it was drenched in dust.

Casually, I tried pushing it aside but it was too heavy. So I stood up and with both hands, grabbed the edges to pull it away. Thankfully it complied, but by then alarm bells were already going off in my head, asking me what the hell I thought I was doing and why I wasn't running away from this place. But I just wanted to see what was beneath the rug, so I promised myself I would leave as soon as I discovered it.

As I suspected, it was a trap door. And it was also time to leave, but I wasn't going to. My curiosity wasn't going to let me, so ignoring my inward struggle for reason I pressed on.

Holding the latch attached to the door, I pulled firmly but was met with resistance. Then I tried pushing it down, and it instantly gave way.

My breath caught as I peered through it, but I couldn't see what was down there because again, it was too dark. I did however notice a ladder leading downwards, so as I stared down into the darkness, I thought hard about what I was about to do.

It was a stupid idea, I knew, but even if I didn't go down today, the fact was that I now knew that it existed and the knowledge was going to bring me back. So I might as well just get it over with. I mean, what could possibly be down there? The school had probably examined the entire premises, and I was sure they wouldn't have allowed anything to exist that could cause any potential damage or harm to the lives of their students.

I swallowed, and at that moment, tried really hard not to think of Hogwarts as I reminded myself that there was a reason the room had been shut off and hidden behind a bookcase. Nevertheless, I managed to push past that. I did wonder who had opened it today and thought it possible that maybe Nathan had also found it. Either way, it encouraged me to think that someone else might be down there already. So as gently and as slowly as I could, I climbed down the dirty and rough, but thankfully firm, wooden ladder.

After about fifteen steps, my feet finally connected with a hard floor. I didn't look backwards or wait to assess my surroundings. I just moved forward because I was on the brink of climbing back up, and returning. Strange thoughts kept recurring in my mind, especially since I could barely see. My mind started to paint pictures of monstrous and unforgiving creatures who were just watching me in pity, but thankful for the meal that had been sent their way. I shivered, and then shook my head to dispel the thought.

I continued meandering down a narrow path - it seemed to be a tunnel – and after tripping and falling on a few stony edges and surfaces, I learnt to be more careful. After a few steps, I started hearing sounds – more like brief whispers.

They would come and startle me, but then just flutter away like they never actually existed. It was creepy, and it made me to start questioning my sanity which seemed to be leading me in all the wrong directions lately. Luckily, I hadn't stumbled on any bones, or worse, flesh, and no animal or beastly grunts either so I figured I was still okay. But the darkness was overwhelming; murky and portent.

As my eyes adjusted, I became aware of the long passage stretching out in front of me. The darkness made me want to turn back so badly and return to safety, but I hadn't looked back since I began this craze and I didn't want to now. Not because of the fear of a hampering on my 'unshakable courage', but because I was scared of what I would see, or better yet what I wouldn't see. For all I knew, the ladder had disappeared, and I didn't think anything could spook or zap me into a frenzy of obscene panic more than that. My only source of safety, gone … I was sure I would collapse.

So I walked on, even though the tunnel somehow seemed to be getting darker, and creepier. The whispers had translated into full voices now, but no words. I was trembling, and the bite from the cold that rushed over me didn't do my bruises any good.

After a long while, I got to a part of the tunnel that seemed less dark. The walls were also a little bit wider as I didn't have to press my arms to myself anymore to keep them from brushing against the wall.

Eventually, I saw the end of the tunnel, and an indescribable relief rose up within me. Its wide opening was set ablaze by the sunlight beyond its walls, so I increased my pace to reach it. I still didn't have the courage to look back because there was no need to get ahead of myself in determining my fate- the day had still not ended.

« CHAPTER 7 »

Nervously, I stepped out, relieved to be out of the tunnel but afraid of what I might meet here. Before me, was a thick forest. And although it was very visible from the school grounds as it rose up beyond its tall walls, the only thing I knew about it was that it was called the Bowland Forest.

Now that I was in it, I wondered why I'd never been more curious about it. I suppose it was because it was so shut off from the premises and too far away to bother me, but now that I was here, I was fascinated by it.

It was so surreal because as I looked around, I found it hard to believe that I had just come through a tunnel that led me to it. I was so overwhelmed that I felt like I needed to sit down, but instead, I just continued to stand there and stare, until eventually, the darkness from the tunnel got to me. So I took a few more steps forward, before turning around to see where I had emerged from.

It looked like the entrance to a small cave, and appeared to be constructed of stones and rocks placed haphazardly against each other. However, the moss, algae and plants that littered the entrance rendered it almost nonexistent to the untrained eye.

The forest was not as bright as I would have liked because the sunlight was held at bay by the canopy of the trees, however, I decided to go a little further. I had to at least justify putting myself through all this by exploring some of it, *but you can't go too far,* I cautioned myself. Only a few steps, otherwise I doubted that I would be able to find my way back.

Walking straight ahead, and as softly as I could, I ensured that I kept on a straight path – despite the obtrusive plants and trees – in order to ensure my safe return. I was still too tensed to relax, darting my eyes around me to limit as many surprises as I could. But it didn't stop me from noticing how loud the racket of the birds here were, compared to the ones we heard in school. It felt like I was in an entirely different world, similar but different.

It was so calm that I could hear every tap of my feet against the ground as I walked, and although no distinct scent stood out from all the plants and trees that surrounded me, the air felt a little bit more fresh and clean. It slid in and out of my nostrils so smoothly, like I had just consumed peppermints and washed it down with cold water.

I had only been walking for about fifteen to twenty minutes, and was about to turn back when I heard it; the unmistakable whooshing of water and its lapping on rocks. Every nerve in my body rose to attention and I stopped, stilling myself as much as I could so that I could clarify my suspicion.

But despite the deafening racket the birds made, I still heard it – the rushing sound of a stream or river. Instantly I was overcome with intrigue, but instead of being excited, I sighed deeply. It was truly beginning to feel like someone somewhere really wanted me to get lost today, or get into whatever trouble was lurking in this forest.

The gushing sound seemed to be coming from the east so I walked a few steps ahead to avoid colliding with a tree, and then headed towards my right. Locating a lean, crooked branch amidst the weeds and small plants, I picked it up and used it to navigate my way onwards. I walked as fast and as carefully as I could, paying as much attention as I could to the path I was taking so that it would be easy to find my way back.

So I trailed on and on, maneuvering through obtrusive plants with the help of the branch I had found earlier, all the while whispering silent prayers for protection. Everything around me was overwhelmingly green, so apparently spring had been generous to the forest, but not to me. I was getting colder with each passing minute, even though I had my blazer on and buttoned up.

After a while, thousands of scurrying sounds and a million crackles, I finally reached it. And the exhilaration at sighting a lighter part of the forest from afar, where there were no trees to shade the sun was nothing compared to seeing the stream.

It was, of course, beyond beautiful. Utterly breathtaking, and it was also noisy, but that I could overlook. I gazed in awe, transfixed to the exact spot that I had stopped in. The stream was not too wide, but it was a little rocky. That however, didn't stop the waters from gushing heartily over it. The serenity it promised drew me in, and I needed to be even nearer to it so I tossed my branch aside and walked closer.

The banks were sprinkled with shrubs and fallen trunks, but thankfully, I wasn't on the most abundant side. The side I was on, although having numerous trees, was more bare and easier to tread through. Walking forward, I eventually reached the banks of the stream.

The ground dipped slightly, so I had to be careful as I slipped gently down onto the rocky shore. My shoes were already muddied, but I didn't want to damage them completely so I slipped them off, and carefully laid them on the smaller rocks. My hands and pinafore were soiled from clinging to the earth as I crawled down, so I held my hands on the surface of the water, wincing in delight as it erased the traces of dirt off my palms.

Straightening, I found leveled rocks situated consecutively against each other, slightly beyond the edge of the stream. So I walked over them until I came to the biggest one, and then settled on it. Bringing my knees up to my chin, I watched the stream, and as my eyes caught a particularly low tree trunk that loomed over it, ideas began to form in my mind about how it would be possible to swing from it and brush against the water. I shivered at the thought of falling in, and dispelled the notion from my mind.

Inhaling the crisp, clean air, I sighed and wondered at how I could feel the silent and equally boisterous presence of everything. It felt as if I was drugged, and I wished so much that I didn't have to go back. But after only just a few minutes in my blissful state, I was interrupted.

"Lenora!" someone yelled, and I froze. Instantly, I knew who it was and at first I was relieved; the burden of finding my way back and braving the walk through the tunnel again now gravely reduced, but I cursed under my breath when I remembered how angry he'd been with me earlier.

If he hadn't felt like killing me then, he was definitely going to want to now. But how the hell had he found all this in the first place? There was no doubt now that he was the one that had left it open, and it all made sense why I hadn't been able to find him in the library.

Rising to my feet, I turned around but almost lost my balance when he barked out my name again. With a frown, I steadied myself and then carefully made my way up the bank. When I emerged at the top, I immediately saw him so I stopped a considerable distance away. He had his hands folded across his chest and looked like he couldn't believe what he was seeing.

"How the hell are you even *here?*" he asked, in a tone that suggested that the question was directed more at himself than at me. But still, the wind carried it over to me. I didn't think a reply was expected so I just moved my eyes away from his, and down the length of his body.

His hair was disheveled, shirttails hanging out of his trousers, collar button undone and sleeves rolled up to just below his elbow. He looked very different from his otherwise usually well-put-together look, but I could have sworn that I almost preferred it. I did though, still note the unmistakable air of superiority and control that hung around him, and that was what kept me from lowering my guard.

"I don't think you can even begin to fathom the level of grief that you're giving me," he said, every word heavy with restrained anger. "How did you find this place?" he asked, a hint of panic in his tone. It would have elicited a bit of remorse on my end but I wasn't sure if it reflected his concern for my safety, or if it was simply because I had found the place.

"It doesn't matter," I said.

Tired of his harassment, I began to walk ahead with the intention of finding my way back on my own since I didn't expect that he would want to help me. However, just before I moved past him he caught my arm in a grip that showed more than anything, his fury. I looked up to meet his eyes but they were closed in anger. A vein throbbed at his temple. He reopened them, and then looked at me.

"What is wrong with you?" he said, and even though I was turned off by the rebuke in his tone, the emotions of frustration and genuine concern that he allowed to show on his face made me hold my tongue.

"What do you think this is?" he asked. "Do you think this is a joke? A million and one things could happen to you out here. What if I hadn't seen you? This is *exactly* what we just fought about."

"It's none of your —" I started but he interrupted, shaking his grip on my arm with a ferocity that intensified the pain.

"Why do you keep doing this? You have no sense of care for your wellbeing and it is driving me crazy."

"I can take care of myself," I said, and I jerked my hand away from his.

"Let's go," he said after a deep breath and he took my hand again to lead me forward, but I pulled it away.

"Let me go!" I said. "I got myself here and I'll get myself back, so you don't have to bother."

I started walking, but stopped after a few steps and turned back to him.

"You know me being here in the first place is your freaking fault," I said. Then my tone rose. "I was calling out to you and you just ignored me, so you know what, just mind your own business and leave me the hell alone."

With that, I turned sharply and started to stomp along to find my way back. As I walked on, I vowed to kick him out of my mind and only vaguely realized that I wasn't paying attention to where I was headed. But at that moment, I was angry enough to convince myself that the path looked familiar enough anyway so I continued on, certain that I would find my way.

As I continued to rant about him in my mind, the sounds that I relished when I had first arrived here had now dimmed behind the deafening hum and heat around my ears. He acted like he cared but he actually didn't. All he felt was a twisted sense of responsibility towards me and that was the last thing I needed. I almost wished I could have told him to his face that he needed to learn to look the other way so that his conscience, at seeing me 'endanger myself' wouldn't prick him.

Asshole! I cursed, and continued walking, stumbling a few times on stumps from not paying attention. Soon I had calmed down enough to start looking out for the stumps, as well as where the hell I was heading. A few minutes later, the path, I now realized, didn't seem as familiar as I had previously thought. I should have taken a left by now, but I hadn't. And I shouldn't have been approaching muddy ground, but I was.

Fear started to slowly creep into my heart, especially since the sky seemed to be getting darker by the second. As I walked along the muddy area, I had to cling to the trees by the side to avoid stepping in it but still, one of my legs got stuck. I tried pulling it out, but it became so messy that I finally just had to slip my feet out of the shoe.

Wondering how I was going to continue the rest of the journey with just my pantyhose, I bent down to retrieve it. But just then, I heard a snapping sound from the tree above me, along with a loud rustle of leaves. With a shriek very close to a scream, I took off in the opposite direction without my shoe, and refused to look back.

I eventually slowed down when I figured that my hurried steps would probably attract grumpy animals whose peace I was possibly disturbing, and the last thing I needed was any more misfortune. Ahead of me was a small clearing that kept the greenery a healthy distance away, so when I reached it, I sat down in the middle and thought about how I was going to find my way back.

I should have listened to him, I thought. *I really should have,* but now was not the time for regrets. I didn't know what next to do so I sat there for countless minutes, and kept my eyes glued to my surroundings so that I would be able to pick up on any unusual movements, and follow any unacceptable sounds. My neck moved around quite a lot as it hurried from one point to another, until eventually, I was too tired to remain sitting up.

So I laid down, but on my back so that I could still monitor my surroundings from both sides, and as well as up. Snakes could still fall down from the trees or crawl towards me, and frankly, they were my biggest fear. I hated them more than anything in the entire world.

As I waited and watched, the minutes seemed to drag on until I began to literally shake with fear.

What's going to happen to me? I wondered.

Out of despair I sat up, and with my arms hugging my knees, continued watching all the available paths, hoping that somehow, Nathan hadn't left or that even if he had, he would be concerned enough to notice that I hadn't yet returned.

But oh, how I prayed that he would notice immediately and not in another ten minutes from now, or an hour, or God forbid, the next day. Thankfully, the darkness had been temporarily chased away in this part of the forest so I could see, despite the canopies, a quite healthy and jubilant sky.

Suddenly I heard rustling, and with my heart in my throat, turned to search for its source. It was coming from my right and sounded as though it was heading towards me, so I rose to my feet, ready to take off if need be.

I hoped with all my heart that it was Nathan, so the moment I saw him coming towards me, my heart dropped into my stomach.

Tears gathered in my eyes as I watched him, feeling so relieved that my knees felt like they would give out. I wanted to cry, or at least throw myself against him in a hug, but I chose to stay where I was and waited until he reached me. When I saw that he had my shoe in his hand, the tears rolled down my cheeks. Turning away, I quickly brushed them away before I turned back to face him. I avoided his eyes, but then wanted to say something when I saw that he wasn't going to.

"How did you find me?" I asked, but he didn't respond. Instead, he just dropped down on one knee, and placed his hand on my left leg. With a damp handkerchief that he had in his other hand, he gently wiped off as much of the mud as he could from the feet of my pantyhose, and then slipped the clean shoe back on. It was a little damp but at that moment, that was the last thing on my mind. Taking my hand off his shoulder, I quickly wiped away another tear as it fell, just before he rose to meet my gaze.

"Are you ready to go?" he asked, and at that moment, I didn't care that I had lost. So with all my heart, I nodded a definite yes.

There was no talking as we headed back, and even when we reached the intersection that led to our different houses, he didn't say goodbye. He just headed off towards his own direction, while I went the opposite way towards mine.

« CHAPTER 8 »

Three days later, I had come to a conclusion. It was Friday, and the assignment that had given so much grief in so many ways was done, but I was aggravated.

With time to mull over the ordeals of that day, I had somehow managed to skip over the shock of all that had happened and to only focus on the fact that I had been subtly mocked- Nathan had let me stew in my fright for an entire hour, before coming to my aid.

It shouldn't have mattered, I knew, but given the terror that I had experienced in those moments when I was lost, it was more than enough to conclude and be irritated by the fact that the boy was completely evil. This was precisely why I needed to run into him again, so I could tell him just that, and a couple more things I was sure would come up when I came face to face with his pompous self.

Loud angry voices that currently rocked my floor had pulled me out of a much needed nap, so as I angrily pulled on my house t-shirt and a pair of shorts, I thought of how I was in the perfect state of mind to be completely enraged with him. But that would be if I ever saw him again. In the three days that had passed, there had been no trace of him.

The corridor seemed to quiet down as I locked my wardrobe and headed down towards the dining hall. One would have thought that after almost three years at L.A., I would've found a fixed seat for my meals, but I hadn't. I'd sat with Kate a few times, but her table was always too noisy and I needed some element of quiet as I ate. And since I didn't keep any other 'friends', I was forced every time I came in, to browse through the myriads of people, just so that I could find a seat that had not already been taken or reserved, and was at the end of the wooden benches.

I doubted I would have any luck since I was late, so when I arrived at the hall, I stopped at the front of its majestic oak door and just stared. It was twice my '5 ft. 8' height, and had square wooden-framed windows, stacked upon it, and all the way up to meet a huge stone archway. I was thinking of what I was going to do because as soon as you entered, most eyes turned on you, and you had to know where you were headed otherwise you appeared pathetic and lonely.

As others continued to stroll past me, laughter and idle chatter ringing in the air, I reminded myself that I didn't care about such things. *I shouldn't care*, I reemphasized, so after a deep breath, I walked in to meet the gigantic hall packed with rows upon rows of innately carved wooden benches, and tables filled with students all happier than I was.

No one seemed to have thought it reasonable to miss Friday dinner, so the entire 1,900 students of the school were present and babbling, each one trying to be heard over the next. Resisting the urge to cover my ears with my hands, I stood to the side of the door and focused on the still pressing problem of where I was going to sit.

I took a quick look around, praying to find a direction that I could quickly escape to. However, after a few minutes had passed and I found myself still standing there, I lost hope. I was about to turn around to leave when a swinging arm high in the air, caught my attention.

Upon closer inspection, I realized that it was James- Nathan's cousin, and instantly, I breathed easier. I was sure he was calling out to me, so before my mind could convince me otherwise, I headed over to his table. His was at the extreme end to the right, and about two tables from the first. I reached it and to my relief, he moved further down the bench so that I could take a seat on the edge. I was more than grateful.

"Hi," he greeted with a bright smile, but was still so shy that his eyes were barely able to hold mine for more than two seconds. It amused me enough to temporarily forget that I was upset, and I returned the greeting with a genuine smile of my own. But the sight I met as I turned from him, instantly wiped the cheer away from my face.

Nathan was sitting directly across from us.

He had a book on the table and was reading, his head casually balanced against his palm. I was stunned enough to keep my gaze on him for at least ten seconds, but when he suddenly moved to turn a page, I darted my gaze away.

It landed on the couple beside him, a curly blonde and an Asian boy, their faces a little too close together for comfort. But absent-mindedly, I left my gaze on them, still reeling from the shock of seeing Nathan, until their lips met and they started kissing. It took me a few more seconds to realize what was happening and when I did, I moved my eyes away, a deep frown carved into my forehead.

Laughter from my side drew me to see two other boys beside James chatting away, but when I took my eyes away from them, Nathan's eyes caught mine.

"Are you alright?" James asked right then, and I was more than glad for the save. I turned to him, my heart pounding in my chest.

"I am," I answered.

"I wanted to apologize for what happened on Tuesday," he said. "I had no idea that you'd left your book. I would've brought it to you."

"Its fine," I quickly dismissed, and looked down to the hands I didn't realize I had been wringing. I untangled them, and took a deep breath. I wanted to get out of there.

My gaze drifted to Nathan again, but thankfully, his attention was back on his book. Earphones were plugged into his ears, and to an extent, I was glad that he wasn't listening to James and I.

"Do you live in the UK?" James asked.

I shook my head. "No, the US," I said. I thought it was quite obvious but he was probably trying to fill up the silence so I didn't mind.

"Oh," he said. "No wonder your accent's all messed up."

I smiled.

"So, how did you end up here?"

"Long story," I replied, as I looked towards the buffet line. It was going slower than I would have liked.

"Alex mentioned that you two met earlier," he said, and that instantly caught my attention.

He talked about me? I thought, and my entire body tingled with excitement. I turned to face James but only realized moments later that my eyes had been boring into his, willing him to say more. I looked away from his confused expression and back to the buffet line to hide my shame.

"Another long story," I said, and thankfully, that severed our communication enough to get myself under control.

What's wrong with me? I wondered. Right now, I was sitting with my hands underneath the table to hide the fact that I couldn't stop wringing them, and was even consciously trying to control my breathing, afraid that it would be too loud and that Nathan would notice. What was happening to the hardened girl I had cultivated for close to three years?

Soon, it was our turn to head to the buffet counter, so I instantly got up to escape and James followed. Yet somehow, I managed to end up with Nathan beside me as we went through the steaming hot plates of spaghetti and tomato sauce. Acting for all the world like the food I had now lost interest in held my complete attention, I tried not to notice that I literally trembled from my awareness of the unbelievably attractive boy that stood to my left. His earphones were still plugged into his ears, so at least he wasn't able to hear the pounding of my heart, which in my opinion, should have been loud enough to be heard across the noisy hall.

I wondered where the rage I'd worked up over the last two days to pour on him had gone to. Now he was standing right beside me, and I had all but forgotten my name, including, I realized, the tomato sauce that would go with my spaghetti.

Without thinking, I turned to retrace my steps, but instead stopped when my disconcerted grey eyes met his cold blue ones. Something cool, yet warm at the same time, slithered down my spine.

"Do you want something?" he asked, but I had already spun right back from the embarrassment. It was several moments later before I realized that I hadn't even answered him.

"No it's fine," I said without looking back, hoping he would catch it. Grabbing a piece of bread, I gave up on my dinner altogether and returned to my seat. I was angrily tearing at it, disappointed in myself, and intending to eat as fast as I could so that I could get the hell out of there, when a small bowl of tomato sauce and meatballs was placed in front of me. Surprised, I looked up, but Nathan had already turned to leave. I watched him return to the counter to pick up his plate, and continue with his serving.

What is wrong with you? I cried to myself, so distraught by my actions that I felt an almost desperate need to escape, and hide until I managed to regain the lick of sense that I had somehow lost during the course of the evening.

Looking down at the bowl of sauce, I considered ignoring it so that I could save my pride and insist if he asked, that I had actually planned on eating the spaghetti on its own. That, I realized, would be even more idiotic, so I just took what I needed from it and started eating.

The rest of the table soon returned, and we were all quietly going through our meals when the racket started. It began with increased tones around the middle of the hall but at first, everyone ignored it.

"So," James started, "I really want to hear the story of how you two met."

I stopped and rolled my eyes. "*James* ..." I complained but he rushed to explain himself.

"It's just that when he mentioned you broke a tray on his back, I've just been so intrigued. And he's refused to tell me any —"

"Wait, he said I broke a tray on his back?"

"Yeah. Isn't he right?"

"No! ... I mean yes, but he pushed me to the floor."

Without thinking, I reached forward and tapped Nathan's arm. He looked up at me and took the earphones out of his ears.

"You told James I broke a tray on your back?"

He kept his eyes on me, and then moved them to James before bringing them back to me again, unhurriedly, like he had all the time in the world. I told myself to bring my temper down a notch.

"Didn't you?" he asked, and my mouth fell open.

"How can you say that? You pushed me to the floor," I accused. He straightened, an eyebrow slightly arched.

"Excuse me?" he said, and my mouth snapped shut. Embarrassed at how intimidated I felt, I lowered my head in annoyance and returned to my food.

To my surprise, he reached across the table and put his fingers on mine. My eyes widened, both at the contact and at the coldness of his fingers, but as soon as he pulled them away, my fingers burned with a sweet warmth.

"I bumped into you," he said. "And I apologized."

The fight had gone out of me, and I wondered why I was even bothering when my mouth opened to reply to him.

"You ruined my lunch," I accused, and I tried to add a little harshness to my tone but it sounded as if I was flirting with him. I cleared my throat.

"And I replaced it," he said. I found my temper again, but it was barely flickering; the flame had gone out.

"Still, you can't just go around saying that I broke a tray on your back. It makes me sound like I'm crazy."

James chuckled then, and the sound gave me the distraction I so desperately needed. I turned to frown at him and he reigned in the smile, but when I returned to Nathan, he had plugged in his earphones and was eating again. I thought to tap his arm, but I had absolutely nothing left to say so I just returned to my meal too. James however, wasn't done.

"I just knew there had to be an interesting story behind it," he said, the loud crunching sound he made as he chewed on what I assumed had to be metal nuts for it to be that loud, digging into my eardrums like tiny needles. "You're the only girl I've seen him actually relate to, and you didn't chase him down. At least I hope you didn't – you did pretend not to know him the first time *we* met."

I shoved his elbow and he laughed. "Shut up," I said, worried that Nathan would overhear. "Why would I chase him down?"

"Oh you haven't heard?" he said. "I don't blame you. I didn't believe the craze over him either until Valentine's Day earlier this year. His room was filled with gifts from apparently *every* girl in school. A lot of guys developed a grudge for him that day."

I smiled despite myself. "Are you serious?"

"I should be asking you that," he said. "Why is this news to you? Everyone knew about it."

"Well *I* didn't," I said, and his surprise dissipated. He popped another handful of roasted almonds into his mouth. I cringed when he started chewing and returned to my food.

"He's called the Italian *bong*," he said in a voice just above a whisper, and instantly, it pulled a laugh out of me. I couldn't help it.

"What the hell does that mean?" I asked as I struggled to keep my amusement under control.

"I have no idea," James said "And he's not even Italian!"

From the corner of my eye, I saw Nathan look up. He asked James what was going on.

"Lenora just learned of your nickname," he said, and I turned just in time to see Nathan frown at James before he returned to his meal. The fact that he didn't even look at me quickly killed my smile.

"Anyway, so far, you're the closest thing to a friend he has so –"

I interrupted, "Trust me, we're not friends."

"Trust me, you've come farther than most."

"I wasn't looking to come anywhere."

With a smile he nodded, and returned to his meal.

A few moments later, the racket that had been slowly rising over the last few minutes erupted, and we all looked up to see two girls towards the middle of the hall on their feet and at opposite sides of the table, yelling at each other. Everyone else was of course interested, so all eyes had turned to them. I saw two teachers get up from their respective corners of the room and start to approach them, but they weren't quick enough.

The insults came next – which I couldn't hear clearly above the noise – punctuated by cheers of encouragement, especially from the boys. I returned to my meal, uninterested in the drama until all of a sudden, the gasping sound of almost two thousand people brought my head back up.

One of the girls had the top of her head completely covered in spaghetti, and was dripping with tomato sauce. Her hands were up in the air in shock, and everyone watched to see what she would do.

Not surprisingly, she picked up a handful from her own plate, but of course her opponent dodged the hit and it met the excited face of a boy a table away from them. They were unlucky because the table was full of boys, and so more excited than offended, they rose and aimed food back at their entire table.

And so the mess began. As I watched, horrified, I couldn't help thinking of how this was too much of a perfect day for a food fight. It was hurls of tomato sauce and soup all the way, and soon, the whole hall had turned into a sporadic scene of flying food.

The boys from our table, including James, eagerly got up and rushed to join the scene, which was rapidly spreading out towards us. Not sure whether to be upset or irritated, I grabbed the piece of bread I had saved to devour later in the night, and I stood up to leave the hall.

Others that felt the same way as I, got up to escape too, but most of them were gunned down with food before they could leave. I prayed that they would miss me, and was about to run out when a sharp tug on my arm pulled me back.

The loaf flew out of my hands as I tried to land on the bench, instead of the floor. Shocked, I turned to see Nathan staring at me as if he had just said *hello* instead of almost injuring me.

"Where are you going?" he asked, and my mouth hung open.

"Are you crazy? Or are you not seeing what's going on?" Somewhere along the line, the couple had left the table so we were the only ones there, and as soon as I noticed the mischievous, glint that was flashing in his eyes, I suspected that I was in trouble. I wasn't sure whether to completely believe it, so I slowly straightened, but before I could even turn to face him, a cup of orange juice was thrown in my face.

« CHAPTER 9 »

My eyes remained closed as I tried to take in what had just happened. A few seconds later I reopened them, intending to bring down hell against him but when I saw the grin on his face – my breath caught in my throat.

I remembered imagining what it would look like to see a full and genuine smile from him, and now that I did, I wanted to melt into a puddle on the wooden floor. I was now very excited so I rose, and started to go around the table towards him.

However before I could take more than two steps, he was up and out of his seat. I grabbed a handful of spaghetti from his plate, and continued approaching him. He was backing up now with his hands held out to protect himself, and a devastatingly beautiful smile on his face. I couldn't believe it.

"Stop," he said. "I was kidding."

"Oh were you now?" I mocked, unable to control my own smile which had stretched my lips painfully taut. When his back reached the wooden wall, I rushed at him but was abruptly stopped when his hands came out to still mine in mid-air.

He started laughing as I struggled to lower it enough to reach his face, but when he still wouldn't let go, I just flicked the food at him. He swerved his upper body to the right so that he could avoid it but it was too late. The sauce soaked spaghetti hit the side of his head, and trickled down onto his shoulder.

Laughing, I immediately started to move backwards as he slowly wiped the food away from his face. He reopened his eyes and watched me as I continued to retreat, but when a sharp scream from across the room briefly distracted me, I turned back to him, only to find that he had moved. Instantly I turned on my heels so that I could get away, but I wasn't quick enough.

The next thing I knew, his hand had caught mine and I was screaming in delight as he pulled me against him. With one solid arm around my middle, he glued me to him and stretched his free hand so that he could reach the nearest plate. I continued struggling to get away, trying my best to pull his arm from around my waist until my legs had practically left the floor.

But it was of no use. He was able to keep me against his tall frame, until his other hand came up to show me the food he had in it. With a loud shriek, I shot my hands up so that I could protect my head.

However he wasn't aiming for my head, but I didn't realize what he was planning to do until I felt the warm food on my legs. Before I could react, he had rubbed it all the way up my thigh. Almost jumping out of my skin, I flew out of his hold and started to swipe at it while he just watched me with a wide smile, entirely too pleased at my horror.

I started to reach for the bowl of sauce that he had gotten for me but out of the corner of my eye, I saw him move so quickly that one minute I was reaching for the bowl and the next my hands were held together in his.

"Nathan let me go!" I said, in a tone that I had hoped would sound stern enough for him to comply, but instead the words came out in a giggle. He shook his head and held on, our gazes firmly fixed on each other until my back finally met the wall.

Suddenly, the deafening shrill of a whistle rang across hall and we stopped, our faces ablaze with amusement. But slowly, and as a semblance of order began to fill the room, the magic dissipated and he let me go. Our smiles waned, gazes faltered and soon, he had turned away to face the houseparent who now stood at the entrance of the hall.

"Wow! Dogs of Lancaster Academy. You respond well to whistles," Mr. Dwayne Cart said, and my head snapped up at his bitter tone. He was Grizedale's houseparent. Low-toned giggles broke out from every corner of the room, but I was done smiling- this wasn't going to end well.

He gave the hall a dark look that instantly quieted it down, and then in a yell, low enough not to offend but loud and angry enough to spike dread through our hearts, he said, "Are you all out of your minds? Where do you think you are? Who started this mess?"

As expected, no one answered him. He smiled sardonically. "It's good to see that you're all united in vandalism. As young adults, one would expect you'd have developed enough sense to act like proper human beings, even without supervision, but I can now see that I was deluded."

The murmurings heightened to a deafening buzz, but again quieted down when he turned his hostile gaze around the room. Three of the other house parents who had been around but unable to stop the fight, scowled behind him. Bowland's Mrs. Lucy Ryan, Lonsdale's Margaret Hetcher and Cartmel's Michael Beveridge. An assistant I'd seen around also stood a little ways away from them but I couldn't remember what house he belonged to. Our Pendle's Mariam Kempster was absent, as well as Mr. Cassidy Maine. What an amiable house we were.

"Thank God it's Friday," he said as he looked around, a wicked smile stretching the corners of his lips. "This hall could use an overnight scrubbing."

Gasps erupted throughout the room. Someone muttered in disbelief behind me; "he wouldn't", but as he continued, we came to realize that he actually would.

"The halls have been locked, so don't even dream of going back anytime soon," he said. "As you all know, there are taps behind the hall in the kitchen. The stewards will provide you with buckets and other cleaning materials. Scrub this place until it's clean enough to eat from the floor."

The murmuring turned into full-blown complaints, but Mr. Dwayne Cart ignored it. "Everyone cleans the area in which they sat – from the tables to the benches and to the plates and cutlery you used. If there are any stains on the wall, wipe them clean. If no one on your table is tall enough to get to any of the spots, get a ladder. You're welcome to break your necks in the process."

Muffled laughter was hard to miss. He went on, "There were at least seven of you on each table, so one of you should have enough sense to know how to divide the chores amongst yourselves."

He glanced at his watch. "We'll be back in two hours, and if the work's not complete by then, I'll give you an extra two. So if you prefer, take it all as a joke. You'll end up staying here till morning."

He turned to leave, but then stopped and turned back to us. "One more thing," he said. "There's extra duty. So any table that doesn't meet my satisfaction in anyway, will stay up and clean all the hallways ... in all the houses. Tonight. And trust me, there will be some tables that I don't like. And since you are all smeared like rats, I wouldn't want your filth messing up my hallways as you return to your rooms now would I?"

He gave a dry smile. "Have fun," he said before he walked out, the other three filing out after him.

"Is he allowed to talk to us like that?" I heard someone say from behind me, in a deep Russian accent. I rolled my eyes in disgust; *Like that was what mattered now.*

With a heavy heart I took a good look at the hall, no longer with a quiet admiration for how exquisite it was, but with a serious dread for how long we were all going to spend cleaning it. Thankfully, the wooden walls on our side didn't look as bad as some of the others further down, and better still, the stone walls that extended to the roof from its eight-foot glory, also looked untouched.

The rows of portraits that hosted past headmasters seemed to be smiling down at us in mockery. I sighed, and like most people, wandered off in search of the taps. I couldn't stand one more second as soiled as I was.

Nathan had left the hall as soon as Mr. Cart had finished speaking. In my years at Lancaster, playing with him the way I had during the food fight was the first time that I'd actually let my hair down enough to enjoy something, especially something as senseless as a food fight. I was reminiscing about his arm around me when I met the impossible crowd that was already gathered at the taps. That quickly wiped any more fantasies out of my mind as I tried to find a way to help myself.

After waiting for a while, I got my turn and I immediately loosened my hair so that I could wet my fingers with the gushing faucet and run it through them. It was a little damp when I was done, but it didn't bother me. I moved down to my leg and as I washed the grime away, I remembered the brief, but fiery thrill that I had felt when he had rubbed his hand along it. *God...* now that I was thinking about it, it had been a fairly inappropriate thing to do, but then I hadn't been thinking straight. Now I was, and I wished he'd have taken his time.

I washed my face when I was done, and dusted at the front of my t-shirt. Anymore and I'd be thoroughly embarrassed since the shirt was white – or had been before Nathan had decided to splash orange juice all over it. I caught myself smiling at the thought as I walked away, and then I frowned when I realized that I shouldn't have been amused.

Straightening my back, I returned to the hall to see that everyone on my table was present. James looked like he had bathed in tomato sauce, but it obviously didn't concern him as much as it did me because he was standing in front of the table, and speaking. Nathan, on the other hand, was leaning casually against the wall with his arms folded across his chest. Apart from a small stain on his shoulder and his slightly damp hair, he looked almost spotless and it made me wonder if I had only imagined his participation in the fight.

He started to turn towards me – or at least I thought so – so I removed my eyes from him and focused on returning to my seat. The couple were leaning against each other, while the other two boys looked like they'd rather be idly gazing at stars than participating in the chore we were about to embark on. James was just finishing when I got to them.

"Lenora," he called out smiling, and everyone turned to look at me. It made me feel uncomfortable, so I quickly sat down. James however continued to stare at me but he snapped out of it when I started to frown.

"What?" I asked.

"Uh, nothing. We just thought you'd bailed on us." he said. I didn't think I needed to answer that so I just waited for him to address me.

"We've just divided the chores," he told me. "We'll handle the tables, while Eric and Seth will head over to the kitchen to wash the dishes. Alexandre will handle the walls since he's tall while they –" he pointed to the couple, "– will handle the floor. Are you okay with that?" he asked.

I nodded. "Yeah. It's fine."

"Okay. Let's get to work," he said. He turned to the boys to ask, "Can you guys come help me get the materials?"

They took a couple of moments before rising, but even that I suspected, was just because James was a year above them and a prefect. I didn't miss the dark scowl Nathan gave to them when they started to complain. As they walked away, Nathan pulled himself away from the wall and took a seat on the bench. With his back against the table, he brought out his ear phones and plugged it into his ears.

If I had had any doubt about his intention before, I had none now. He had literally turned his back on me. Trying not to become upset because that would just be ridiculous, I looked away from him, and focused my attention on the rowdy hall. However a few minutes after, the couple drew my attention back to the table when they stood up, and started to leave.

"Where are you going?" I asked.

"We'll be back soon," the boy answered, but when I realized that their absence would leave me alone with Nathan, I tried getting them to stay.

"James will be back soon," I said, but it didn't stop them.

"We won't be long," the girl said. "Plus our chore is the last one so you guys won't need us till later. We'll be back," she assured me before she ran off with her boyfriend.

Nathan of course ignored me, which made me a little ashamed that I had even bothered trying to keep the couple with me. He had probably forgotten I was even seated there.

James came back a few minutes later looking almost angry, and it was surprising since I'd never even seen him frown before.

"Bad news," he said as he reached us, surprised to see the table almost empty. "There's not enough utensils for everyone so we'll have to wait our turn. The punishment isn't the cleaning, it's the wasting of our goddamn time. Do you mind us getting started on the table?" he asked me.

"No, it's fine." I answered.

He tossed a damp dish cloth to me, so after moving our tableware to a corner by the wall, we started to wipe down the furniture. Not long after, Nathan was able to get a bowl of water so he started on his chore too. I had finished with mine and was seated, when I heard Nathan call my name. James had gone to the kitchen to check on Eric and Seth.

"Do you want to go to the stream tomorrow?" he asked, when I turned to him.

"Uh … I don't know," I replied, surprised that he was asking me. Then I remembered that I was supposed to have confronted him about letting me stew in my fear. I decided to let it go.

"Well, if you want to, I'll be going in the morning," he said, and he returned to wiping the wall.

"Thanks, but when I want to I'll just go on my own.

"You can't." he said. "Because I have the key to the place,"

I frowned. "Why do you have the key to the place?"

"It's not exactly a common area is it?"

"Then how do *you* have access to it?"

"It's none of your concern. You weren't even supposed to find out about it."

"But I did, didn't I?" I sneered. "And I wouldn't want to go with you anyway since you enjoy letting people stew in their fear when they get lost."

He didn't even try to look surprised. He knew exactly what I was talking about.

"You *chose* to get lost," he said.

I scoffed. "And so that gave you enough reason to let me almost die there?"

"I didn't leave." he said, looking almost bored. "If I had you might have actually not found your way back, and then the whole school would be searching for you. Shouldn't you be thanking me for that?"

"I should, but I won't. You probably would have been happier if I'd stayed lost and never came back."

The coldness returned to his gaze when I said that, and I instantly felt his withdrawal like a shadow at the appearance of light. He turned away from me without a word and continued with his task.

« CHAPTER 10 »

We left the hall around 10:30pm, after almost three hours of waiting. Tables that hadn't met the acceptable standard were set on extra duty until about 11:30pm, since they had to clean the hallways that we stained as we returned to our rooms. No one had any strength to do anything else that evening, so most people just collapsed on their beds. Only a few remained awake to chat about the events of the evening. I was more than exhausted, but still, I couldn't sleep.

I had made the statement about him not caring if I came back, not because I had actually meant it but because some part of me had wanted him to refute me and insist that he would have cared. But instead, it had annoyed him.

He'd been civil enough until we'd all gone our separate ways, but now I felt like one of the many other girls that he never paid any attention to, and it made me ponder religiously on how to rectify it.

His offer still stood I supposed, and I wanted to take it, but I didn't imagine that he'd want me there anymore. I tried pushing the whole issue out of my mind and completely forgetting about him, but when hours later, my eyes were still wide open and thoughts were still coursing through my head so much that I forgot to blink, I decided to take another approach.

Maybe I could be just his friend, and wipe away any notions I had conceived of it being anything more than that. That would mean that I could accept the offer and if I got to the storage room and he told me that he had withdrawn it, I would feel absolutely nothing whatsoever, and casually return to my house.

Yet, by 10:30 the next morning, as I pushed the door to the storage room open, I wondered why my heart was pounding so painfully in my chest.

As expected, the door behind the bookcase was locked so I leaned against the wall beside it to wait, and eventually just slid down to the floor. I was considering leaving about forty-five minutes later when the door to the room opened, and he came in.

He was dressed just like me with our house's white jumper, and dark jeans. He also had what looked to be a small white cake box in his hands, and his backpack was slung over his shoulder. He offered his hand when he reached me and I held it to pull myself up, but ended up being too close to him.

"How long have you been here?" he asked. I decided to exaggerate.

"Two hours," I answered. He just stared at me.

"You're lying," he said after a few seconds, and turned to slot in the key

"What makes you think that?" I asked, and moved inside after he pushed the door open. He shut it behind me and handed the box over, then went ahead to pull the rug aside. He opened the trap door, and then stood up to face me.

"Let's just say I know when you're lying."

For some reason, my heart fluttered.

"Well, that's just not true," I said, but he ignored my response, and moved on to the topic that I'd hoped that he wouldn't bring up.

"You gave me the impression that you weren't going to be here today," he said. It sounded like an accusation.

"Well I changed my mind."

He didn't say anything else, and I didn't know whether to be relieved or angry at him. I wanted so badly to know what was going through his head.

Taking the box from me, he headed down the trap door while I waited until I was certain that he had reached the ground, before I followed. I was about midway through when I felt one of his arms encircle my waist, and lift me off the ladder.

It was startling and unsettling, but not until he had placed me on the ground did I complain.

"I can take care of myself," I said, my voice bouncing off the tunnel walls, creating an echo.

"Probably," he said in a lower tone. "However I don't want to spend forever down here, because just in case you haven't noticed, this tunnel is kind of creepy."

"That's exactly what I thought when I first came here," I said, pleased that my initial fright had been validated. "I thought I was going to get eaten or something."

He switched on a flashlight and shone it directly in my face. "So even though you were terrified, it didn't occur to you to return to school?"

I squinted against the rays and swiped at it to get him to move it away. Taking my hand, he started to lead me through the tunnel, and I couldn't resist the smile that came to my face.

"Do you know how this tunnel came about?" I asked.

"Yeah," he replied. "The soldiers used it during World War I."

"Now I'm even more terrified. So the school knows about it?"

"Of course they do. It's just been ignored, I assume."

"So how did you find it?"

"I searched for it. I read about its history and found it at the end of last term when I came down with James to sort out some storage inventory."

"So he doesn't know about it?"

"No. No one was supposed to,' he said, and with his hand on the small of my back and an accusatory look in his eyes, he led me forward until we reached the end of the tunnel.

We emerged outside and into the forest, then immediately began our walk towards the stream. It was a warm day as the bright sun shot its rays through the openings the trees provided. So although there was a slight chill in the air, the breeze was warm enough to be accommodating.

"How many times have you been here?" I asked, when I saw how confidently he made his way through parts I could barely remember.

"I spend most days after school here ... and sometimes during school." he answered.

It explained why I never saw him – he was never in school.

We arrived at the stream, and for a few seconds I even forgot he was with me. It was just as breathtaking as it had been the first time, and as I rushed over to the rocky banks, he yelled out to me to be careful.

Finding my way over to the huge rock that I'd sat on last time, I removed my tennis shoes and socks, rolled up my jeans, and lowered myself onto it. The rush of the clear water was powerful today, and as I watched it hiss along the beautiful array of rocks and plants that threatened to hold it at bay, I couldn't remember ever feeling more peaceful. It was fascinating enough to hold my attention for a few minutes but soon, my eyelids began to grow heavy. Nathan's sharp call however, snapped me out of it.

I looked up to see what he wanted but when I couldn't see him, I left the rock and made my way to the land. He had spread a blanket on the ground, close to a massive tree and was sitting, his ankles crossed and his back against the trunk. He had a book on his lap, and a pair of dark-rimmed glasses sitting on the crook of his nose. When he saw me approaching, he slipped a bookmark between the pages he was currently on, and then closed the book to rest it by his side.

"I didn't know you used glasses," I said as I reached him, and crossed my legs to land softly on the blanket. I would have never considered myself to have 'a thing' for glasses, at least not until now, but with the way they framed his beautiful eyes, I knew that a fetish for dark rims had just been planted in my heart. *As well as a fetish for silliness*, I added, appalled at the thoughts that were popping up in my head.

He just smiled in response, and dragged his backpack towards him. He brought out a little black bag, and unzipped it to retrieve a cutlery cloth roll. Next, he got out a small pack of cake candles and a lighter, before he took off the lid to the box.

I was rendered speechless as I watched; the loud chirping of the birds above us, and the increasing pace of my heart thumping in my ears as he started to stick the candles in a whipped cream cake, decked with strawberries and with the message- *HBD Nora* written on it.

My breath caught at the back of my throat. And as he battled with the wind that kept on putting out the flames he was trying to use to light the candles, I felt an ocean of tears fill my eyes and then roll down my cheeks. He turned then to look at me, but I instantly turned my head away, and used my hands to wipe the tears off my face.

"Are you alright?" he asked. I nodded and gave him a reassuring smile.

"How did you know?" I asked as he lit the last one.

He answered without looking at me. "I filled out your clinic form the first time you fainted in the corridor," he said as he straightened.

Instead of meeting his eyes, I watched the tiny flames flicker as the breeze harassed them. Then I laughed out loud when they all finally blew off, and he turned to see his hard work destroyed. He just shook his head and gave up.

"Why did you bother?" I managed to ask, amidst my heavy amusement, but he thought I was talking about the candles.

"It's supposed to add effect or something," he said, but he realized when he turned to me that it wasn't what I was referring to.

"I don't know," he answered. "I just felt like I should. And I know it's late," he continued, "But it's been a hell of a week and I didn't think about it early enough."

He handed one of the sandwiches to me and I said quietly. "I still hate you."

"Of course," he nodded and then smiled, that genuine, breathtaking grin that I was beginning to fool myself into believing he brought out for just me. He retrieved a table knife, and thrust it into the middle of the cake.

"So, how are we doing this?" he asked.

I shrugged.

"Do I have to sing?" he asked, and the dread in his voice made me laugh.

"Actually, you do,' I said.

He shook his head. "Never."

"You have to," I insisted, but he ignored me and took my hand to place it on the handle of the knife. I started to move my hand away but he pushed it down, and the knife slid smoothly through.

"You cheated," I accused, but he just chuckled.

"Happy Birthday in arrears," he said in a whisper soft voice, and with a look that he'd never given to me before. It was sultry and moved from my eyes down my body, in a tease that made my cheeks flush with heat. He looked away to cut out two humongous slices while I raised my hands to my cheeks, afraid that they had turned visibly red. *What was that?*

"Thank you," I said when he handed a paper plate to me.

"So when is *your* birthday?" I asked, after I had begun to pick at the frosting. He handed me a fork, which I refused, and when part of the frosting dropped down to my lap, he retrieved a sheet of tissue and handed it to me. He took another, and to my surprise, he wiped the cream off my jeans. He offered me the fork again.

"Use it," he insisted, but I refused. Shaking his head, he put it away and continued to eat his slice.

"When's your birthday?" I asked again.

"Don't worry about it."

"Don't do that," I said.

He sighed. "It's on the third of June," he said, and I immediately stored it in my brain.

"Thanks again," I said, and he nodded.

"You know, you should use your hands," I suggested. "It's sweeter this way."

He seemed amused. "Probably, but I can't stand the mess."

"Interesting," I said. "Given the fact that you thought nothing of soiling me yesterday, and somehow ended up spotless."

"I wasn't. I had stains on my shoulder."

"And I was stained all over."

He chuckled, and I thought of how much he sounded like a patient elder when he did that.

"So where did you order the cake from?" I asked.

"Cornish," he said. "It's a little bakery in town. It arrived this morning."

"Ooh, you mean that place close to Domino's? On your way to the Town House?"

"Yeah. It's on Penny Street."

"I've been there once. Couldn't make up my mind, so I just left and went to McDonald's instead."

"*Hmm*," I groaned as the cream and red velvet cake melted in my mouth. "This is *good*."

He nodded his head in agreement.

We started talking and laughing about our pastry experiences, until eventually we got tired of eating and just laid on our backs to stare at the sky. I shamelessly ate more than half of the cake while he struggled to finish just one slice. It turned out that he didn't like sugar as much as I did, but preferred spicy foods.

"So what made you so upset that day?" he asked softly, and the grin I had been nursing, shrunk.

"I'm always upset," I said with a small laugh, but after a few minutes had passed, and he didn't say anything else I decided to just tell him.

"It was the day my mom died," I said. "Three years ago."

He was silent for longer than I would have liked before he asked, "How? If you don't mind."

"No it's fine," I said and took a deep breath. "It was a car accident. She'd just had a fight with my dad and was going away to her best friend's house," I said. "They used to fight a lot. I was in the car with her and then I asked her a question. One moment she was looking at me, and the next… I was on a hospital bed, and the doctor was telling me that I'd never see her again."

An eagle shrieked in the distance.

"Why didn't your dad tell you himself?" he asked.

"That's a whole other story."

We were silent for some time, and then I said. "I used to blame myself at first, because I reasoned that if I hadn't distracted her with my question, then she would have kept her eyes on the road."

"Don't do that." He said.

"I know." I responded. "I chose not to think about it when I realized that if I did, it was just going to eat at me until it destroyed me. It doesn't mean I don't believe it, but I've just chosen not to dwell on it."

He turned to face me. "Are you an only child?"

"Yeah … you?"

I could feel the smile in his voice when he responded. "We're four – all boys. I'm the last," he said. "I always wondered what having a sister would have felt like though."

I could sense him trying to shift the topic and I appreciated it. "I always wanted a brother, and I know exactly how it would have felt. It would have been awesome. Boys I think, are the coolest people ever. Girls are too complicated."

"Says the girl who has given me more hell in a few days than I've known in an entire year," he said, and I laughed.

We spoke for a while after that until we ran out of neutral topics of conversation. I began to feel drowsy but just before I shut my eyes, he rose and walked towards the stream.

Lying on my side, I watched him go, my eyelids heavy with exhaustion. With his hands in his pockets, he just stood on the banks and gazed straight ahead for more minutes than I could count.

Even in my drowsy state, I was still basking in the euphoria I felt from being with him and communicating with him. It felt like every dream I'd ever had, had come true, and that was beyond silly because I didn't have any dreams. But I was sure that if I ever did, and they came true, this was exactly how I'd feel- excited and awed and content, all at once. Like I needed nothing more to make me happy.

I realized it was a dangerous reaction that I was letting myself indulge in, but he made me want to just throw away my reservations and learn to lean on somebody else for a change. Having to be strong and act hard when I knew I was anything but was exhausting, and I wanted more than anything to let go, even if it was just for a little bit.

A little over an hour later, I opened my eyes to meet the view of a dull sky. Instantly, I remembered where I was and turned my head to meet Nathan's gaze as he sat with his back against the tree. He was watching me, and it was uncomfortable, so I sat up and subtly checked for drool signs at the corners of my mouth.

"I'm sure you realize how creepy that is," I joked, trying to smooth out my hair, but he didn't say anything.

"We need to get back," he said, and I wasn't too happy to hear that.

"Already?"

He nodded, and then got up to start putting his things together. I helped, and in no time we were back to school.

When we reached the residences, we met the sports field packed with students watching a football match that was going on between the Lonsdale and Cartmel boys. Others who wanted to just enjoy the day were either sitting on the pews, or laid out on blankets by the corners of the field. It was a cool afternoon, and everyone seemed to be making the most of it.

After a light brush of my hand, Nathan headed towards his dorm while I went to mine. On my way, I thought back to our day; his battle with the candles, his surprise and my complete and utter tranquility. He'd left the cake box with me, so as I repeatedly glanced at it, I couldn't help the smile that rose to my lips.

« CHAPTER 11 »

I headed straight to my room to change into more comfortable clothes. However, Kate bounded in a few minutes later in her full volleyball attire and her hair in a tight ponytail.

"Oh thank God you're here," she said, and I immediately grew wary.

"What do you want?" I asked suspiciously.

"We have a game in twenty minutes," she said. "Get dressed."

"What is that supposed to mean? Don't you mean *you* have a game in twenty minutes?"

"No, *we* both have a game in twenty minutes," she said, as she threw open my wardrobe to look for the jersey I'd been given for the society at the beginning of the year, and had only worn once. "I've been coming here all day but Olivia said she had no idea where you'd gone to. I wasn't at dinner last night so I couldn't tell you then."

I stood up, glaring at her. "And how am I suddenly playing volleyball in twenty minutes?"

"Well, I volunteered you," she said, as she turned to face me. "The society planned a friendly game with the boys and we were short of a player. Don't worry, it's not a big deal. It's just for fun."

My face darkened. "Well, I am definitely *not* going. If I wanted to play volleyball I would've been active for the last eight months."

"Lenora, don't do this," she pleaded. "Everyone's expecting you."

"But I suck at the game!" I cried.

She sighed. "That's why I volunteered you, because it's not a real game. I suck too, but I want to have fun."

"Right," I said. "I'm sure you're on the school team because you *suck*."

"C'mon. It's a society thing not a team thing," she said as she pulled my shoes out from the bottom of the wardrobe. "We're late and I'm not going without you. Unless you want Elka to take my head off later," she added, referring to her house prefect. "Please Lennie."

"Fine," I said, and pushed her away from the wardrobe so that I could search for my things.

Ց

We arrived at the court ten minutes later to meet more people present than I would have liked. It was of course, better than the mayhem that was currently taking place on the field, but having more than half of the bleachers on both sides filled, was just as nerve racking. I headed to the locker room to quickly change, then returned to see that the teams were already huddled together.

Dragging my eyes away from the excited male spectators that sat watching, I followed Kate as we met up with the rest of the team. I knew why they were there of course. The spandex shorts female volley ballers were obligated to wear hugged our behinds like a second skin, and in most cases, were so short that they rode high to almost the top of our thighs.

The uniform always bothered me, which was why I had gotten mid-thigh spandex shorts to replace the much shorter ones I had initially been given. I stood out immediately from the rest of the team as some even had their butt cheeks proudly sticking out. Boys on the other hand wore loose above-the-knee shorts, so I had always wondered what the deal was with the female uniforms.

My hair was still wild so as Elka started to lay out some basic instructions for us, I tamed it to the back of my head with a black hair tie. We were going to have a best-of-three sets match to twenty-five points each, and there was no catch— just plain, hard fun or in my case, hard torture.

I still didn't understand why I had agreed to this. Usually, an unyielding 'no' was the easiest word for me to say, but nowadays, it was almost as if my shell was melting. Most things got to me now more than ever, and it was beginning to scare me. I decided to just survive this one and then revisit my resolve to become a robot.

Kate grabbed my hand and dragged me along as we headed over to meet the boys. She seemed to be jumping out of her skin with excitement and I had no idea why, but all that faded when we stood face to face with the six boys … and Nathan's blue eyes, locked with mine.

He was at the extreme end with James by his side, and averted his eyes as soon as they had locked with mine. James said something to him as Elka called out the girls that would be collaborating with their team, and he smiled, the heart-stopping grin that I had been subject to all morning. Unlike the rest of us with jerseys, he had on a white t-shirt that although loose on his lower body, clung perfectly to his sturdy upper body.

Kate's small squeal startled me as her name was called, and she, along with two other girls went over to join the boy's team. I didn't recover early enough to feel disappointed that I wasn't chosen to be on his team, until we had taken our positions on the court with me at the extreme right corner of the back row. The pressure was on, now more than ever, and I was so sure that I was going to completely humiliate myself.

With a loud shrill of the whistle from Elka, who was now the referee, the game began. Kate served excellently from her side of the court. It flew through the air, bounded off the arms of the two players in our team that were supposed to receive it, and was sent back by the third to Nathan's team. It came back almost immediately with a dizzyingly fast block that was played by a really tall boy next to the net, and of course, hit the ground of our court to the delight of his teammates – a point to them and none to us.

The point of the game was to earn points by grounding the ball on the opposing team's court or having them commit a fault, which I did more than twice by both touching the ball consecutively, and completely missing it when it was passed to me. After the first set, which brought the other team to twenty-five points to our thirteen, I started to consider pleading with the team to let me go. I was doing more harm than good.

They all spread out to retrieve their water bottles as soon as we had a break, so I was left standing and looking lost in the middle of the court. I did manage to find my hair tie, which had flown away during the game, and used it to secure my sprawling hair- more tightly this time around.

Heading up to the bleachers, I sat behind the team as they talked and drank, thinking of how to bring up the subject of my leaving. I could always say that I had developed a headache or that I was sick – anything, but I just had to get out of there. I had caught Nathan's gaze on mine only once during the game and it was when I had let the ball, that had been clearly aiming for me, pass through my outstretched arms. It had been humiliating, and I had quickly looked away to hide my shame.

Another loud shrill brought us together, and Elka addressed us. "Some people have brought the obvious fact to our attention that some of you are suffering out there." She said. I quickly looked away, but turned back when I heard everyone laugh as she pointedly looked at a red-haired boy on Nathan's team. He was apparently worse that I was. I had been too occupied with my own failures to notice.

"So we're switching members ..." she said, and she raised her voice to speak over those who had started to grumble, "... *since* this is a friendly game and we're supposed to have fun and help each other!"

"Alexandre and ... Kate, would you exchange with ..." She turned to examine our team. "Marcus and James." She looked again. "Laura and Sam, please exchange with Joseph and ... Lenora. No! Stacy." She examined her damage. "I think that should do. Hope everyone is okay with that. We begin in three minutes guys," she said, and the new teams returned to their seats to get acquainted.

Kate immediately latched onto me as we walked back, but I was too nervous to pay attention enough to scold her for getting me involved in this in the first place. We took our seats and to my surprise, Nathan came over and sat next to me, a sports water bottle in his hand. Kate tightened her hold on my arm, but when I turned to ask her what was wrong, she just stared straight ahead, her neck stiff and lips tightened.

"Are you thirsty?" Nathan asked, and although I for some reason couldn't meet his eyes, I nodded and took the bottle he offered.

"You're doing well out there," he mocked, and this time I met his eyes with a murderous glare. He grinned. I raised the bottle to my mouth and after a good, long drink, handed it back to him. He immediately raised the bottle to his lips and took a good long drink for himself.

The lower part of my stomach tightened in response to the familiarity of his act, but there was no time to dwell. It was time to get back on the court. However, just before we split up and took our positions, he briefly held my hand and whispered into my ear, "Just have fun."

I shook my head. "Impossible."

He let go with a smile, and headed to his front row position while I headed to the back. I met Kate's frown as she headed to the front too, and I wondered what her problem was.

Nathan got me to serve the ball, twice, and each time he came to my side and softly spoke instructions to me. It was uncomfortable because a lot of eyes were on us, but there was too much pressure all around for me to dwell on that. The game was too quick for him to guide me in playing properly, but each time I played in a weak way, he mouthed corrections as quickly as he could.

Time for dinner drew dangerously close and so we decided to end the game after the second set, which brought us to a win over the other team with twenty-five points to twenty-two. A tie in total, and I was more than happy when the whistle shrilled the game to an end. Nathan walked off toward James without a word, leaving me subtly staring after him until Kate came up to me.

"What the hell just happened?" she asked, and I turned a puzzled gaze on her.

"What do you mean?"

"Alexandre," she said. "How do you know him?"

"Uh, we just met a while ago."

Her voice rose. "He's the one I've been telling you about. Why didn't you tell me you were friends with him?"

I noticed a couple of heads turned to us so I frowned at her. "How was I supposed to know he was the one that you were talking about? And we're not friends. I just know him."

"How can you say you aren't friends, or did I not just watch the both of you practically play the game together?"

I was surprised that she seemed so upset about it. "I didn't know he was the one you were talking about, okay?" I said, but she scoffed in disbelief.

"That can't be true."

"I'm serious," I insisted, wondering why I was even bothering to convince her.

"I told you he was Italian."

"Nathan's not Italian Kate, he's Portuguese," I said.

She was confused. "Wait, what? Who's Nathan?"

I realized my error. "I mean Alex. Nathan's his middle name."

Her mouth dropped open, and I wanted to slap it shut.

"You already know his middle name?" she yelled, and I cringed from the noise. More heads turned.

"Kate you seriously need to stop yelling."

"But why didn't you tell me?"

"Again," I repeated, close to snapping. "I didn't know he was the one you were referring to."

"When did you guys meet? How did you start talking to each other?"

With an irritated look at her, I turned around and walked away.

"Lenora," she called and she came after me. I tried to think of the best way to end this fuss.

"We're family people," I said and she frowned.

"What's that supposed to mean?"

I didn't know what to say so I just ignored her, and grabbed my bag to head over to the locker room to change. She did the same.

"Tell me," she insisted.

"I'm really tired Kate, I'll tell you some other time, okay? Trust me it's not that interesting," I said.

"Fine then, but could you introduce me to him ... tonight at dinner?"

I groaned. "Kate, don't push this, I can barely stand the boy."

"Well it's not for you Lenora, it's for me. Can you please do it or not?"

"Fine," I muttered, needing her to drop the issue. She squealed in delight. I couldn't believe he was the one that she and Olivia had been pining over. I wasn't overly surprised, but I did feel stupid. It should have occurred to me.

We changed quickly and were soon on our way to the dining hall, but I couldn't help thinking- *what the hell had I just agreed to?*

ഇ

Kate made me go earlier than I would have to the dining hall, and we secured a table not far from the one Nathan had been at the previous night. We weren't too close, but at least we would be able to see him if he sat there again. Her friends were all on our table too because apparently, Nathan was the object of many a teenage obsession. I didn't realize I had started to wish that he wouldn't show up, until he strolled in with James a few minutes later and I'd felt depressed. He had now changed from his sports attire and was in a white hoodie, and dark jeans.

Returning my gaze to the novel I had since lost concentration in, I wondered how I was going to tell a boy I was barely acquainted with to come over and play Casanova. I was dreading it, and barely held myself from snapping at Kate when she called me to alert me to his presence.

"Go bring him over," she mouthed, and I gave her a 'you're-out-of-your-mind look'.

"Lennie," she urged.

I asked her if she was joking, "You want me to go over there and speak to someone that the whole school apparently has eyes on?"

"Come on."

"No way," I said. "I don't want to be labeled the next obsessed idiot – no offense. I'll try to get him to come over instead."

Turning my head, I tried to make eye contact with him but he was talking to James, and after a few minutes, I realized with a sunken heart that he was never going to look my way. I had to get up. I first of all made sure to tell Kate how much I hated her, and then I walked over to his table with a stern face, just in case anyone thought I was going there because I was smitten.

I was met with his soft gaze as I approached, and I sighed at how impossibly attractive he was. His hair was now slicked back from his face, and his eyes were intense enough to burn. I didn't blame Kate or any of the others waiting for him at the table. The first time I had laid eyes on him I had felt incredibly stunned, of course it hadn't held me back from breaking a tray on him and for that I felt braver than all the others. I hoped he wouldn't humiliate me too much as I reached his table, but before I could speak James looked up at me and smiled.

"Hey Lenora," he greeted, and I smiled back at him.

"Hey James," I responded before turning to Nathan. He was sitting on the edge of the bench.

"I need a favor from you," I said, low enough so that only he could hear what I was saying. He arched an eyebrow in surprise.

"Okay?" he said calmly, and I didn't fail to notice how the hall had suddenly become less noisy. Why was I just realizing all this now after I'd all but doused his face with spaghetti the previous night? I groaned as I took a quick glance around to catch the curious eyes on us. He noticed my distress.

"What's wrong?" he asked.

"Apparently half the school's in love with you," I said.

"That's not true," he said and I fought a smile.

"So," he continued, "what's the favor?"

"Someone wants to meet you," I said, eager to get this over with. He studied me for a moment.

"Why?" he asked, his voice back to the chilling calm I was familiar with.

After considering the question for a moment, I said, "I don't think it'll be proper to explicitly tell you why, so could we just take it as a favor? Please?"

He continued to watch me and I began to squirm under his gaze, at a complete loss on what was going through his mind. I expected that he was surprised, but what I prayed that he wouldn't be was offended, or rude if he did want to turn me down.

"Okay," he finally said, and my head snapped up in surprise.

"Are you serious?"

"Yeah," he said, like we were just going for ice-cream instead of going to prostitute him. Now I really wanted him to say no.

"Why didn't you say no?"

He was just about to get up as I said that, so he sat back down.

He sighed. "What do you want?"

"What do *you* want?"

"I just want to eat my dinner."

"Well I thought you'd say no."

"I thought so too," he said. "Do you want me to say no?"

I considered this for a moment, and finally said, "I don't know. I think we should just go and get it over with. It's not a big deal."

"Okay," he said, and he rose to go with me. James was watching us, probably wondering what was going on but he didn't ask so we left without speaking to him.

What the hell are you doing? I kept asking myself as we headed towards my table. I wasn't even certain that I could come up to talk to him whenever I wanted and here I was, acting the pimp. And worse, he obliged. *It has to be out of pity*, I thought, and shook my head at how pathetic I had become.

When we reached the table, I immediately went to my seat while he took the one that Kate had reserved for him beside her. I sat across from them and gazed at Kate, but she refused to look at him. She was trying to pretend like she didn't even notice that someone was sitting beside her and that aggravated me. Nathan smiled.

"Kate!" I called sharply, and she looked up at me, but shifted slightly away from Nathan.

I couldn't believe it. I had embarrassed myself for her and she was acting as though she was mute. I didn't know whether to slap her or flat out abuse her.

"This is Nathan," I eventually said, my voice thick with contempt.

It got her to raise her head to him, and mumble a greeting. Nathan, instead of being as irritated as I was, smiled and looked at her like she was the cutest thing since Oreos. He asked her a question, she answered, and they took it from there. I looked away and left them to it.

Nathan participated more fully than I would have expected him to. He spoke in his usual quiet voice, but it was more than enough to continuously draw giggles from Kate. It sounded like they were having so much fun that at a point, I had to look up from the book that I had been pretending to be engrossed in to see what was happening.

He was saying something about volleyball and she was grinning like an idiot, all traces of shyness gone.

He had completely charmed her, making little jokes that made her laugh and made my eyes widen.

He can actually be this warm? I wondered. Three seconds after meeting Kate he was acting like they were best friends, but it took us countless accidents to get to the point where we could even be civil with one another. The distaste and look of betrayal was apparently obvious in my gaze, because he smiled as he glanced up at me and said, "You can't blame me. She's cool."

Kate giggled again and I made sure to send her a look that warned her to control herself. I picked up my novel and tried to shut them out.

"Ahem," I heard him clear his throat, and I looked up to meet his gaze, and Kate's sparkling eyes.

"Um, *My Blood Approves*?" he asked, referring to the title of my novel.

"Do me a favor and mind your own business Nathan," I said.

He smiled, but Kate on the other hand was shocked at my tone; she couldn't seem to understand how anyone could be rude to Nathan.

"Lenora ..." she chided and I thought about pounding her head into the table. They returned to their chat, but when Kate said something to him and he bent down to plant a soft peck on her cheek, everyone froze, especially me. Somehow, my book left my hands and clattered noisily as it landed on the wooden table.

Nathan got up immediately after that, and without even a glance at me he walked back to his seat. Kate on the other hand had turned every shade of red. I felt a pain come into a corner of my chest that made me feel as if my heart was splitting into two.

Ignoring it, I picked my book back up, and told myself that she had to have been the one that had requested the kiss. Her friends however didn't think so; they were barely able to keep their excited voices down as they jostled her.

She was the star for today; Alexandre Roque had kissed her.

« CHAPTER 12 »

The weather was warm the next Monday morning, so at lunchtime, I was sitting in the courtyard and getting ready to dive into my meal. Class had barely registered in my memory since I hadn't been able to stop thinking about the kiss that Nathan had given to Kate, and how he'd properly ignored that I existed.

It bothered me more how much it had plagued me since then, but no amount of control on my part had been able to reign in the disheartening thoughts. Now however, and for a change, I was more than happy to focus on my beautiful golden French fries. But five minutes later, I was interrupted.

"Nora," I heard Nathan call. I turned around and saw him coming towards me. My mouth was loaded with fries so to salvage some shred of dignity, I looked away and chewed faster so that I could send the food down my throat before he reached my table.

"Don't call me Nora," I said when he reached me. I tried not to notice how good he looked.

"Oh, so we're back to that?" he asked, but before I could answer, he sat down and drew my tray to him.

"Hey, give that back," I said as I reached for it, but he held it away and parted his lips to give me the most beautiful smile I had seen yet. I cringed.

"What is wrong with you?" I complained. "You're all smiles these days."

He chuckled and grabbed my drink from the tray before returning it to me. I watched him take a sip from *my* straw and my insides began to melt. I should have been irritated but at that moment, all I wanted was to take the cup back and wrap my lips around it too.

You're crazy! I yelled in my head, and shook it to dispel my lunacy so that I could work up an appropriate reaction.

"Eww, that touched my mouth," I said in a flat tone.

He let go enough to reply to me, but wrinkled his nose first. "I know right." And then he teased. "You know, in a way, we just kissed."

I gave him a dry look, but the way he'd said the last word made me swallow. Unrepentantly, he returned his mouth to the straw and took a long slug before he pushed the cup back to me. I pushed it aside.

"So," he started, "why are you always alone?"

"Because I want to be," I answered sarcastically before smiling at him. "Could you please leave?"

He gave me a hurt look. "You chase me down for weeks and now you can't stand my presence?"

I gaped at him. "What do you mean I chased you down?"

He just chuckled and continued, "Kate is the only one I've ever seen you with and you're still not very close. It'd be nice if you made an extra effort in getting to know people."

I pushed more fries into my mouth, and slapped his hands away when he reached forward to grab some. He tried again, but this time got away with it.

"I don't need anyone Nathan, I'm fine on my own."

"Maybe, but you're definitely not fine on your own," he said, amused. I shook my head and looked away from him, only to meet the curious stares of a few people all over the yard.

Why am I only just noticing this now? I complained under my breath and I frowned when I saw his hand again reaching for a fry. I slapped it away, but he ignored the smack and came away with a few that he put straight into his mouth. Sparkling with a wicked glint, his eyes caught and held my glare, but neither of us looked away.

My breathing became ragged when seconds later, we were still staring at each other as we silently chewed our food. I turned away, and dragged the cup to myself for a drink.

He put his hand on mine, intending to say something but just when he started to speak, he looked up and saw something that made him stop.

Moving his hand away from mine, he lowered his eyes for a second and when he raised them up again, he had on another smile. It was a small one, and was so different from the ones I was accustomed to, that it surprised me.

It seemed genuine but there was a restraint to it, and as I heard the soft giggles that came up behind me, I understood why. I returned my mouth to the straw to hide my smile.

His blue eyes moved upwards and so did mine as Kate came to stand by our table, three other girls with her.

"Hi Alexandre," she said with breathy excitement, and I almost laughed out at the mouthful. I was so used to calling him *Nathan* that it seemed weird when people called him *Alexandre*.

"Hello," he said in a very quiet voice that had the right effect on all of them, including me. Our faces heated up, and Kate, feeling incredibly welcomed by his politeness, slid in next to him. The other girls came in after her and she somehow forgot to acknowledge my presence, as did the others.

They looked up at Nathan as though he had created the world, while he had his head casually turned away, looking as though even if he did, he regretted it. It warmed me how wary he was of attention and I almost began to pity him. But I reserved my concern when I saw how well he was able to mask it.

To them he probably looked the same but I could see his unease – the tightness of his lips as he smiled, and the stiffness of his shoulders. He heard my chuckle and turned to see me lift the straw to my lips. He snatched the cup out of my grasp.

"Nathan!" I complained, but he just ignored me and put his lips over it.

Kate and the girls watched with widened eyes as he took a sip, and then returned it to me. They hadn't realized that we were *that* familiar, not that I'd realized it either but at that moment, I didn't mind. He took the opportunity of their surprise to get up from the bench.

He held out his hand to the girls, who quickly recovered from their surprise, and took turns in introducing themselves; Beatrice, Ana, and the last one's name I didn't bother to catch. He shook Kate's hand last and then nodded at me.

I frowned at him as he walked away, while the other girls giggled and whispered amongst themselves. Kate, now recovered from her post-Nathan dazzle, finally noticed me.

"Lenora," she said, in a breathy voice.

I gave her a surprised look. "Oh, so you see me now," I said, and the smile left her face. "Are you sure I'm still not invisible?"

"Don't be silly," she said. I just shook my head and placed my mouth on the straw but tried not to make it obvious that I lingered on it.

Kate's narrowed gaze met mine so I took one last draw, and lifted my lips from it. "Alex just placed his lips on that." she said.

I shrugged. "So? It's mine."

"Well, it's just weird," she said. "Especially from you."

"Leave me alone Kate," I groaned, and returned to my now cold meal.

Her roommates said their goodbyes to her, and left the table.

"So," she said when they'd left. "Do you think he likes me?"

I stopped chewing. "Are you kidding me?" I asked, and she cringed from the show of mashed food still in my mouth. "You did this all through last evening. Do you want me to start avoiding you?"

"Well you know him," she continued sorely. "And I was just wondering if he's said anything today."

I sighed and tried to dull the harshness that I knew was going to be in my tone. "No Kate," I answered. "He hasn't said anything."

I watched her face turn somber so I added, "He doesn't talk to people much, and so far he's been open with you, so I'm sure that's a good thing."

I said *'thing'* instead of *'sign'* because I didn't want it to prompt her to start expecting anything. But from her delight, I doubted she noticed the difference.

"Are you serious Lennie?" she squealed, and she started her jabber again.

When I couldn't take it anymore, I stood up and with my tray in hand, found my way out of there. I returned to my classroom to eat my lunch, finishing it just as the bell rang and our chemistry teacher walked in.

« CHAPTER 13 »

I got a message from Carlie, my best friend back home in Miami, as soon as I got in that afternoon. She was upset that I hadn't contacted her in so long so when I saw that she was online, I immediately sent her a message. She replied a few minutes later and I was just starting to tell her about Nathan, when I was interrupted. Beverly had come into the room.

"Hi," she said with a bright smile.

"Olivia's not here," I immediately announced, hoping that she was searching for her sister and not me.

"Oh I'm not looking for Olivia," she said, and my heart sunk. "We have a meeting in the common room and we need your help. Do you mind?"

"Uh ... I sort of have a headache. I don't feel very well."

Her smile disappeared. "Well, I'm sure you'll feel better when you're with us. I expect you there now." She said, and turned to leave the room.

I said goodbye to Carlie after she left and minutes later, walked into the common room to find about seven of her friends lounging on the couches that surrounded the television. There were some students from my year playing a board game at the window seat, while some others were in the kitchen. Beverly called me over when she saw me.

"Mrs. Kempster said that she wants these books color-coordinated," she told me. I turned to see the huge bookcase that was built around the television and my heart sunk; I was going to be stuck here forever.

"I really don't feel well," I insisted, but she gave me a dirty look. It was clear then that I didn't have a choice, unless I wanted her and her friends to turn on me and that was the last thing I needed. So I headed to the bookcase and lowered myself to the carpeted floor to begin.

"Is she one of the girls that are all over Alexandre?" one of them asked a few minutes after I'd already started the chore. I briefly closed my eyes and exhaled; the hope I'd nursed that they'd at least ignore me now lost. I didn't hear Beverly's response but I assumed that she did, because almost immediately, the same girl spoke again.

"Eww," she said, and they all laughed.

"You guys shouldn't laugh," another said. "There's hope for them. This one took him over to their table last night."

"You're joking." A third girl said. She had a nasal voice that made me cringe. "What's he even doing hanging out with them?"

"It's a pity," Beverly said. "And that girl ... uh ... what's her name?

"Kate," supplied the one with the nasal voice.

"Kate. She got him to kiss her on the cheek last night. She's lucky she's not in Pendle but then again, it was this idiot that organized it."

"Hey, idiot!" she called, but I didn't respond. Almost immediately, a throw pillow hit my back. I turned then, and she spat. "Bring it back!"

Taking a deep breath, I reached for it and then slid it across the carpet to her.

One of the girls snorted, "Do you really expect her to pick it up?"

Sighing, I crawled over to the pillow and picked it up to hand over to Beverly. She didn't acknowledge it, but was now laughing with her friends over something funny that had come onto the screen.

I could barely contain my fury anymore, but I kept it in check because I lived in this house. And if I wanted to remain peacefully in it, I had to keep from starting a fire. So I decided to just do whatever they wanted, with the hope that this would be the last time.

I dropped the pillow on the stool beside her, and returned to the bookcase.

More than an hour later, I was nowhere near finished but had now sort of relaxed into the chore, since I kept on finding a lot of interesting books that I'd never expected were on the shelf. The insults had continued, and now all sorts of crisps and nuts that had been thrown at me to get me out of the way or to answer a question, littered the area around me.

It was humiliating, but getting the work done and over with as quickly as I could was more than enough motivation to keep me from reacting.

I had assumed that this was punishment for forgetting Beverly's errand the previous week, but it turned out that she probably would've forgotten about it if she hadn't repeatedly seen me with Nathan. The fact that she liked him was apparent as she talked with her friends on how she found reasons to spend time in his classes, just so that she could watch him. She had tried speaking to him on various occasions, but he'd always just smiled politely and walked away. She wondered why he was so distant, and since she had a boyfriend, there was only so much that she could do to find out.

I couldn't believe a lot of things they said as I worked. If I'd known weeks ago that all the care I'd taken to avoid any unnecessary attention was going to be burnt into a pile of rubbish, and all because of a boy, I'd have laughed my head off. But now here I was, and I didn't know what to do.

It did surprise me though that I wasn't as angry as I should have been. Maybe it was because the chore involved me working with books, which I naturally didn't have a problem with, or maybe it was simply because my life had become a little bit interesting. The highlight of my post-Nathan drama was still finding the forest, so as I sat there discovering more novels that I was excited to take upstairs with me to read, I also pondered on when I'd see him again so that I could ask him to the stream. It seemed that that was the only place I would ever have peace in.

§§

I didn't finish with the bookcase before dinner, but Beverly had long left with her friends so I put the uncoordinated books back in their place, and headed upstairs to get ready. Minutes later, I walked into the hall yawning, to see Kate at the table we had sat at the previous evening.

Luckily it wasn't full yet, so I walked over and sat next to her. I was just about to tell her what had happened when Nathan walked in with James. He wore his white house shirt over navy blue sweatpants and looked more than worth the trouble I had gone through. I sighed. This boy was complicating my life more and more by the minute.

I held my breath when he started to look around like he was searching for something... or someone, and eventually, his eyes came to rest on me. But still, I wasn't certain I was the one he was looking for so I stayed put. He raised his hand to flash the book that he had in it, and my heart jumped at the confirmation; he wanted to see me.

However, the last thing I wanted was to get up in front of everyone so I waved, and tried signaling to him to come over by pointing to my table. But he just stared pointedly at me. I got the message and rolled my eyes to let him know what I thought about his stubbornness, and then calmly made my way over to him.

Unfortunately for me, Beverly and two of her friends chose that exact moment to walk in. Again, I rolled my eyes at how complicated my life was indeed becoming. As soon as she saw me and noticed who I was going to meet, her smile broke. But I didn't expect it when she brushed my shoulders with hers as she walked past. I stumbled back a few steps but Nathan's hand was already on mine to steady me.

"Are you alright?" he asked. I nodded, but kept my head lowered so that he wouldn't see the anger in my eyes.

"What was that about?"

"It's nothing, just ignore it." I said and tried to focus my attention on him.

I forced myself to let it go, but the sound of their mocking laughter ringing in the air as they walked away drove even more nails into me. Nathan tightened his hold on my arm to get me to meet his gaze and I did, but I was already so upset my breathing had turned ragged.

He was studying me intently, trying to decipher what was wrong, but all I could think about was how I hadn't even done anything with him, and already I was a target. They'd ruined my afternoon, and now in front of everyone, embarrassed me. I decided right then to put on a little show for them; to give them something to really frown about. I took a step closer to him.

"Could you please put your arms around me?" I asked.

He blinked. Then as an amused smile slowly curved his lips, I felt a hot flush in my face. But I couldn't back out now- I didn't want to anyway.

"What?" he asked, and I repeated the request.

He took a brief glance around, then took what seemed like an unconscious step closer to me. Bringing his face closer to mine, he asked.

"Can I ask why?"

At that moment I completely forgot about Beverly; the feel of his warm breath on my face drove a steady frenzy through me as he held my eyes in a captivating hold.

"Please just do it," I eventually said, annoyed at how much he was able to affect me even when I felt hundreds of eyes boring into my back. When he still didn't seem convinced, I just closed the distance between us and lifted myself up on my tiptoes to wrap my arms around his neck. But still, he didn't move.

"Nathan," I whispered, fear rapidly filling me since it would soon become obvious that I was the one forcing myself on him. We were standing in front of an audience of more than a thousand for Christ's sake.

"Tell me why," he insisted again, and that hurt me. Letting my feet rest completely on the floor, I started to pull away from him but he surprised me when with a small laugh, he tightened my arms back around his neck, and wrapped his around my waist in a fierce hug. My feet completely left the ground.

"Hey!" I protested at his exaggerated display, and gave him a hard tap on his shoulder.

He released his hold, but not before planting a quick kiss on my forehead which I doubt anyone saw, but either way, it struck me dumb for a few seconds.

"That's two favors now," he again leaned in to say before handing the book over to me. I recovered enough to take the old but neat copy of J.R.R.Tolkien's *The Fellowship of the Ring*.

"Don't tell me you've read it already." he said. I shook my head.

"Well it's one of my favorite books, and dare I say it, but it should be an upgrade from your vampire novels."

"Hey!" I scolded. "Don't hate on my choice of literature."

"Those are *not* literature," he said with a soft tone, so I couldn't even take offense. Grateful, I took the book from him but when he gently brushed my hair away from my face I froze, because suddenly, I remembered exactly where we were and the eyes that were probably on us.

"Thank you," I said, and returned to my seat with my eyes lowered, refusing to check how much curiosity we had garnered. Sighing heavily on how I continued to make myself the subject of attention, I slid into my seat, only to meet the glares that the entire table gave to me.

I ignored them, but only realized later and well into the meal that Kate hadn't said a single word to me. I turned to see her toying around with the lasagna on her plate, and her eyebrows furrowed in a frown. Not wanting to make any assumptions as to why she was upset, I gently tapped her on her arm to ask, but she wouldn't look at me.

"Kate?" I called, but she took her time taking a sip from her glass of water, before finally turning to give me a cold stare.

"What?" she asked flatly. I was taken aback.

"What's wrong with you?"

"Nothing," she said and returned to her meal. I watched her for a few more seconds and then decided to mind my own business. I still refused to assume, but I hoped that it wasn't in any way related to me hugging Nathan, because if it was, I was going to be very disappointed.

So I kept to myself through the rest of the dinner hour, hoping she'd snap out of whatever was upsetting her and talk to me. She didn't, so I left the hall when it was time, alone and irritated.

℘

Kate came into class the next morning and although we didn't usually exchange greetings every time, our eyes did meet from time to time and she always offered a sweet cheery smile.

Today however, there was nothing from her, so when it was time for lunch, I hurried out of my seat to catch her before she could leave. When I caught her hand, she surprised me by pulling it away. Then she folded her arms across her chest.

I frowned at her, offended that she would act this way.

"Kate, I can't believe you're acting like this," I said.

When she still didn't respond to me, I went on to relieve her fears just in case that was what was bothering her. "There's nothing going on with me and Nathan, you know that right?"

Instantly, she reacted. "Are you kidding me, or did I not see him kiss you last night?"

"He didn't kiss me," I said. "And it was all an 'act' for Beverly; she bullied me because of him."

"What?"

157

"She made me color-coordinate the common room bookshelf yesterday, and as if that wasn't enough, she hit me when I stood up to collect a book from Nathan. I got angry, and that was why I put the show on. He just played along."

She seemed calmer now, but it was obvious that she was still upset.

"I don't think it's just that," she argued. "I see the way he is with you. He's so comfortable. I won't be surprised if he actually did like you."

"Don't be silly Kate," I said, but her tone increased.

"I'm *not*. How can you not see it? He does stuff for you, he listens to you. Out of the entire school you're the only girl he allows anyone to see him with and he's been here for a year. Tell me I'm being stupid again."

I was surprised. "So if you see it this way then why are you upset with *me*?"

"Because you're encouraging him by always being there. And it's so unfair because you don't even like him."

"But I introduced you to him."

"That's the thing- it doesn't even matter because he did that for you, not because he really wanted to know who I was and that's the problem right there. You're ... *there*, so he doesn't look anywhere else."

I couldn't believe this.

"So what do you want me to do?" I asked. "To not be there?"

She seemed reluctant, but that didn't stop her from saying it. "Yes," she said. "If you can manage it."

Suddenly none of this was interesting anymore, and at that moment, I wanted so desperately to put an end to all of it.

"Kate," I said, hurt at how selfish she'd just shown herself to be. "He can't be in love with me."

"Really?" she said sarcastically. "And what makes you think so?"

"Because we're related."

Her eyes widened. "Are you trying to be funny?" she asked, sounding offended that I thought her stupid enough to believe such a lie.

"No, I'm not, and it's the truth. We're cousins," I said, and tried not to imagine Nathan's face when he eventually got wind of this lie, because he was definitely going to find out.

"Really? How?" she asked, still skeptical. "Because in case you haven't noticed, he's from a different continent than you."

"His mom is American and she's my mom's aunty." I said, wondering why I couldn't have just said sister instead of aunty. It sounded too complicated even to my own ears. She watched me, and for a moment there I was sure that I had overdone it.

"I'm sure I've mentioned this to you before," I went on to add, hoping that her need to believe me would help her latch more easily onto the tale. It was wrong, I knew, but I didn't know how else to handle what was rapidly beginning to feel like chaos to me. I didn't keep myself out of the limelight for so long only to be brought into it for something as ridiculous as receiving attention from a boy.

When I could see her shoulders eventually relax, and acceptance gradually come to her face, I threw in another fable to solidify all the others. "That's why he helped me out, and that's why you see me with him sometimes." I dug a nail into the skin of my thumb to get me to shut up; I was overdoing it.

"I'm sorry I overreacted," she finally muttered. I forced a smile.

"No problem," I said, and then I turned around to return to my seat. I was pissed as I gathered my things and left the class.

₰⊕

Nathan called me when I got back to my room after school. I'd just returned from the bathroom to meet the incoming Skype call, and was surprised when I saw that he was the one calling.

Stunned, I just stared at the screen until it disconnected, and that pulled me out of my daze. However, when seconds later he called again, I rushed to grab the hairbrush off my table and roughly ran it through my hair. I was wearing a sweatshirt over my tank top so I was decent, but before I could get back to the call, it disconnected again. So with a racing heart, I plugged my earphones into my ears and called him back. He picked it up on the second to last ring. My eyes widened slightly as his face came into view.

"Hi," I said, but my voice sounded hoarse. I cleared my throat and repeated my greeting. I could see that he was seated at his desk and scribbling away, but only when he turned did I realize that he didn't have a shirt on. That drew a small cough from me.

"Hey," he replied, without looking up and I waited a few seconds before he finally did. "How was your day?" he asked.

I rolled my eyes.

He chuckled. "That bad huh?"

"That bad."

"Anything you want to share?"

"Nah. I did tell Kate we were cousins though."

"I've heard," he said flatly.

My jaw dropped. "Already?'

He shrugged. "What prompted it?"

"I don't feel it's appropriate to tell you," I said with a sigh and somehow, he either understood or just didn't care.

"Okay," he said, seemingly eager to get off the subject. "You have a math test tomorrow."

The reminder immediately depressed me.

"How do you know?" I asked, curious as to why he even knew that.

He frowned half-heartedly. "Does it matter?"

"It does," I teased, but he ignored it, and went on.

"Are you ready for it?"

I shook my head. "I hate Math."

"I've heard," he muttered, but I heard it.

I scowled at him.

"Get your notebook, let's do some work."

That surprised me. "You're kidding right?"

"I'm not," he said. "What did you get on your last test?"

I got a 'D' but I wasn't about to tell him that. He narrowed his eyes. "Let's pretend I don't know. Come on, get your books."

"But, on Skype?"

"Yes Nora, on Skype. Or would you rather see me in person?" he teased.

I cocked an eyebrow at him, and fetched the notebook from under my desk. He scribbled the problems down as I recited them to him, and then patiently went through each one- explaining until he was sure that I understood them. Sadly, he had to repeat himself a lot because I barely had the basics down, but at the end of the hour, we were almost done revising the concentration areas that Mr Barron had given to us.

I grew drowsy towards the end and in consideration, he finally let me go. I fell asleep immediately and got up just in time for dinner. Walking sluggishly, I found my way to the hall but was accosted at the door by a couple of girls I had seen with Kate on varied occasions. They dragged me away to sit with them and quietly, I watched as I suddenly became more important to them than whatever had made them ignore me for the last three years.

Kate was already seated when we reached the table so as soon as I sat down, they started with the attack. "Kate tells us you're cousins with Alexandre," one said.

"Oh my God," another squealed, "you're so lucky. You get to like talk to him a whole lot don't you?"

"Uh ..." I began, but another interrupted me. I didn't have concrete answers to their questions anyway so I just responded in grunts and nods, until I finally felt too uncomfortable to continue. I looked away and it was just in time to see Nathan walk into the hall.

He didn't look in my direction but just headed over to his table, and sat down quietly. He had an unusually dark expression on his face and I wondered why.

James started speaking to him as soon as he sat down, and as I continued to sneak peeks at them, I wished more than anything that I could ditch the nightmare that I was in at this table, and go over. It did hurt me a little though that he still hadn't bothered looking around to find me; no one would have guessed that we had practically spent the entire afternoon together.

"Lennie, please introduce us to Alex," one of the girl's finally said, and that brought my full focus to rest on all of them. *What?*

"He's in a bad mood," I replied.

"He seems fine to me," she said, and I turned around to see what she was talking about. Nathan was now smiling as James spoke to him and it surprised me; a moment ago he had seemed gloomy.

Before I could respond, Kate was already out of her seat, the girl that had asked me to introduce her to him with her, and they were heading towards him. I wanted to slap my palm against my forehead.

"What are they doing?" I asked, but turned when I didn't get a response to see the excitement on the faces of the remaining two girls as they watched their friends go up to him. Apparently I didn't exist anymore, so I just turned to watch what he would do.

I expected that he wasn't aware that they were heading towards him, so when he stood from the bench before they reached him and started to make his way towards the exit, my eyes widened in amusement. He did stop though, when Kate called out to him. They hurried over when he waited and although he didn't stay long, he seemed polite enough and flashed soft smiles at them before he finally excused himself, and went on his way.

Both Kate and her friend looked sour as he left, while I turned away to gloat silently. I did hope that he would be able to get something to eat before he slept since they had obviously made him miss dinner, even though as they returned with beaming faces, I didn't think they realized it. I logged into skype on my laptop as soon as I got back to my room so that I could confirm, but he didn't come online. I fell asleep waiting.

℘

My test was bad, but not horrible. At least I had had an idea of the problems; I just didn't remember the steps Nathan had laboriously explained to me. It darkened my mood and kept me wondering about what excuse I was going to come up with when he asked me about it. I really hoped he didn't.

When lunch came, I sat in the cafeteria at the far end of an empty table and silently ate. It was a bit silly but I was avoiding him, just in case he came by the courtyard. I was almost done with my food when Beverly came over with two of her friends. They had their trays in their hands.

"Move!" she said, and I raised my head to frown at her. Before I could do anything else she picked up my tray and carelessly dropped it on a nearby table. Its occupants looked up to see what was going on.

I was sick of the harassment, but the cafeteria was the worst possible place to lose my cool. So without a word, I took my tray along with me and finished my lunch in the courtyard. I refused to feel anything, but when I opened my locker a few minutes later to see that Nathan had left a note for me, I eagerly tore it open. It read:

Do you want to go to the stream on Saturday? 2pm.

Instantly, a wide, heartfelt smile broke out on my face. *Finally*, I thought; *I will have a little peace tomorrow.*

« CHAPTER 14 »

On Saturday, my hands trembled as I approached the storage room and it wasn't because I was more than twenty minutes late. I found him seated on the floor, but he got up as soon as he saw me. I sensed immediately that something was wrong with him, but I held my peace until we arrived at the forest. He laid a blanket on the cool ground for us and I sat on it, but watched as he walked quietly away from me and towards the stream. After a few minutes, he called out.

"How was your test?"

I blushed, and was glad that he was too far out to see how uneasy I'd gotten. I didn't respond but instead, began racking my brain to think of a way to change the subject. Then it occurred to me that I could use the woes of my failed test to tease him into lightening up, since there was obviously something that was bothering him. Assuming of course, that it wouldn't make him more upset than he already was.

Either way it was worth a try, so I removed my sandals and walked over to him. Today I had a pair of khaki shorts on, with a thin, white, extra-large shirt that hung off my right shoulder. My hair had been tamed into a very loose bun on the top of my head.

I had taken extra care with my appearance today so although it was casual, it wasn't as careless as it usually was. He watched me as I walked over to him and it made me feel thrilled at the appreciation, - whether it was real or imagined-, that I thought I saw in his eyes. I glowed under his scrutiny but for both our sakes, paid attention as I treaded carefully down the banks.

He took my hand when I reached the wide rock that he was standing on and gently led me from his side until I was facing him. Looking into his eyes, I took a deep breath and stepped closer to him until our chests were pressed against each other. His eyes widened slightly when he saw what I was doing, but he didn't say anything. He just watched to see what I wanted to do.

Wondering what the hell had come over me, I took my eyes away from his and hoped that for both our sakes, he wouldn't mock me too much because it was surely going to ruin the afternoon if out of annoyance, I pushed him off the rock and into the stream. Still avoiding his gaze, I lightly poked at his chest with my forefinger.

"You made me fail," I accused, and looked up to watch as the amusement that found its way into his eyes, replaced his previously dour look.

"You flunked the test?" he asked.

My frown deepened, but I didn't nod. There was still hope.

"I didn't flunk ... yet," I said and he laughed softly.

"You're a bad teacher," I accused, but he shook his head.

"I am *not*," he said, and surprised me by encircling his hands around my neck. He drew me even closer and rested his chin on my head. "You're just a very bad student."

An overwhelming warmth came over me as I encircled my arms around his waist, and leaned into him. It should have been inappropriate that we held each other like that, but in that moment, I couldn't have objected even if I wanted to. And besides, we were supposed to be 'cousins'.

We remained like that for longer than I expected and in those few minutes, I was able to hear the gentle beating of his heart; although the rush of the stream and the chatter of the birds overhead were almost loud enough to drown it. Tightening my hold around him, I eagerly breathed in his clean scent and relished his warmth as I was reminded of what contentment felt like.

"You didn't practice it, did you?" he asked.

I smiled sheepishly against his shoulder. "I was sure I'd remember how to do it."

"You only understood it when I explained to you. Knowing math takes practice."

"I know that," I said.

He loosened his arms from around my neck and with both hands on my shoulder, pulled me slightly away so that I could meet his eyes.

"I can't have you flunking your tests," he said, and tucked the tendrils of escaped hair that were now blowing across my face behind my ear.

I couldn't respond; I was too busy trying to remain sane from the way he was looking directly into my eyes. "I'll do better next time," I eventually said, and he nodded in agreement. "You will."

We continued to stare at each other until the thought occurred to me that if I just reached up on the tip of my toes, I would be able to kiss him. As soon as it did, it felt like my breathing slowed down. So I took my gaze away from his, and took a deep breath as I tried to think of something to say that would change the suddenly tense air around us.

His gloom from the previous night and earlier immediately came into my mind, so I returned my gaze to him and asked.

"Was something bothering you? Earlier you seemed a little... distracted."

His eyes narrowed in surprise.

"What makes you think that?"

I shrugged. "I don't know, you just seemed a little down. Is everything alright?"

Lifting his hand to my face, he gently stroked my cheeks and shook his head. "It's fine," he said. "I'm fine."

"Okay," I said, the dismissal of my concern a little disheartening. I started to pull away from him so I could head back to the clearing but he refused to let me go. Instead, he took my hand and slowly guided me to the rock closest to the water. We sat down on it and watched as the clear water lapped noisily against the rocks, and rushed downstream.

"One of my brothers sent me a message on Tuesday," he said, "just before dinner. He told me that my dad had a heart attack late last week..."

My breath caught as soon as he said that, but he hurried on to relieve my concern. "It's fine... he's fine; luckily it was a mild one, so he's already recovering. They didn't tell me immediately because they didn't want me to be unnecessarily worried about it."

"I'm so sorry," I said, feeling absolutely useless because that was all I could say.

"He's strong," he said. "So he'll be fine. Come to think about it the only times I've seen him weak were in his dealings with my mother, and that, I could not understand. She practically ruined him."

"What do you mean, 'she ruined him'?" I asked, and his eyes roved over my face. I assumed he was trying to decide whether to reveal this part of himself or not but I didn't want him to feel uncomfortable. I started to tell him not to bother, but he began before I could speak.

"My dad loved my mom. I always knew that, but not until she left did any of us realize just how much."

"She didn't love him back?"

"I want to believe that she did, to an extent at least, but it wasn't enough."

"How?"

He sighed heavily, and even though he stared straight ahead so I couldn't see the pain that was no doubt in his eyes, I heard it in his voice. His tone had become harsh, and it was obvious that he was still so angry about it.

"He wasn't rich enough for her." He stated plainly, and the statement immediately drove a chill down my spine. "Her dad hadn't been wealthy either so she saw it as a cruel repeat of history. She left when I was thirteen, but my dad still let her come over anytime she wanted to see us. At first I was mad at him, but when she only came once or twice a year, I didn't mind so much. She went back to the States and married some guy – I never really bothered to find out all the details."

"Wait, your mom *is* actually an American?" I asked. He turned to me, wondering why I seemed so surprised.

"Yes, why?"

"Nothing," I said, but couldn't stop the sheepish smile that found its way to my face. He understood then.

"Your little lie about us seems to hold," he said.

I smiled shyly at him, while he just shook his head.

"Your dad didn't get remarried?"

"No, he never wanted to. Not after her, and it's scared me in a way." He turned his face so that he could meet my eyes. "I feel like I'm going to make the same mistake; fall for someone so deeply that I don't recover from it."

"That's not a bad thing," I said, but he disagreed.

"It is, because if it goes south you can literally not be able to function. And from what I've seen so far, that's almost always the case. I don't want to ever get to that point where I have no control over myself in that way; it terrifies the shit out of me."

"Well, you do have a point, but I still believe you can choose who you give that kind of power to."

"Maybe, but that's the thing; everyone is an angel right now. But what about ten years down the line when life is not as sweet anymore?"

"Well, that's the big question, and how do you know that you won't be the one to flip out?"

"I don't, but I've come to trust myself enough to know what I will and will not do. And like my dad, if I ever come to the point where I promise my heart to someone, I'd never want to be able recover from that."

"So in other words you don't want to be as unlucky as he was."

"Exactly." He said and it made me chuckle.

"My dad's relationship with my mom scared me too,' I said. "Especially since that didn't end well. So sometimes I think about it and I get really scared, but then there's also a solution to the whole mess."

"Really? And what is it?"

"Don't get married," I said, sounding like a game show host announcing a million dollar win.

He chuckled. "So you don't plan to get married?"

"I hope I do, I'm just not planning for it. If it does happen, it happens and if it doesn't, oh well. It's not a big deal."

He took a moment to consider what I'd said but when it didn't look like he was going to share what he thought about it, I nudged him so that I could get a response.

"So, what do you think?"

"I don't know," he said. "I guess I've never really thought about it, because even though it became bad, I did see it when it was good. I don't know if I want to miss out on that."

"Well, I never saw that, and the parts I did see, I'm more than ready to miss out on."

"I understand," he said and ruffled my hair. I playfully slapped his hand away.

"Do you want to take a swim?" he asked, but before I could answer he was already on his feet and taking off his shorts. I immediately turned away at the glimpse of his dark boxer briefs, a low heat spreading rapidly across my cheeks.

Lowering himself, he slipped in one foot after the other before finally letting his whole body go in. Ducking his head to completely submerge himself in the water, he came up a few seconds later and shook the water off his face.

"Come on," he said to me as he ran his fingers through his hair. And although I was tempted, I shook my head, content to just watch.

"I'll pass. If I want a swim I'll go to the sports complex."

"Come on," he urged. "Why swim there when you can swim here?"

"Because I don't know what's in this water, and isn't it cold?"

"It's not, and it'll only be for a few minutes."

I shook my head again but he reached me, and began to tug on my shirt.

"Nathan, no!" I said, but only had time to gasp when he suddenly grabbed my legs and pulled me to the edge of the rock. With his arm behind my knee and the other around my waist, he lifted me up and out into the water. I screamed as I hovered over the water, holding onto his neck and pleading for him to take me back.

Laughing at how hysteric I'd gotten, he lowered me just enough to wet the back of my shorts before he finally complied, and took me back. As soon as he settled me back on the rock, he swam away before I could attack him. I watched him go and it wasn't long before I began to feel the chill of being left alone.

After taking a few more minutes to make up my mind, I stood to take my shorts off but left my shirt on. I tested the water with my hands and then feet, before eventually slipping in as slowly as I could. But in the end, my efforts did little to dull the bite of the cold water as it came up to cover my waist. However, I quickly adjusted to the temperature and began to move further out so that I could search for him.

"Nathan!" I yelled, when a few seconds later, I'd still not sighted him. Still a little paranoid with what could be lurking underwater, I moved as quickly as I could and was about to turn back when he called out to me. I followed his voice, swimming a little further out before I eventually saw him studying something against a rock. He turned when he heard me and with a broad smile, disappeared underwater and towards me. He came back up when he reached me but his face was just a few inches away from mine; I forgot to breathe.

"You wore your shirt in?" he asked and I nodded shyly. I saw him reach down but before I understood what his aim was, his hand was already on my thigh. I reacted immediately.

"Hey!" I shrieked as I slapped water in his face to get him to move away. He ran his palm over his face to clear it.

"Would you relax?" he said, amused. "I was just checking."

"Well don't," I said. "Ask me instead."

"Okay," he said, but since he still looked amused by my reaction, I moved closer to him and without any warning, reached down to touch his thigh too. He moved back.

"Hey!" he protested. A laugh escaped from my lips.

"*See.*" I gloated, but when he started coming towards me, I turned and around and swam away.

It didn't take any time at all for him to catch up with me and when he did, he grabbed a hold of my legs, forcing me to stop. I laughed as he turned me around but was surprised when he lowered himself to wrap his arms around my knees, and lift me up till only a part of my legs were covered by the water. I squealed excitedly as he moved with me to a deeper part of the stream and then he let go, sending me through the water with a loud splash.

I came up laughing and without thinking, threw my arms around him while his automatically went around my waist. Seconds of pure delight passed before I realized how we were. I started to pull away but he held me to him, and with his free hand, brushed the hair out of my face. Moments passed and soon our heads were inching closer together, our breathing ragged.

But at the last moment, he lowered his head and rested it against my forehead. I was disappointed, but apparently a little more than I thought I would be because before I could stop myself, I slanted my head and placed a small peck on his lips.

Immediately I swam away, not even waiting to see his reaction and as I lifted myself out of the water, it felt like my heart was going to explode out of my chest. I quickly picked up my shorts, and headed back to the blanket.

He followed shortly after, his shorts now back on and his shirt in his hand, but I avoided his gaze. I was now seated on the blanket and finger-combing the tangles out of my hair, but all I could focus on was the picture in my head of what I had just stupidly done.

"Oh my God," I cried under my breath. "Lenora what did you just do?"

"Here," he said when he reached me, and I looked up to see that he was offering me his jumper. I declined for absolutely no reason which was incredibly stupid of me because I was shivering from my damp shirt.

"Take it off." he insisted, and dropped the jumper beside me. With a sigh, I pulled the shirt over my head and handed it over to him. I quickly put his jumper on and watched as he left to spread the shirt on a small rock, not too far away from us.

"What about you?" I asked, when he returned.

"I'm fine," he said and took my hand to pull me up.

It brought me closer to him than was appropriate but in my effort to avoid his eyes, my gaze became involuntarily glued to his chest. And then at the vein that throbbed on the edge of his bicep. Only when he cleared his throat to get my attention did I realize that I'd been staring for longer than I had thought.

With a gasp, I started to babble an apology and immediately turned away, but he held my shoulders and turned me right back.

"This way," he said. He then bent down to retrieve a Canon camera from his backpack which he slung over his shoulder. "I found something on Tuesday."

"Really?" I said. "What?"

"Be Patient," he teased and it made me smile. However, I still felt so embarrassed by all the ways that I'd managed to effortlessly fool myself within the last thirty minutes.

He led me through barely visible paths, and the thick green scenery of huge trees and countless plants. The canopies of the taller trees did an excellent job of almost completely shielding the sunlight, so when the rustling that constantly sounded around us continued to drive me even closer to him in fear, he eventually noticed and took my hand in his.

My hand *burned* from the feel of his hand in mine, and when I looked down my arm, I wasn't surprised to see that it was covered in goose pimples. His action revealed the care for me that he had in his heart, and it made me feel so insanely happy.

After walking for quite a while, I started to get an inkling of where he was taking me. At first, I heard the rushing sound from far away but as we continued on, it gradually became louder. Excited, I started to softly bounce on my feet, but he tightened his hold on my hand and pulled me along.

"How did you find it?" I asked.

"You're ruining the surprise; at least pretend you don't know," he said. But I continued bugging him just for the fun of it, until the deafening roar of the water dimmed out my voice.

Carefully, we headed up a small rocky incline and when we got to the top, the sight that I met completely took my breath away. A powerful cascade of silvery white water rushed down rocky outcrops, and plunged majestically into a calm pool. Nathan stilled my hand to stop me from going any further, but from where I stood I could see the mists as they rose up and shadowed the rocks, as well as the moss and wildflowers that surrounded the entire waterfall.

It wasn't huge but it was powerful, and when I saw the lily pads with white and pink flowers, anchored far off to the opposite ends of the calm pool and close to the banks, I felt the urge to shout out my joy. This had to be heaven, surely.

I glanced back at Nathan, my eyes bright with awe and appreciation. He understood, and sent back a soft smile.

"Thank you," I said and hurried over to throw myself in his arms.

He caught me. "You're welcome," he said with a small laugh, and leaned slightly away to look into my eyes. As he softly stroked my cheek with the back of his fingers, I saw the complete admiration for me that shone in his eyes; I threw myself back into his arms.

He held me as tightly as he could and so did I. My heart was melting inside my chest and at that moment, I didn't want to be anywhere else or with anyone else in the entire world. The moment was consuming and priceless, and one that I knew I'd never forget.

"Do you want to take some pictures?" he asked, after we'd stayed like that for a few seconds.

I nodded, and released him so that he could use his camera. He took some of the scenery first while I continued to stare at the waterfall until he came to get me. He led me to a high rock, and after making sure I was steady, started to click away.

Spreading my arms, I threw my head backwards and wanted to yell out the overwhelming joy I felt, but the roar of the waterfall would have overpowered it so I didn't bother. In as long as I could remember, and especially in the last three years, nothing had made me feel like this, and I wanted to remember every moment of it.

Nathan continued clicking away as I struck comical poses and made funny faces at his camera from where I stood. Eventually, I moved towards him but he kept clicking until I pulled on his arm to let me take some photos of him. He nodded, but kept on taking random shots even as I complained.

I was really starting to get uncomfortable so I reached out to take the camera from him, but he raised it up in the air and out of my reach. Grabbing one of my hands, he whirled me around to fall against him and I happily did, a high-pitched squeal escaping my lips.

He positioned his arm and then took a shot of us together, surrounded by the beautiful waterfall, trees and wildflowers; I was leaning against his bare chest, my grin ridiculously wide and eyes ablaze with joy. His arm was around my waist and as I turned sideways to glance at him, I saw that he too had a wild grin on his face.

He pressed the shutter button on the camera, and that memory was captured forever. It was a magical moment, and I would never forget it.

« CHAPTER 15 »

We arrived back at school almost two hours later. With a smile, he said goodbye before heading to his house while I headed over to the dining hall. He wasn't going to come in for dinner today and when I arrived at the hall to meet it already filled, I wished that I could skip it like he had. But I was way too hungry so I ate as quickly as I could, and then went straight to my room.

I was exhausted when I got in so after a quick shower, got into bed so that I could fall asleep. However, I couldn't stop replaying the scenes from the stream over and over in my mind, especially when I'd purposely complained of being tired and he'd piggybacked me for a few minutes as we'd returned to the clearing.

It had been amazing, and as I continued to reminisce over it, it brought the most powerful of emotions coursing through my body. I hugged myself underneath the covers feeling the overwhelming warmth and drugging thrill that I still felt from the day and from him. I knew I was digging a very dangerous hole for myself but at that point I didn't mind at all. The world was taking me on a ride and it was more than what I could have ever imagined.

He left me a message online the next afternoon saying that I was to bring my test materials to dinner that evening, and I thought him insane for two reasons; a) that he would for even a second, consider the idea of us sitting together with the entire school's population watching.

And b), that I would be willing to do any studying when I was supposed to be eating. Nevertheless, I indulged him and took my note book with me.

However I was a little late, so I had to go further down the hall before I could find a vacant seat. To my annoyance, the only one that I could settle for was so far away from the front of the hall, that I could barely see him. I was worried that he would think that I'd skipped dinner because I was so impossible to spot out, but that wasn't enough to make me do anything stupid- like go over to his table to announce myself.

So I stayed put, but grew more depressed when I realized that this part of the hall didn't even get their food from the same buffet counter as his did. Here, I was surrounded by first and second years shooting petty insults at each other, and laughing too loudly. They were still too young to be self-conscious about anything so more than once, I caught the nauseating sight of mashed food in their mouths.

I was moving the creole rice around my plate, and wondering when this nightmare was going to end when a boy came up to me. He was small, and bore a similarity in appearance to all the others beside, so I knew immediately that he was in his first year.

"Here, this is for you." he said shyly, and handed a folded note to me. I took it from him but before I could ask him what it was about, he turned around and took off.

I opened it and instantly recognized Nathan's scribbly handwriting. It read:

Nora...

▷ You just missed James singing Kesha's 'Tik tok' song- It was disturbing.

▷ And, remember to wait a few minutes after dinner. James will come get you.

Instantly a laugh escaped me, startling the people on my table who had probably since concluded that I was mute. From then on, I couldn't stop imagining how James would have sounded and *looked*, while singing the song. I wished I had been there to watch.

As I reread the note again, my heart swelled with the sweet ache that came from knowing that he knew exactly where I was seated, and had taken the trouble to send me the note.

Suddenly I regained my appetite and hurried through my meal, anticipating the hour when dinner would be over and everyone would start leaving. Of course most of the first years around me left as soon as they were done so in no time at all, it became obvious that I was still there for some other reason.

The entrance of the hall however, was still filled with seniors whom had now come to value social relationships, over the video games and social activities that were no doubt waiting for the younger students back in their houses.

It couldn't have been more than ten minutes after the majority of the seats around me had been vacated, but being there alone and waiting, made it feel like forever. I was just about to get up and go over to Nathan's table when I saw James heading towards me with a huge smile on his face. I let out a sigh of relief.

"Hi." He said when he reached me.

"Hey" I responded, and got up to face him.

"So, I hope you're excited."

My smile waned. "About what?"

"The library club." He replied, with a look on his face that showed that my question was unexpected. "We have our session in the library now. Alex said you loved reading and wanted to come along."

"Um, isn't the library closed by now?"

He started to laugh, until he saw my face and realized that I wasn't joking. "Please tell me you know that when you guys have prep in your rooms, fifth and sixth years are allowed to have theirs in the library – until 11pm even."

"You're kidding!"

"How long have you been here again?" he asked, and turned around so that we could start walking towards the entrance of the hall.

"Oh please." I scoffed. "How am I supposed to know that when we're not even allowed to stay up till then?"

"Of course that's a perfectly reasonable explanation for why you don't know the routine of a school that you've been in for three years."

"I'm more of a 'live in the moment kinda girl'." I said.

"Uh huh, definitely." He said, unmoved by my attempt to excuse my ignorance.

"I really am though."

He chuckled. "Okay."

When we reached his table, I was surprised that Nathan was nowhere to be found, so I asked James where he was.

"He went back to his dorm."

"Isn't he coming with us for the meeting?"

He snorted. "Of course not. He has his own library in his room- the snob."

My face instantly fell. *What had Nathan just gotten me into?* It barely even registered in my brain as James picked up his bag and we started to walk out of the hall because I was trying to figure out what was happening.

"How did you know I was back there?" I asked James.

"Alex told me. He was the one that told me to come get you since you wanted to come along."

"And you're sure he's not coming?"

"Yeah, I mean, he never does. Did he say something to you? Is he going to stop by? I've been trying to get him to accept our invite for months."

I shook my head. "No. *No* he didn't."

ॐ

The library club took place in the section of the library that allowed for a quiet chat, and leisurely reading. It was usually decorated with huge navy blue sofas, but for today's meeting, a few more single chairs had been added around it to make room for the surprisingly large number of people that came. From where I sat on one of the single chairs by an extreme corner, I had counted up to forty-five people.

James was in his element as he led the discussion about the classic literature book that they had read for the week. I'd never heard of it, but apparently reading it automatically made you sound smarter because everyone that stood up to give their reviews did it pretentiously. They used such unnecessarily complex words that I was certain I wasn't the only one in the room who had trouble understanding.

It no doubt made them feel smarter, but it made me hate Nathan even more than I already did. I still couldn't believe that he had thrown me in here with no intention of bringing me out. It would have been funny, but I was too angry and disappointed that he was still so inept at dealing with me. Anyway, it had only been fifteen minutes since I'd been here so there was still a possibility that there was a punch line to the joke. I just couldn't accept that there wasn't because I had to believe that he knew better than to forcibly thrust me into a situation such as this.

At twenty-five minutes past eight, I almost fell out of my chair when I happened to glance backwards, and saw Nathan arrive. I watched as he took a seat and started to watch the Slovakian girl that was now giving her review. With my mind, I willed him to turn so that he could meet my gaze and see how pissed I was, but when almost a minute later he still hadn't, I turned my head back to the girl.

I gave myself *and him* until 8:30, because if he hadn't made a move to get me out of here by then, I was returning to my house immediately. By 8:30 however, he still hadn't done anything so I got ready to leave. Just as I was about to excuse myself, the girl finished with her review and James stood up to announce the next phase of the meeting.

"Now we go for the *'hunt and discover'*." He said with exaggerated excitement. "And for the new comers it simply means that you go around the literature section and find any fascinating book that you would want to be our read for next week. The point is to enjoy discovering new books with little to no distraction since we're the only ones here. Have fun, and I'll see you all back here in half an hour."

Everyone got up after that and so did I. I didn't turn to look at Nathan again but I knew when he came up to me. He stood behind me as I took my time to brush off whatever imaginary lint particles I felt were on my clothes.

"Are you going to talk to me anytime soon?" he asked calmly, sounding as if he was ready for whatever hell I was going to raise at him for sending me here. It made me smile, and although I was still pissed, I had to admit that his plan was brilliant. I couldn't have thought about it if I'd tried, but it did made me wonder why he felt that it wouldn't be a good idea for us to be seen together. Did he perhaps know something about Beverly and the bullying? I hoped that he didn't because it made me anxious at what his reaction would be.

Before turning to him, I tried my best to wipe the smile off my face and replace it with the scowl that had been on it all evening.

"Do you plan to warn me next time you decide to send me to a library book club?"

"No." he replied unrepentantly. "Societies like this are good in molding young minds like yours."

"And let me guess, you're not part of these young minds"

"I am not." He said, and then surprised me when he gently brushed my hair away from my shoulder.

"Uh," I cleared my throat. "How old are you? I've never thought to ask."

"I'll be nineteen next month." He replied, and then took my hand in his. "Come on, let's go. We have work to do."

I grumbled half-heartedly as he pulled me along with him. "I'm not in the mood for math anymore."

"Don't worry, I'll get you in the mood." He said, and I was sure that it was an innocent comment but I couldn't help the fake cough that escaped my lips. It made him laugh.

"Those vampire novels are ruining your mind." He said as we reached my usual table. After pulling out a seat for me, he pulled out another for himself and sat down.

"They're not," I disagreed. "And you've only seen me with one so far. What makes you think that that's all I read?"

He took a moment to consider the question. "I don't know." he said, "Anyway, let's get started. I heard most of your class failed the math test."

I smiled.

"You're pleased?"

I shrugged. "It got Mr. Barron to give a retake."

"Well then, let's make sure you do better this time around."

"Don't you have your own studying to do?" I asked.

"I'll do that later." He said, and we began.

After I showed him the problems I had difficulties with, he put his glasses on, and started going through them with me.

We were at it for almost two hours and by then, I had forgotten about the library club. I wasn't even sure they were still around because the book cases that shielded my table from the rest of the library prevented me from seeing anyone else.

It was now getting close to 11pm and we were almost done because he had gone through almost all the calculations that I had covered since the beginning of the term. He was so focused throughout the whole thing that I was almost too scared to make jokes. I did try though; little dumb remarks here and there, to which he only supplied a light smile if I was lucky, but most times he totally ignored them.

I knew he was serious, but I didn't expect him to be this single minded. It was so different from how I was because I had a low attention span, so my mind wandered away easily. But he just stayed on what he was doing and only turned to me when he wanted to ensure that I understood what he was saying. I was tempted more than once to ruffle his hair or peck his cheek, but I'd already surpassed my flirting limit for the day and quite possibly the month. I cringed when I remembered how I'd kissed him in the stream.

I'd succeeded in convincing myself that it wasn't a big deal, and that he'd probably just taken it as a friendly kiss, but I would have liked it if he'd at least mentioned it, even if it was to discourage me from repeating it in the future. That would of course be a huge blow to my self- esteem but it was better than completely ignoring the fact that it had happened.

After another half hour of making me run through the problems again, but this time listening to me as I explained them to him, he finally let me breathe.

He excused himself for a few minutes to check on James, but then came back and wrote out a question that he wanted me to try out. I rolled my eyes but picked the pen up to start on it. He leaned forward to watch me as I worked but it was too distracting so I kept stumbling around, trying to find the solution. He was just too close to me now. So close that I could feel the warmth from his body. I really tried to concentrate but when he went on to drape an arm across the top of my chair and leaned even closer, I dropped the pen.

"What is it?" he asked, looking confused when I turned to scowl at him. When I didn't say anything, he picked the pen back up and prodded it into my hand.

"Come on," he urged gently. "We only have a few more minutes here."

Then back up because I can't think, I wanted to say, but didn't.

Eventually I made a mistake and didn't realize it, so when I kept on going, he pulled the pen from my hand and told me where I'd gone wrong. This time I watched the gentle movement of his lips and the soft way his eyelids moved as he spoke. When he caught me staring, he frowned.

"What was the last thing I just said?" he asked.

I had no idea. "Uhh…" I started and he watched, his eyebrows furrowed into a frown as I tried to make something up. He got up then and started replacing my things into my bag. Then he pulled my chair backwards with me on it. I giggled.

"Let's go." He said, and I was more than happy to.

ॐ

The next morning was the test, and it ended up being amazing. I had revisited the problems we had studied last evening several times before I had gone to bed, so I was convinced that I was prepared. However I had been so nervous at first that it had taken me a few moments to reacquaint myself with the first question. I almost stumbled on the final question as well, but I was able to recover quickly and complete the problem.

When I was done, there was still fifteen minutes left so I went over everything again and still found myself early. So I waited until the majority of the class had left, and then stood up to submit my paper.

I walked out of the door, trying but failing to keep the joy off my face as I headed to my locker. When I saw that Nathan was waiting by it, my nerves joined in so by the time I reached him, I was sure that my face was now a bright red.

"How was your test?" Nathan asked.

"It was fine," I answered with a breathy voice, and an excited smile. Both stunned me. Only then did I notice the quiet uproar we stirred along the hallway in curious stares and light whispers, as everyone no doubt wondered why we were together, yet again.

We're cousins! I wanted to yell at them, but instead I directed my upset at their intrusion on forcefully prying my locker open. When I turned back to look at him, I found him watching me intently.

"Are you alright?" he asked, but I suspected he knew why I was upset.

"I am." I replied anyway. "Any news about your dad?"

"Yeah, he's doing well now so he'll be out of hospital soon."

"That's good," I said, relieved for him.

"Are you returning to the States for midterms?" he asked.

I shrugged. "I probably will, I always do. I don't know anyone in England. What about you?"

"I'm not sure yet." he said. "So, was the test *that* good?"

I nodded. "It was."

"You still need to wait for the results though," he said.

I frowned at him for attempting to lower my expectation. "Can't I at least enjoy this?"

"You can," he said, and rested a hand on my shoulder. "But still ... wait." Then with a smile, he walked away.

I stared after him until he finally disappeared above the stairs, wondering when I'd be able to see him again and away from prying eyes. Shrewd laughter behind me brought my attention back so I retrieved the things I needed from my locker, and headed back to the dining hall for lunch.

ઐ

Later that afternoon, I had just finished the cup of raspberry yoghurt that I'd brought back with me from lunch, and was heading to the bathroom to wash my hands when I heard someone sobbing quietly.

True enough, I walked in and met a girl at the sink with her head lowered. She turned the faucet on to begin washing her hands as soon as she noticed me come in, but I could still hear her sniffing as she tried to control her tears.

I proceeded to wash my hands but even as I turned the faucet off and then went on to the dryer, I couldn't stop watching her. There was something very familiar about her frame that I couldn't quite place, but when she glanced at me and caught me staring, I finally remembered who she was.

She was the one that had been at our table with her boyfriend, on the day of the food fight. I hadn't noticed it then, but she was very pretty. She had big brown eyes, and shoulder length, dark blonde curly hair.

When I didn't do or say anything after holding her gaze for a few seconds, she turned the faucet off and left the bathroom. I took a deep breath, knowing what I should do but wishing that I didn't have to. I probably wouldn't have even bothered a few weeks ago, but now I wanted to believe that to an extent, I wasn't so bitter and uncaring anymore.

So I quietly followed her until she walked into her room and closed the door behind her. I knocked softly, and when she told me to come in, I did. She was sitting on her bed, and looked puzzled when she saw that I was the one.

"Do you need something?" she asked.

I shook my head. "Uh, I–I just wanted to find out if you were alright."

"Do I look like I'm alright?" she asked, and I was sure that she intended it to be sarcastic but it came out sounding like an outright question. I didn't know whether to answer her or be offended, so I just took a few steps further into the room until I was standing close to her bed.

"What's wrong?" I asked, and was fascinated when a thousand emotions crossed her face in the minute that it took for her to assess me, and make up her mind on whether to talk to me or kick me out.

"It's nothing," she eventually replied. "Just boyfriend problems, which has now caused hazing problems. Stupid Natalie had me serving her table all afternoon."

"I'm sorry," I said, fully able to relate. "He's a senior right?"

"Yeah," she said.

"Well, it's expected." I said. "There's an instant hate from them when you're suddenly in their waters."

"That's not even the worst part," she said, her eyes filling up with tears again. "The boy aspect is just driving me freaking crazy."

"The guy that was at the table with you right? The night of the food fight."

"Yeah," she answered. "Matthew."

"Do you want to talk about it?" I asked, hoping she wouldn't hear me, or at least decline the offer.

"Not really..." she started. I rolled my eyes and waited.

"It's just that he used to be so psyched about us, you know. But now he acts like I'm a burden- like he's tired or something. This was a boy that begged me to date him, and now that I am, it's like I don't matter anymore."

She looked at me, and I was prepared to listen to her rant as long as she wanted to, but her next comment stunned the breath out of me. "I bet Alexandre doesn't treat you this way." She said.

"Excuse me?"

"James's cousin- Alex."

"Um, we're just friends," I said. "Cousins too, in fact."

She looked genuinely confused. "Are you serious? James never mentioned that to me and I heard you were dating him."

"Well, I'm not," I said, wondering how many other people thought we were dating, and why the cousin story had not spread widely enough.

"Well, with the way he was with you at the table and a couple of other times I've seen you guys around, I could have sworn you were. I'm sorry."

"It's okay." I said, wondering what everyone was seeing that made them think we were a couple, because I sure as hell wasn't seeing it.

"Anyway about your boyfriend," I said, so that we could change the topic. "Do you still like him?"

"I do," she answered. "But with the way he acts sometimes I'm beginning to think that I should just forget about him and move on."

That, I didn't have a response to but after a few silent moments, she looked at me, expecting one.

"Oh, I have no idea," I said with a shaky laugh. "I don't know how these things work so I'm probably the last person you should ask."

"Probably," she said, and I felt relieved. She, however still hung her head low, so I thought of something neutral to say.

"Don't worry about all of this though," I said. "I mean, if it's meant to work out it will, and if it doesn't, then don't be sad about it either. You'll have to let it go and wait for something better."

"What if there isn't anything better?" she asked.

I scoffed away her question. "There's always something better."

"Okay. Thank you." She said, before introducing herself. Her name was Elisa Watton.

ജ

I felt elated throughout the entire afternoon, and when by dinnertime, I walked into the hall and spotted Nathan, I went straight over to his table. I sat beside him, but with my legs on both side of the bench so that I could face him directly.

"Guess what happened today?" I said.

"What?" he asked as he looked up from the book he was reading- and that was all it took for my brain to turn to mush. As I stared at him, all I could hear was my heart pounding in my ears, along with a nervous excitement that ran up and down my body, and made it a little harder to breathe. It was the stupidest thing to be able to feel like this because of one inconsequential look, and I sure as hell didn't want to end up hurt like Elisa. Worried, I took a cookie from the packet in front of him.

"Are you alright?" he asked, and lightly touched the side of my arm.

"I'm fine," I replied, and put the cookie in my mouth. I used that time to retrace my train of thought and it would have helped greatly, if his eyes weren't so fixed on me in concern.

"Did you beat someone up?" he teased, and it amused me. I flicked the crumbs on my fingertips at him. Grinning, he shifted slightly to the side to avoid it and then lifted his left leg over the bench so that he was sitting across just like I was.

"You know for all my temper, I can't fight to save my life." I said.

He chuckled. "I know," he agreed, and then fake coughed when I glared at him.

He looked so adorable acting wary of me, but of course I wasn't going to tell him that.

"So, what happened?" he asked.

I shrugged. "I was nice to someone today."

His eyes widened in feigned wonder, but then narrowed almost immediately. "Was it Kate?" he asked.

"No, you ass. It was Elisa. She sat with us the day of that food fight."

"Isn't she Matthew's girlfriend?"

"Yes, she is." I said, surprised that Nathan knew who Matthew was. "She was crying."

"Why, what happened?" he asked, as he took another cookie from his packet.

"I don't know if it's proper to tell you."

"Okay." He said.

"But I want to."

"I understand."

"Like I *really* want to."

"Lenora?" he called.

I answered. "Yes?"

"Make up your mind, would you?"

"Fine. She thinks he doesn't love her anymore."

A thoughtful "hmmm" was all he offered.

"And what did you tell her?"

"What could I say? I know nothing about things like that."

"But you read romance novels."

"Yeah, because that's how we want it to be, not how it actually is in real life."

Just then, I heard someone call my name and we both looked up to see who it was. It was Elisa, and she was waving to me from the entrance to the hall.

Surprised, I waved back, and swung my right leg over the bench to sit properly when I saw that she was coming over.

"Hi," she said a little out of breath as she reached us. She took a seat on the opposite side of the table.

"Hey," I answered while Nathan smiled at her. She took a few moments to recover from him, and then turned to me with slightly widened eyes.

"So about what we talked about earlier," She started, but was a little hesitant because Nathan was right beside me. She decided to speak anyway because he had brought his book down to the bench and wasn't looking at her.

"I just spoke to him," she said, "and he told me that he had no idea about what I was talking about because we're fine!"

"Do you think you guys are?"

"Of course not. We're not fine. It's not like it used to be and he's not like he was."

"It'll be okay," I said, trying to console her, but she just continued to look dejected.

"I know, but it's not supposed to be like this." She looked up at me. "What would you do if you were in my shoes?"

"No idea." I said with a shrug.

"Can we ask him?" she mouthed to me, referring to Nathan.

I mouthed back. "Why?"

"Because he's a guy."

I sighed, and turned to him. "Nathan, what do you think?"

He lifted his head from his book. "Pardon?" He asked.

"Elisa thinks Matthew doesn't love her anymore but he thinks she's being paranoid."

He turned to Elisa, and I could immediately tell that I'd put him in a very uncomfortable position. Taking another cookie from his packet, I got ready to watch how he would get himself out of it.

He straightened. "I really don't have an answer for that, but Nora you should have an idea."

I scowled at him for turning the question back at me. "Well, I don't."

"Well, I think you do." He said.

"I don't!" I argued, and watched as crumbs flew out of my mouth and bathed him. I snickered as he took in the damage. His patient elder voice came out.

"Nora, it's impolite to speak with your mouth open."

I responded by spraying him with more crumbs. "It's also impolite to delve into other people's problems."

"I don't mind," Elisa said, clearly enjoying our banter.

"Thank you," Nathan told her and she blushed.

I shoved him playfully, and got up. "I'm going to my table," I announced and pretended to leave, but a sharp tug on my shirt pulled me back until I was sitting on the bench again. I turned to hit him but he leaned away.

Just then I noticed Elisa wringing her hands. She'd suddenly become nervous. When I looked up to see Matthew walking towards our table, I understood why.

He nodded to Nathan and me when he reached us, and then turned to Elisa. He didn't seem happy.

"We need to talk," he told her in a quiet voice, and she nodded. We watched them leave and then Nathan nudged me to rise because it was our table's turn to get food from the buffet counter. We got our food quickly amidst curious stares and at one point, I became so nervous that I started wringing my hands. He looked down at me and asked what was wrong. I shook my head to indicate that it was nothing, but he wasn't fooled.

"Relax," he said as I stared up at him, and I smiled in response.

Everything went well after that, and soon we were laughing about favorite meals, and stealing food off each other's plates. Some strips of chicken breast still remained on his after he was done, but when I reached forward to help him with it, he slapped my hand away.

"Ow!" I said and I rubbed the sting, but when he looked away a few minutes later I quickly grabbed the pieces off his plate and put them in my mouth. He turned back to see them missing, and raised an eyebrow at me. I beamed like an excited toddler while he just shook his head, and used a tissue to wipe the oil from the corners of my mouth.

I tensed at the gesture and he noticed, but didn't comment. He grabbed my drink in retaliation moments later and I started to complain when I saw Elisa returning to us.

"Is everything sorted out?" I asked as she sat down, but she just shook her head and then stood back up to get her food. She had just returned and was about to sit down when a tall girl with short black hair came up to us. She had a light dusting of freckles spread along the swell of her cheeks.

"Hi," she greeted, but I didn't see Nathan's response. I was too busy watching what she'd do because I suspected that this was Natalie; the senior who had been making Elisa serve her table.

True enough she bent down to whisper in Elisa's ear, and Elisa went on to look even more depressed than she already was. She was just about to get up when I quickly said. "Elisa aren't you going to help Nathan?"

She looked confused. "What?"

"The stuff you said you were going to explain to him. Have you changed your mind?"

"She'll be back," Natalie said, and I was about to respond when Nathan stilled my arm from underneath the table.

"Natalie, do you mind if Elisa remains here for a while? I really need her help," he said.

I was surprised he knew Natalie's name, but then I remembered that they were both in the same year.

"On what?" she asked, sounding curious. But he just smiled, and somehow that made her forget that he hadn't answered her question.

"That's fine," she said, and she turned around to leave. Nathan took his hand off mine.

"Thanks Lennie," Elisa said in a tired voice. "But I think you just made it worse."

"Why haven't you reported her?" I asked.

She shook her head. "It'll just become worse. I'll become the number one target. I'm just hoping she gets tired soon because it's really beginning to frustrate me."

"Why don't you tell Matthew to talk to her?" Nathan asked, but again her response was that she didn't want to escalate the situation.

"She'll get tired," she said, but I doubted it. Beverly didn't seem like she was going to get tired of me either, and I also didn't want Nathan to know about it.

We were quiet for a few more minutes, until I happened to glance back to see Natalie and Beverly getting up from their seats. They started to head towards us.

"Argh," I groaned. "What's happening? Why can't they freaking leave us alone?"

Elisa raised her head to see them, and then looked at me with widened eyes.

When they reached us, they ignored both Elisa and me and acknowledged just Nathan. I turned my head away in disgust, but Nathan put his hand on my knee to caution my reaction. I still refused to turn back to them.

"We were wondering if we could join you." Beverly said, and as I opened my mouth to speak he tightened his hand on my knee. But that didn't stop me.

"We were just about to leave," I said, my contempt for her apparent in my tone.

Her face darkened, and she snapped at me. "Excuse me, but I don't think I was talking to you,"

Nathan stepped in. "We were actually about to leave," he said. "But you can join us of course."

She blushed.

"You're Beverly right?" he asked. She could barely contain her flush while I just turned to look at him with amazement. Was he joking? I wasn't going to share a meal with the both of them. I started to say that I was leaving but again, he pressed down on my knee, and whispered to me to stay put.

Grudgingly, I agreed. Natalie took a seat across from me- next to Elisa while Beverly came over to join Nathan and I. She made Nathan move from the edge of the bench so that she could sit next to him.

Just then, James arrived with his dinner plate and came to sit beside me. I spoke to him and Elisa, trying my best to ignore Beverly and Natalie as they spoke to

Nathan. But eventually, I just wanted to get out of there. After about ten minutes of giggles and shy smiles, Nathan finally excused himself and asked Elisa and I if we were ready to leave. We nodded, but had to wait a few more minutes for James to finish his meal.

As we left, we all kept silent until James and Nathan reached the front of our house.

"See you guys later," James said. I immediately started to head into the building when Nathan took my hand, and pulled me aside.

"Why are you upset?" he asked.

I sighed. "I'm not upset, I'm fine."

I knew he knew better, but since I wasn't ready to speak, he let me go.

"I think he did okay," Elisa said as we climbed up the stairs to our floor.

"Really, how?"

"If you hadn't spoken, we'd have probably been able to leave. But you did, and so to save us later he allowed them to stay for a while."

"I know that," I muttered. "And he's not the one I'm mad at. I just wonder when being a senior automatically made you a tyrant?"

"Everyone catches the disease when they get there," she said.

"Well, let's just hope they'll leave us alone now."

« CHAPTER 16 »

That evening, Beverly sent for me. Olivia had come in with a smug smile on her face and informed me of the call. I took my time in getting there, hoping that Beverly would already be asleep and I'd be able to get away with it until the next day, but I wasn't so lucky. I walked into her room at about eleven-thirty to find her room filled with her friends.

The two beds in the room had been joined together to create one huge one in the middle, and on it they were all lying down and chatting. The door was left open, so as soon as they noticed me standing at the threshold, the room quieted down.

Beverly was the last to notice me because she wasn't facing the door, but when she turned to see what had caused the quiet, a scowl appeared on her face.

"Come in," she said, and she introduced me to the others – there were six of them on the bed.

"Guys, this is my *friend* Lenora," she said, and the others laughed like she had just issued an insult. "I hope I'm not intruding in on your plans for the night." she asked in a sickeningly sweet tone, but I refused to answer. She waited a few seconds, and then yelled so loudly that some of her friends jumped. "Answer me!"

But all I could do was shake my head, not trusting my mouth to not dig a deeper grave for me than I was already in. With a disgusted look, she turned away from me and started to speak to her friends. They gossiped about everyone they knew, mimicked people and argued about silly things that I'd have wished in a million years that I wasn't present to hear.

An hour passed, and then two, and I just stood there watching them, until I was almost certain that she'd forgotten about me. Just when I was about to ask for a bathroom break, she turned towards me.

"My clothes are in the dryer," she said. "5b. *Please* go get them for me."

Straightening, I moved away from the wall, and walked out of the room. She had added a '*please*' so even if I wanted to report her now, her defense would be that that she had asked me politely as a '*friend*', and that I had willingly agreed. There were six witnesses to verify that. And if I just decided to go to my room now like I was immensely tempted to, they could come together and pound the hell out of me. Olivia was my roommate, so there would be no witnesses to back up my tale later. And since I wasn't particularly close to anyone else, no one would be ready to put their necks on the line for me.

Furious, I headed down to the basement and retrieved her clothes from the dryer as she had instructed. When I returned to her room, the next chore was to iron all of them- from her dress shirts to her sheets. I'd never even *ironed* my own sheets before, but there I was, at two a.m. in the morning, ironing those of someone who I was now fully convinced I completely hated.

When I returned and she offered my services to two more of her friends, I was past reacting. With a blank look on my face, I did all I was asked and by past four, returned to my room and closed the door behind me. I gazed at Olivia as she slept soundly, and for a few minutes I considered pouring all my anger on her.

It was a quiet anger that I felt, I realized, when I couldn't even feel the blinding heat that usually accompanied my fury. Or maybe it was because I was just too exhausted.

Dragging myself off to bed, I fell asleep thinking of ways to make Olivia's life a living hell.

ళ

I went through the next day with a soreness behind my eyes that constantly reminded me that I hadn't gotten enough sleep. By lunchtime, Elisa joined me in the courtyard and by the time I was done morosely narrating the tale to her, she was more upset that I was.

"Oh my God!" she gasped. "Have you told Nathan?"

"And what good is that going to bring?"

"I don't know, but he might be able to do something about all this. He'll be freaking pissed."

"*He* is the cause of it," I said. "And like you said, getting him involved is just going to make things worse, just like you didn't want Matthew to get involved."

"Yeah, I guess you're probably right," she said with a sigh, and drew her soda cup towards her to take a sip.

"When I was about to leave, she warned me off Nathan," I said and her eyes widened.

"Did you tell her that he is your cousin?"

"No," I replied, and carelessly dropped the white chocolate chip cookie I had picked up from the dining hall earlier at breakfast. "At that point I didn't really give a damn about what she thought. I was too exhausted."

"Well, maybe you need to find a way to tell her then."

"Maybe, but I'm sure she's already heard. And even if she hasn't, I don't think it's going to make any difference. She's stupid enough to not care even if it was his mother in her way."

"Well, I still think you should. It's worth a shot," she insisted, but I didn't think so. Telling her would feel too much like selling out, and would just inflame the lie.

"Nathan's coming," she warned, and from my groggy position against the table, I straightened.

"He'll notice something is wrong," I said worriedly. "I look too tired."

"He won't, and you don't look too bad," she said.

But when he came to sit by me, within seconds he asked why I looked so exhausted.

"It's nothing, I'm fine," I said, and then added a small smile when it was obvious that he didn't believe me.

He let it go, and left almost immediately after that.

೮ಾ

A week passed and I barely saw Nathan.

Beverly on the other hand, made me take apart the bookcase that I had color-coordinated. Again! This time around she wanted it organized by topic. So my Tuesday and Wednesday afternoons had been unwillingly dedicated to her. After that however, she left me alone and seemed to have forgotten about me, or maybe she'd just gotten tired of making my life a living hell.

Nathan's distance however, posed another problem that I didn't want to have to deal with. He'd come for dinner about twice during the week, but had left each time without even a glance in my direction. I'd racked my brain for what could possibly have gone wrong, and thought at first that it could be related to his dad. But when he'd laughed with James during one of his rare appearances in the dining hall, I'd concluded that he was okay. I had previously only seen him when he wanted me to, so the fact that he had ignored me for the entire week brought up a lot to think about.

The result of my Math test came in the next Monday, and although I was happy that I'd gotten a B+, it was short-lived because once again, he was nowhere to be found. I wanted to share it with him but I couldn't, because I had no idea where he was. When Elisa came over to ask me to lunch with her, I shared my concern.

We were waiting in line in the cafeteria and she was listening to me talk about his absence when she suddenly stopped me and said, "There's Nathan."

I followed her gaze to see him sitting at one of the tables, with a coffee cup in front of him. But he wasn't alone. I tried to see who the girl was but Elisa saved me the trouble.

"What's he doing with Marilyn?" she asked. I kept my eyes on them for a few more seconds, and then forced myself to turn away.

"Who is she?" I asked, trying to keep the edge out of my voice.

Elisa looked surprised. "She's the head girl, and she's in our *house*. How don't you know this?"

I shrugged. I didn't care.

"Do you want to go over?" she asked.

"Of course not!"

A few seconds passed.

"Do you think I should?"

"Well, I don't know," she said. "You *are* pretty close to him, aren't you? *Cousins* even."

The way she said "cousins" sounded like she was mocking me, but I ignored it to glance back at them again. There was no doubt that I wanted to go over just so I could confirm that we were okay, but I was scared of what I would see in his reaction.

What if we actually weren't okay? I found myself thinking. *And that somehow in the last week, he had managed to outgrow me.*

Almost immediately, I cringed at how pathetic the thought was because even if he had, so what? It'd be easy for me to do the same. So with my heart in my throat, I threw all caution to the wind and headed over.

Nathan didn't see me, or at least he pretended not to until I reached him and he was forced to look up. I needed his acknowledgment before I could turn to the girl, but when he raised his eyes to mine and I saw nothing, I knew instantly that me coming over had been a terrible decision. It was official; I had been tossed into the crowd of unwanted females.

"Hey," he said in his usual cool voice, but it was devoid of the affection that I had grown accustomed to. The difference was dazing, and it felt like I was talking to a stranger.

"Hi," I responded, the word coming out sounding like a question. I wasn't sure what I was waiting for, but his narrowed gaze eventually forced me to explain myself. I said the first thing that came to mind, "My test results came back."

He nodded. "Okay."

"I got a B." I added, feeling more stupid as the seconds passed, but I still managed a smile. He on the other hand just stared at me, until I was forced to turn and acknowledge the other girl.

"Hi," she greeted, with what looked like a genuine smile, but I couldn't even bring myself to respond.

I nodded at her and then with a frown, I looked back at him. "I'll see you around," I told him, and then

I walked away without even waiting for a reply. By then, I didn't even expect one.

"How was it?" Elisa asked as I met up with her, two steaming cups of tea, and a brown paper bag between her teeth. Shrugging, I thanked her as I took the bag from her, and walked out of the cafeteria. She followed closely behind.

⇛⇝

Elisa came over to my room just before dinner and by then, I was so strung out from turning over the cafeteria incident continuously in my mind that I needed to talk to someone before I completely lost it. I left out the details and just glossed over my concern at his distance.

She listened, and afterwards asked if I was bothered that he had been talking to someone else instead of me. I wasn't about to admit what I knew was a very big part of the truth, so I just brushed her suggestion away and reminded her that we were cousins, so I couldn't be jealous of that. She gave me a leery look that showed she didn't buy the whole relation thing anymore, but I ignored it.

She asked me if I didn't think I was overreacting, and although I denied it immediately, I went back to consider it. I had to believe that I was because there was no other reasonable explanation for my distress.

Maybe Marilyn was a classmate of his and they just happened to meet at the table. Maybe he had a lot on his mind so he was too distracted to pay me any mind. But that was part of the problem, because I would never have been too distracted to pay him the attention I believed he deserved from me.

I cared too much and it was a problem, but despite this, I went early to dinner that evening hoping to catch him. He was at his usual table with James and to an extent that relieved me, because at least he wasn't missing meals like he had been the previous week. I snuck peeks at him throughout the entire dinner hoping he would turn to seek me out, but when I never caught his stare, I completely lost my appetite.

It was only when Elisa kicked me beneath the table and asked me if I had a death wish, that I realized that I had been outright staring at him, my emotions completely bared on my face. I straightened and continued moving my food around.

"Do you think I should go over to say hi?" I asked Elisa.

She looked up from her plate.

"No, I don't think so," she said, almost sarcastically.

"But why?" I argued. "Last week I was able to do that."

"That was last week, and you know why." Then she looked to his table. "It doesn't even matter now because he's leaving."

"What?"

She was right, and after he left, I turned back to her.

"He didn't even look for me," I said. She didn't know how to respond.

ॐ

The week passed much too slowly and by the end of it, I felt like a mess. Thrice more I had seen him in the dining hall – once more with Marilyn and the rest with James. So when I had woken up on Saturday with the urge to cry, I had finally realized that my infatuation had gone too far. My resolve was to completely toss him out of my mind, so I started working at it.

When lunch time came on Monday, instead of going out to the courtyard like I would have if I'd expected to see him, I went up to the library to continue the reading rituals in my secluded corner- a routine that I'd almost forsaken. Elisa had said she'd stop by before lunch ended so when I felt someone approaching, I expected to see her. But instead, I looked up to see Nathan walking towards me.

I was transfixed in surprise as I watched him approach, and could do nothing but stare until he came to stand right in front of my table. My heart was hammering away in my chest.

"Hey," he greeted, but I was too stunned to respond. I eventually took my eyes away from him, and calmly returned to my novel.

I could no longer see the words, but it didn't matter. I kept my eyes on the pages because at that moment, I had nothing to say, and it was surprising. The previous week, I could have written a book on the insults I'd have loved to throw at him. Seeing him now, I was speechless and nervous. My hands were beginning to tremble.

"Aren't you going to reply me?" he asked.

I turned a page and said, "Please go away." I was astonished at how steady I sounded when my insides were frying in turmoil.

Pulling out a seat from the opposite side of the table, he placed it in front of me and sat down. I still refused to acknowledge his presence until he took hold of the sides of my chair, and turned it so that I faced him.

"Nathan..." I complained, and had a frown waiting for him as soon as he refocused his gaze on me. I stared at him; the brilliance of his beautiful blue eyes and the way his hair, now longer than I'd ever seen it fell in thick dark brown waves, past his ear and to just below the edge of his collar. Despite my awe at seeing him this way again, the hurt and anger over his neglect for the past week rose up to overthrow my delight at his presence.

"What's this?" I asked. "You ignore me for weeks and now all of a sudden you show up?"

"I didn't ignore you."

"Really? Okay."

I started to turn away but he held me still with his hand on my arm, and urged my gaze to return to his.

"Nora," he said, but I brushed his hand away.

"Just leave me alone," I said half-heartedly, but inwardly, I screamed at him not to listen to me. I wished he would notice the pain in my eyes without me having to say anything, because I had missed him.

Suddenly he leaned forward, and the next thing I knew he had slanted his head to take my mouth in a soft, but ardent kiss. My eyes flew open as soon as I tasted him, and reflexively, I pulled myself away from him.

He refused to give me a moment to recover, so sliding his hand around my neck, he brought my head closer to his and kissed me again.

"Nathan," I breathed, stunned at the thrill that shot through my body. Liquid fire began to burn low in the pit of my stomach. I couldn't move, and when I closed my eyes again for another kiss, my lips trembled as his met mine.

It started as a slow caress, and each time his lips graced mine, I fought to savor the taste before I let go. Then I felt his fingers under my chin to hold it in place just before he slanted his head again, but this time, kissed me deeply.

It enraged the fire inside of me, making me almost fall out of my chair, but without stopping, he reached out to steady me. Then with one hand around my waist, he pulled me up and led me to the wall. My legs had turned to rubber so I leaned against it, partly conscious of what I was doing. Then I lifted up on tiptoes to reach his mouth again.

I could feel his smile as he bent his head to meet mine, and kissed me again. The feel of his body pressed against mine was driving me insane, and as I gripped the lapels of his blazer to bring him closer to me, I could not believe that this was happening.

I was actually kissing Nathan, not the senseless peck he had given to Kate, but a full, mind blowing kiss that was sucking all the life out of me.

I couldn't get enough of him, and as the fire found its way to my brain, I threw my hands around his neck to bring him even closer. He widened his legs and with a palm flattened on the wall behind my head, pushed against me to do the same.

"Ahem," I heard someone clear their throat from a distance, but I didn't care. Nathan on the other hand was more alert. He turned to see who it was and then let me go, his breathing as ragged as mine. Thankfully, it wasn't the librarian standing there but Elisa, wide-eyed and cheeks flushed a bright crimson. She looked amused.

I turned back to him and watched as he ran a hand through his hair. He took a deep breath to help calm himself before turning to face her. His cool mask was now back on and once again, he was in control. I, on the other hand, was barely managing to stand still.

"Elisa," he said with a small smile, and her cheeks turned brighter. He then turned to me, gave a small nod and walked away.

We both stared at him as he left until Elisa turned to look at me, her eyes still round with surprise.

"What was that?" she asked, sounding every bit as dazed as I felt, but I couldn't respond. After a few minutes of mindless staring and deep, heavy breaths, I was finally able to remain upright without the help of the wall. She came closer as I started to slowly gather my things and said, "Isn't there a curse attached to kissing relatives?"

I shot her a fiery look, but she wasn't deterred. She went on, a little too excited. "I knew it! I knew that you guys weren't related. That whole cousin stuff was just plain rubbish, and *God*, that kiss …"

"If you don't shut up I'm going to hit you," I threatened her, but she ignored me and leaned against the table seemingly enraptured in a dreamy state. She straightened when she saw that I had collected my bag and was walking past her.

"You have to tell me all about it," she said as she hurried after me, but I just closed my eyes and ignored her. Her squeal haunted me.

෨

For the rest of the afternoon, my classes passed more quickly than I would have ever thought possible. Through the entire four hours my mind had remained on the kiss, and why in hell I had allowed it.

With the current issues we already had between us, this was the last thing we needed. It was now another reason to wonder where we even stood with each other. We were supposed to be *just* friends, but after today, that obviously didn't make any sense, as well as the 'cousin' story which Elisa now knew wasn't true.

The question now was where we were going to go from here.

Would we return back to how we were initially, go somewhere else or just remain situational strangers?

I grew more confused as each moment passed, and by the end of the day I was more than ready to return to the hall. I was exhausted and tired of thinking, so as I laid on my bed still unable to stop, I decided to write it all in my journal.

It would hopefully help me carve some sense out of the entire episode and probably make for excellent memories even if it all went downhill from here because one thing was for sure – I did *not* want to forget what had happened today.

Retrieving my brown journal from my wardrobe, I flipped it open to the first page. It was practically empty except for some very brief and indiscernible notes. And of course my mother's signature scribbled boldly across the first page.

I recalled the day I had bought it and how she had teased me about the cover.

"It's so boring," she'd said, and she offered to get me a new one. Something that would undoubtedly have looked more like it belonged to a girl, with glitters and bright colors, but I'd refused.

In the end she'd accepted my resolve for it to be plain, but had insisted that her signature across it would give it the glamorous touch that it needed, and she'd been right.

I miss you... I thought, as I ran my fingers across the scribble that seemed to bring the journal to life. I probably would have told her about Nathan, and she'd have known exactly what to do, but now I had to figure it out on my own.

Maybe she'd have wanted me to not overthink the entire situation like I currently was, but I couldn't help it. Some people still had enough room to stomach the pain of getting hurt but over the last three years, I'd been through too much to be careless.

Nevertheless I wanted to remember the memories, clearly and vividly, so I started writing from the kiss in the library and how it all connected – or didn't – with everything else that had happened since I had met him.

Ten pages later, I was still going when someone knocked on my door. Unhappy at the interruption, I pushed the journal under my pillow and told the person to come in. Elisa walked in, her curly hair pulled back in a tight ponytail.

"Matthew and I made up today," she said, and came to sit on the edge of my bed. I was happy for her and told her so.

"He approached me during lunch and we talked, and he apologized. What do you think?"

"That's good. Hopefully he doesn't repeat the same mistakes this time."

"Hopefully," she said.

"What about you and Nathan?"

I scowled at her.

"There is no 'me and Nathan'," I countered. "We're just—"

"Cousins?" she interrupted with a smirk.

I rolled my eyes.

"We're friends. I just told people that to get them to back off."

"I understand. If I had someone like that in love with me, I'd do anything to get them to back off."

I glared at her like she was crazy. It seemed like she was deliberately trying to misunderstand me.

"I wasn't trying to get anybody to back off from him, I meant me. My life was starting to get too complicated."

"Oh," she said and smiled sheepishly. "But still …"

"But nothing. We're friends. There's no love involved, anywhere."

"*Right*," she replied disbelievingly.

"I'm serious Elisa."

"I didn't say you weren't."

I sighed. "First of all, love isn't even on the table here. Ask me about that when I'm in my late twenties and have a lot more sense. Secondly, if at all there would be anything, it would be a 'like', and nothing more."

"A very strong *like*," she added, and I frowned at her. "Excuse me, but have you watched yourselves when you're both together?" she asked.

"What do you mean?"

"I don't know how to explain it, but I can remember how I've felt watching the both of you. Jealous almost, and then I wasn't sure why because you were related, so of course there would be a sort of familiarity and fondness present. But with the both of you it was just... *more* and I couldn't understand why I felt that way. I got my answer today."

I was silent as I pondered her words, then I decided to share something with her. "I'm not sure I want to have anything *more* with him," I said.

"Why?" she asked.

"Honestly, because I'm scared. He's too unpredictable, and I can never quite guess what's going on in his mind or what he's about to do."

"But he cares about you."

"Elisa, even that I'm sometimes not certain of, but yes, I think he does. In his own weird way."

"Well, it's a start. But, do you ever think he might just be messing with you?"

A little fear crept into my heart. "Where's that coming from?"

"The fact that he's a guy ... and these things don't mean as much to them as they do to us."

I looked away. That had never crossed my mind and I didn't like how I felt about it.

"Anyway I have to go, I'm meeting Matthew before dinner," she said. "By the way, was that your first kiss?"

For some reason I was more amused than shy as I replied her. "It was."

"Well, you're one of the lucky few. At least it wasn't a mess."

"No comment."

"Don't worry you don't need to comment. I was there so I'll always be able to remind you that you were still disorientated even after he'd left."

"Go away," I groaned, and she laughed as she walked away.

I brought my journal out from under my pillow and went through my entries again. I read through everything, reminiscing through the accounts I'd written down so far. When Elisa's comment began to echo in my head, I closed the book and took a moment to consider it.

Could it even be possible that he was actually playing with me? For all I knew Nathan might've been doing and saying things behind my back that I wasn't aware of. I wondered why it had never crossed my mind before. Maybe it was because of who he was – he just seemed too mature to act so shady. But then again, I didn't know him. All I knew was the person he'd wanted me to see.

Nevertheless, I felt drugged; the emotions and images of our rendezvous in the library still overwhelming me. I knew I still had to make sure that I kept myself under control, so I wouldn't fall for him, but falling in love didn't just happen overnight. I still had time.

« CHAPTER 17 »

Nathan was at dinner later that evening, and as soon as I got in and saw him, I didn't know what to expect. But halfway through the meal, I knew- because although he had kissed me in the library like I had mattered to him, right here and in the presence of all, a mere glance was too expensive to spare.

The message was clear.

However I continued to steal glances at him, and most times just outright stared- but he never lifted his head from his meal to look anywhere else, except when he wanted to talk to James. It was like he was a stranger, and as I watched him- trying to understand what the hell was happening, it got to the point where

I was staring so much that Elisa kicked me from underneath the table.

She warned me to stop, and I did because I just didn't have the strength in me to keep up with him anymore. But towards the end of dinner, I wanted to go over to speak to him- just to plainly ask what the problem was because nothing made sense. I could ignore him the way he did me, but I just needed to understand what was going on... and why?

I spoke to her about it and she asked me if I was out of my mind. "Have you forgotten what Beverly did to you even though everyone thinks you're cousins?"

"Elisa, I don't..." I exhaled. "He hasn't even looked up once to try to find me here – it's almost as if I don't exist."

"Well that's not true."

"What do you mean?"

"He looks at you when you look away," she said, her tone still somewhat harsh.

She rolled her eyes when a smile broke out on my face.

"Really? When? I kept looking at him but he never turned."

"That's because he's smarter than you."

"Ouch?"

She sighed. "Lennie, you need to be careful, and also, if knowing that he has been stealing glances at you for the last hour is all it takes for you to smile like this, then you're so screwed."

"I am not," I said, as I put a fry in my mouth. I glanced at him again, and this time I caught his stare. It was so unexpected that I froze, and this time, he left his eyes on me for a few seconds before turning away. I had to take a few deep breaths after that to keep my heart from exploding in my chest.

સ૦

I got into bed late that evening, and was almost falling asleep when my laptop started ringing with a video call from him.

I almost went into shock, but recovered enough to accept it just before it disconnected.

"Hi," he said, when his face came into view.

"Hey," I responded, and that was all we said for the next few seconds. He eventually broke the ice.

"You have a chemistry test on Monday," he said.

I frowned. "Why do you know about that?"

He ignored the question and went on. "We need to study for that."

I sighed. "Okay, thank you. But first I want to ask you something."

"Shoot."

"You um … there are times you act like, like you care but then sometimes it's like you don't. Why?"

He was silent for a few moments before he said, "I don't understand."

That made me angry. "You know exactly what I'm talking about."

"Lenora don't do this."

"What do you mean by *don't do this*."

"What do you want me to say?"

"I want you to tell me what's going on, and don't you dare act like it's all in my head."

He sighed. "It's not, but everything's fine."

Just then Olivia walked in, so I told him to give me a second as I reached under my desk for my earphones.

"Can you hear me?" I asked when I'd plugged them in.

He nodded.

"Please help me understand what's going on."

"Nora, there's noth –" he started, but I interrupted. I had to literally clench my teeth to keep myself from yelling at him.

"Why won't you talk to me?"

"There's nothing to say," he said.

"Really?"

"Yes. Really."

I cut the call on him.

⇣

The next day I went to the library to sort out my own chemistry dilemma. It was my worst subject and after the thrill of getting a 'B' on my second worst, which was math, I wanted to give this as much effort as I could. Thirty minutes into the struggle, I'd started to regret that I'd rejected Nathan's offer to help me when I heard soft footsteps approaching.

I looked up to see Nathan walking towards me. I'd hoped that he'd look for me, but now that he was here, I didn't want to have to deal with him, because the confusion that both he and chemistry were bringing to my life was too exhausting.

"What happened yesterday?" he asked when he reached the front of my table. He sounded pissed.

"What do you mean?" I asked, trying to control my own annoyance.

"You hung up on me!"

"Well, you kept avoiding my questions."

"I didn't avoid your questions."

I sighed. "Nathan, you ignore me for weeks and then all of a sudden start caring again, and you don't think I need an explanation? Do you really think I'm stupid?"

"Don't put words in my mouth."

"Well that's the problem right there; you're not *saying* anything. It seems like you expect me to just go with the flow- to just ignore whatever you do and then of course jump to the call whenever you decide that I'm worth your time. Well, I'm sorry to disappoint you. You might think me dumb enough to do that, but I can't. I still respect myself."

Rising to my feet, I gathered my things, and hoped that as I walked past him that he would stop me. If not to say anything, but at least to apologize and promise that he would make me understand as soon as he could. But he didn't.

I returned to my classroom, wondering how I had allowed someone to be able to make me feel miserable.

∞

My sour mood continued until dinnertime, where I made sure not to even care if he was present. I was glad to see James though, who came over to see what we were up to. He noticed that I seemed unhappy and asked me what was wrong.

"Chemistry's torturing her," Elisa supplied with a bright smile.

He turned to me. "Is that really what's wrong?" he asked.

I frowned at her. "Don't pay any attention to her, I'm fine," I said, but he wasn't convinced.

"I could help you with it," he offered. "I'm science savvy…"

"Yay," I said in a flat tone.

He chuckled. "Seriously though, it's not that hard. I'm sure it'll be easier for you when we're done. What time is your test?"

"It's on Monday, but don't worry about it; I'll sort myself out before then."

"Are you sure?"

"I am. Thank you."

"You're welcome," he said, and left a few minutes later when he was done talking to Elisa. They seemed to be more familiar with each other than I'd originally thought.

I returned to my room after dinner and spent the rest of the weekend trying to figure out my chemistry notes, and filling in my journal. Despite the fact that I'd barely ever been able to keep a journal and update it regularly, this one was filling up quite nicely.

I wrote everything I could remember about Nathan and I. At first it was just for closure, but then I got lost in it, and then sad, because as the days passed, I realized that this could very well be the end for the both of us.

ᔕᗡ

My test on Monday morning was as horrible as I'd expected, and that set my mood for the rest of the week. I was withdrawn from everyone, even Elisa, and by the end of the week, I realized I was back to the way I'd been before I'd met Nathan.

My time with him hadn't exactly been blue skies, but at least I'd reacted during that period – I'd laughed and I'd cried and I'd been excited. But now I was just bored and hurt and back to wishing again that I didn't feel.

We had socials that weekend. The party was held in the open field that separated the house area from the main school block, and despite Elisa's pleas to accompany her, I'd stayed in my room and dozed on and off to the soft sound of Simon and Garfunkel's 'The *Sound of Silence'*. It was a really old song that my mum had always listened to, but it wasn't till she'd died that I'd been able to understand, and come to resonate with its lyrics. Now, whenever I felt as heavyhearted as I currently did, I listened to it, and somehow, it calmed me.

By two a.m., the racket of exhausted students as they returned to their rooms drew me from my sleep. The party was over, but my night had just started. I stayed up reading a novel, but my mind constantly wandered back to Nathan. I kept wondering if he had attended the party, and if he had, who he had gone with. A few hours later, Elisa came in and climbed into bed with me.

"Enjoy the party?" I asked, and she smiled before letting out a wide yawn. I got up from the bed and went to stand by the window; it was starting to rain outside.

"How come Olivia isn't back yet?"

I shrugged. "She's probably with her sister."

"Alex was there," she said quietly. "He didn't stay for long though."

I'd decided that I wasn't going to ask- because it didn't matter, but I couldn't help myself. "Did he go with anyone?"

"I don't think so. I did see him with Marilyn at some point but he left before the party was even halfway through. I told you, you should have come."

I returned to the bed. "So now I should plan my life based on Nathan's decisions?"

She frowned. "I always get confused when you use that name. Why not just call him Alex?"

"I prefer Nathan," I said, and dragged the covers over us.

"Anyway, where do you think you'll be spending your midterms?"

"I usually spend it back home, but I'm thinking of staying back this time around."

She instantly shot up from the bed, displacing the duvet that I'd just arranged over us. I sighed.

"Really?" she beamed excitedly. "Who're you planning to stay with?"

"Uh ... I'm not sure right now." I answered, amused at how excited she'd become.

"You could stay with me," she said. "I mean there's plenty of space back at home, well not plenty but it's more than enough for you. And you'd love my family. And my mum will love you, she'll have someone she can boss around and compare me to for a fortnight. And my brothers, they're still little but they're adorable. There'll be work though, both in the house and at the bookstore, but it'll be fun. I promise."

"Your family owns a bookstore?" I asked.

"Mm-hm," she grinned. "It's not huge but it's okay. I'm sure you'll like it."

"I'm sure I will," I said, beginning to feel excited too. "I'll ask my dad and see what he says. I'll get back to you soon."

"Okay!" she squealed, before returning to her side of the bed.

"Let's have a makeover." she said out of the blue.

I immediately refused.

"Come on," she urged. "It'll be fun, I promise – and no funny stuff. You can revert it if you're not okay with it."

"No." I repeated, but she kept on talking about it until I finally agreed. She left to get her things and returned a few minutes later with a huge pink bag. She unzipped it and brought out a hair dryer. Leaning forward for a closer look, I saw that she had almost everything in there; a curling iron, hairbrushes and a couple of smaller bags in the same striped pattern as the main one. I hesitated for a moment, but pushed my concern aside when I saw the sparkle in her eyes as she waited for me to get up and go over to my desk.

An hour and some minutes later, we were in front of the mirror in my wardrobe and admiring my new hairdo. She had first of all straightened my hair and then curled into soft shiny waves that I just couldn't stop ruffling.

"Stop ruining it," she pleaded but I couldn't help it; it felt fantastic.

"It doesn't matter," I said. "I'm going to ruin it before Monday anyway,"

"Obviously, but at least let me savor my hard work for today. I know you're not going to let me do this again."

"Fine," I said, unable to drag my gaze away from the mirror. I looked beautiful. It was amazing how much difference a good hairdo could make.

My mind wandered to Nathan, and I found myself wondering what his reaction would be if he saw me like this. I smiled sadly and ran my fingers through the curls again.

I missed him – a lot – and it annoyed me that life could be so complicated that a simple friendship between two people couldn't even be sustained. I pushed him out of my mind and strengthened my resolve to forget about him.

I knew I'd failed woefully when hours later, I was re-curling my hair in preparation for dinner. I tried not to think of the real reason for the care in my appearance, but I could see a knowing look in Elisa's eyes when she came into my room and saw what I was doing. Thankfully, she kept her comments to herself and soon we were on our way to the dining hall.

When we arrived, the place was as rowdy as usual but our usual seats had been occupied. Elisa spotted Matthew and immediately started to pull me along. I refused to go with her.

"It's Nathan's table." I said.

"You don't have to talk to him." she said, and didn't wait for me to argue. She pulled me along and I ended up sitting next to the spot that Nathan usually sat in. Elisa sat beside Matthew, which was opposite me, and immediately forgot that I existed as she chatted away with him.

James was also at the table and had started talking to me as soon as I sat down. I enjoyed speaking to him, but still felt nervous about the moment that Nathan would come in. I hadn't spoken to Nathan since the day in the library, and I was nervous. Maybe things would be better if we saw each other now, I allowed myself to hope, but when we had already collected our meals and he still hadn't showed up, I finally accepted that he wasn't going to come.

I thought I'd be disappointed but instead I was angry; angry at him, and then angry at myself because once again I'd broken my resolve to never go out of my way for anything, when it came to him.

સ્ર

The next day, which was Monday, we entered the last week of the first half of the term. The day had been good so far, and even though I had done a terrible job of curling my hair, it had still been a considerable change from the familiar jumble.

I had even taken time with my uniform. Both my pinafore and dress-shirt were neat and pressed – ill-fitted though, but still an improvement. No one had stepped on my toes- not even the teachers, I'd had a peaceful lunch with Elisa and Matthew and for the first time, was actually paying attention in my chemistry class.

All this was until Mrs. Zimmerman decided to return our chemistry test papers. I got an F, and it hurt because I'd actually tried and written something down. Apparently it had been rubbish.

I stared dejectedly at the marker board after that, the disappointment seemingly pulling on the strings of the heavyheartedness that had plagued me all weekend long. It overwhelmed me until I literally couldn't breathe. I had to get out of there. So I excused myself and left the class.

I didn't know where to go so I just headed towards my locker, the test script crumpled in my hand.

I really, *really* wanted to have done better. Maybe it was to prove to myself that Nathan being absent in my life wouldn't make a difference, and that I could still be a little happier and successful at my school work. That I didn't need him to tutor me or make me feel like I existed, or give me at least one reason in my *damn* life to be excited about something.

I crumpled the paper in my hand even more, then let out a long breath to steady my rising temper. I was starting to really hate him- for everything. For being present in the first place, and then for leaving- without a word. I didn't need him. I didn't need anyone, but damn it, he'd made me care about myself, and I didn't want to go back to being and feeling so dark that even in my own eyes, I didn't matter.

When I turned the corner that led into the hallway that housed my locker, I stopped dead in my tracks when I saw that Nathan was standing beside my locker. I watched as he slipped an envelope into one of the openings, and then turned to walk away.

I watched him leave, and wanted to call him back but my mouth wouldn't work. So I just stared after him but suddenly, he stopped. Then he glanced backwards and our gazes met. My heart dropped into my stomach.

It seemed like a full minute passed before I finally broke our gaze, and started walking towards my locker. But really, it may have only been just a few seconds. But in that moment, everything seemed to have slowed down. The tap of my shoes against the floor suddenly seemed too loud, and my breathing was ragged. I could hear the pulse of my now accelerated heartbeat in my ears.

He started moving towards me and I grew nervous, because I didn't know what I was going to do or say. I wasn't even sure I wanted him to come any closer. Just leaving without a word like he'd been doing so far would be perfect, but he didn't leave. He reached me just as I turned towards my locker and began to open it. He waited beside me for a few seconds and then I felt his hand touch my arm. I brushed it away.

I continued struggling with the combination for my padlock, but just couldn't get it right, especially since my hands were now trembling. Eventually, I just got pissed and wanted to slam my palm against the stupid locker. Instead I turned, and started to walk away.

He caught my hand and gently pulled me back. I tried with my other free hand to release his grip from around my wrist but it didn't budge.

"Nora look at me," he pleaded.

I shook my head. "Leave me alone."

He took a step closer to me, and it was way too close. I saw him briefly look to his sides to confirm that we were alone and then he lowered his head towards mine, literally forcing me to meet his gaze. I still refused, and kept my eyes at a point above his shoulder.

"I'm sorry," he said. "So please don't be mad at me."

"Don't be mad at you? Let me go," I said, but then realized that he wasn't holding me. I turned to walk away but again, he caught my hand and pulled me back. I didn't see it coming until suddenly, his lips were on mine, soft and moist.

Fire shot through my body.

My automatic response was to hold on to him by the sides of his arms, but when I realized what I was doing, I tore my mouth away from his and pushed him away. I was grateful it didn't move him an inch though because I would have dropped to the floor if he had let me go- I couldn't feel my legs!

"What're you doing?" I whispered. I couldn't find my voice.

"Getting you to talk to me?" he said, sounding like he was trying to convince himself that that was a valid excuse.

"Are you kidding me?" I asked.

He shut his eyes then and brought his hand to rest on his forehead, his chest heaving up and down from trying to control his breathing.

I watched him, and even though I was mad at him, I couldn't control the longing for him that filled my heart. With my hand on his shoulder, I lifted myself up on my tip toes for another kiss.

I was mad at myself for doing this but God help me, kissing him had to be the best feeling in the entire world. It felt like everything had come alive inside of me, and I never wanted it to end. But it had to, so after savoring the taste and fire of him one last time, I finally pulled away.

"I hate you," I said as I leaned back against the locker, and pounded on his chest with my fist.

He chuckled. And then said, "Lenora I really am sorry."

I waited, but he didn't say anything more.

"Is that it?" I asked, and just then, the bell that signaled the start of lunch time rang throughout the school. I didn't care but he did. He let go of my hand and took a step back.

"I'll talk to you soon," he said apologetically, and then turned around to walk away.

I stared after him until he disappeared out of sight, just as people began filling the hallway.

Picking up my crumpled test paper that had fallen to the ground, I turned around to work the combinations on my padlock. It budged this time around so slipping it off the hook, I pulled the locker open and tossed the crumpled test paper into a corner. Then I noticed the cream colored envelope that was sitting on the shelf. I pried it open and brought out the photograph that was inside.

It was the picture of the both of us that he had taken at the waterfall.

« CHAPTER 18 »

I didn't see Nathan for the rest of the week, and by the time Saturday rolled by, I was more than ready to head home with Elisa.

She lived in South Ealing- London, and from the moment we arrived, I was made to feel more at home than I could have ever hoped for.

Her mom, boisterous and warm, had approached me with two small children closely at her heels. She had her hair in a loose ponytail, a spatula in hand and a flowered apron covering her jeans and T-shirt.

At first I wasn't sure what would qualify as an appropriate greeting for her, but she solved that dilemma for me when she captured me in a bear hug the moment I walked through the door.

Her dad had been extremely polite and gentle. We didn't get much out of him on the four-hour ride from school to their place, and not much thereafter either. Elisa's younger sister- Melissa -who was thirteen, had appeared beside her mum as soon as she released me. She smiled shyly at us, and then returned to her room.

The younger two, Justin and Jeremiah, just snuck around me until dinner had ended that night. And each time I would turn to look at them, they would duck and squeal in delight at the stranger they thought they were hiding from.

I played along with them and pretended that I indeed had no clue that I was being followed. They were extremely adorable; Justin, who was four, had dark blond curly hair just like Elisa, while Jeremiah, also known as 'the cherub' because of his pudgy frame was three-years-old, and had his dad's straight dark hair.

It didn't take me long to like Elisa's family, and although her mom's constant screaming was a lot to take in at first, the warmth I felt from all of them was as unfamiliar as it was exhilarating. I shared Elisa's room with her, and since I hadn't brought too much with me from school, it didn't take me long to unpack and settle down.

We were allowed to sleep in, but the constant noise from the ground floor hindered our enjoyment of it. By the afternoon, Elisa's mom's screaming drove us downstairs for a late breakfast. We had to fend for ourselves since her mom had disappeared into her bedroom, and at first I was shy, but by the time Jeremiah had bathed me twice with spoon catapults from his cereal bowl, my reserve flew out the window.

Seizing his bowl, I ran around the kitchen with it while he squealed and pursued me. Justin soon joined in the chase, and before long we were all on the floor, drenched with milk and cereal.

Elisa avoided our chaos and chose to silently make toasts for us, which I later ate with ice cream that the boys had tricked me into stealing for them. Apparently it was prohibited until dinner, but since I couldn't be faulted for breaking rules I knew nothing about, I automatically became their fall guy.

When we were done, we helped Elisa's mom clean out the backyard. She'd been saving it for Elisa to do and it was almost a joy to see the pain on her face, when her mom broke the news to her. We had completed it happily though, and in no time we were finished and in front of the television for the remaining part of the evening. Jeremiah stuck to me like glue all night, so I had to be the one to put him to bed.

He grinned at me and refused to close his eyes, even after I'd gone through three of his story books. An hour later, I woke up with my head on his duvet and thankfully, he was asleep. I switched off his bedside lamp, and returned to my own bed- exhausted, but happy. The next day proved to be even better.

&⊙

The bookstore was only about twenty minutes from the house so Elisa and I got up early, and walked over. I was very excited at what we would meet and the moment I walked in, I fell in love with it.

It wasn't an intimidating bookstore, but a cozy one. It wasn't the kind of place that scared you from rendering any of the books out of place, but one that made you want to cross your legs on the floor to devour a title and then crawl on to explore.

At first it looked too small, but when I got beyond the narrow entrance, I saw that it opened up into a much bigger space. In some areas, the books that weren't on the shelves were stacked from the floor to the ceiling. In a way, it made the place look like a well-kept attic of books stored by members of the family over the years.

We immediately headed to her dad's office, which was at the back of the bookstore. Elisa knocked once on the ancient looking door and without waiting for permission to enter, she dragged me in after her.

Her dad's office surprisingly contained only a few books that sat on a small bookshelf behind him. He was going through some documents on his desk, but raised his head the moment we came in.

"Hey girls," he greeted with a wide smile. Elisa went over to give him a hug while I scanned my eyes around the office. There were some opened boxes filled with books on the floor, so I ignored Elisa and her dad and tried inclining my head so that I could see what kind of books they held. I straightened a few moments later to find them watching me.

"Do you like books Lenora?" he asked with a gentle smile on his face.

I nodded in response.

"Well, Elisa isn't much of a book person but with you here, I'm sure she'll enjoy helping out. Two of my staff took some time off this week so I'm glad the both of you will be around to assist Mark."

As if on cue, there was a small knock on the door. Elisa's dad told the person to come in, and introduced the tall brown-haired guy that entered the room as Mark; he looked no older than twenty years of age, or twenty-two at most.

After sparing I and Elisa a small smile, he handed the clipboard that he had in his hand to Elisa's dad. Elisa on the other hand kept her now enlarged eyes on him, and then turned to me with a 'do-you-see-how-cute-he-is?' look on her face. I just shook my head at her. Her dad signed whatever was on the clipboard and then handed it back to Mark.

"Girls, could you go with Mark- he'll show you what to get started on."

"Okay," Elisa said eagerly, and left his side.

I nodded politely and followed, as she walked out of his office. Mark stopped by a shelf along the way to check on something, while Elisa and I headed straight for the counter. She turned around to make sure that he couldn't see her, and then buckled her knees to lean weakly against the counter.

"Did you see him?" she mouthed like all the breath had been sucked out of her.

"Did I see who?" I deliberately repeated, frowning, because I was certain that she had a boyfriend.

She straightened and slapped my arm, then stretched her neck to get another glimpse of him. "Lennie, I'm just checking him out. It's not a big deal."

"Said everyone who ever got into trouble," I said, and reached out to stroke a stack of magazines that sat on the counter.

Just then, a waft of strong perfume reached my nostrils and I turned around to see Mark behind us. "So, you guys are going to have to help me arrange the new books that just came in," he said politely. "They're in the reading section."

I turned back to Elisa to see her absent-mindedly twirling her hair, so I grabbed her hand and dragged her away before she could become anymore embarrassing. She grudgingly followed me until we reached the reading section, and found the boxes on the floor.

There were no windows in this part of the store, which seemed necessary since the walls seemed to be made out of shelves of books. A beautiful antique chandelier hung from the ceiling and gave the area a warm glow. Two huge black sofas surrounded by a low wooden coffee table sat in the middle of the room, inviting me to collapse on them with a book in hand and a steaming cup of anything.

Saving the mental image for later, I sunk to the floor and dragged a box to myself. Elisa did the same, and after explaining what we were supposed to do, we got to work.

ဆ

Three hours later, Elisa let out a loud yawn as she stretched her arms above her head, and then laid down on the floor.

"I'm tired," she complained, but I wasn't. So far, sorting through the various novels had been exhilarating and more than enough to completely hold my attention.

From the corner of my eye, I saw her suddenly sit up. "I'm going to go ask Mark to come with us for coffee," she said and without asking for my opinion, went ahead to ask him. She came back with a huge smile on her face, and relayed his agreement. Within minutes we were out and on our way, Elisa's dad stationed at the counter until we returned.

⃞

The smell of pastries that assaulted me as we walked into the cafe made me inhale greedily. Although the place seemed really busy, I was able to find us a vacant table by the corner, while Elisa and Mark went over to the counter to place our orders. I took my seat and looked out through the dented, but polished wooden frame of the wide glass windows.

Across the street, the sight of two toddlers tugging on the skirt of their mother as she placed bags of groceries in the trunk of her small car, made me smile as it reminded me of Elisa's brothers. Earlier that morning, Jeremiah had woken up and called out to me just as Elisa and I had walked past his room. He'd made me promise to bring back a new story to read to him tonight and so far, I'd already found two for him.

Just then, the sound of familiar laughter brought me back and I turned to see Mark and Elisa returning. Beside them was ... *James?*

I instantly froze, and only recovered enough to send him a soft smile when he called out to me.

Elisa saw my surprise and immediately explained. "Sorry, I forgot to mention- his dad owns the café." she said.

James placed a tray of Styrofoam coffee cups and a plate of delicious looking scones on our table before turning to me. Elisa took her seat while Mark excused himself to go to the bathroom.

"Wow! It's so strange to see you here," he said, a wide grin spread across his face. "What happened? Where you finally chased out of your country?"

"Ha!" I said dryly. "Even if I was, I wouldn't come here."

His mouth hung open; Elisa arched her eyebrow.

"What's that supposed to mean?" he asked.

"Really, you guys- like you're *so* happy to be in UK." I lifted a scone to my mouth and took a bite.

"Well I am," he said. "What's wrong with the UK?"

"I'm not doing this now."

Elisa laughed. "She does have a point though James."

"What point? She hasn't said anything." He narrowed his eyes at her.

"James go back to work," I said, sincerely pleased to be talking to him but not in the frame of mind to fully engage in the conversation. Come to think of it, the only time I'd ever given him my full attention was the first day we met, and even then it was because I wanted information about Nathan. *What was wrong with me?*

"Well, it's nice to see you," he said and gave my shoulder a fond squeeze. "I'll come over to see you both soon."

"Wow," Elisa said sarcastically. "I never thought I'd see the day."

He snatched away the scone that she was lifting to her lips, and walked quickly away.

"Hey!" she called out, but he didn't turn back. "You owe me a dozen of those when you come over!"

I smiled at their banter as I lifted the Styrofoam cup to my lips. However, a scowl quickly replaced the smile when she turned to face me.

"You forgot to tell me that James's dad owns this place?"

"I really did," she said. "I'm sorry. And besides, if I'd remembered to tell you anyway, you probably wouldn't have come."

"For a good reason," I said exasperated. "What if *he's* here?"

"Would that be so bad?" she asked.

"I don't know," I said. "Still, I'm not saying it makes so much of a difference, but a little heads up would have been nice."

"He's probably not here so, no harm done," she said. "Maybe he went back home."

"Yeah, maybe," I agreed, a little disappointed because I suspected that she was right. It still didn't stop me from looking up every time I heard the entrance door swing open.

Eventually, my compulsion paid off; I saw him the moment he walked into the café.

He headed straight to the counter with the huge carton box that he had in his hands, and passed it over to a staff member who received it on the other side. He'd bunched up the sleeves of the black V-neck sweater that he wore, and had on a baseball cap that kept most of his face hidden from view.

Still, I was able to see him perfectly and as I watched, stunned out of my mind that he was actually standing right there, I didn't even realize when my hand reached out to grab hold of Elisa's.

She had been laughing with Mark about something, but stopped when I touched her to ask me what was wrong. My eyes were still on him, so I didn't have to respond. She traced my line of sight and from somewhere beyond the ringing in my ears that had drowned out the noisy chatter of the café, I heard her gasp.

He seemed to be receiving instructions from the staff member over the counter so we continued to watch him, until he straightened and turned around. My head snapped back so fast that I was dizzy for the next few seconds.

"He's seen us," Elisa said, amused. My heart was pounding painfully in my chest.

"Is he coming over?"

"I don't think so- he just smiled at me though."

"Stop looking at him," I pleaded.

"Don't bother, he already caught you watching him before."

I swore under my breath, and raised the cup of coffee to my lips. Taking a sip, I took a moment to steady myself, and then because I couldn't help it, I glanced back at him as discreetly as I could.

Our eyes met this time around and immediately, I turned my head away. I wanted to leave.

"He's coming over," Elisa said.

"Can we leave?"

She gave a low laugh. "Sure," she said, and turned to ask Mark if he was ready to go.

With a nod, Mark stood to his feet and so did I. I didn't want to but my hand kept going up to my hair-trying to make it less of a mess and tucking the escaped tendrils back into the messy knot on my head. I was nervous, and it showed. Even Mark gave me a concerned look. Finally Nathan came up to us, and I felt his presence even before he spoke.

I was now consciously making the effort to breathe because all the blood in my body had rushed to my head. It felt like I was going to pass out at any moment. My legs had already turned rubbery, but I was used to that whenever he was near. So making sure to maintain a firm grip on the top of the chair, I turned around to face him.

Elisa had already gone ahead to offer him an awkward hug; he seemed genuinely happy to see her. Then he took his cap off and quickly ran his fingers through his hair. He offered Mark his hand for a handshake and introduced himself. Mark took it and did the same. Then it was my turn.

"Nora," he greeted.

I stretched my lips into a thin smile. "Hey."

His gaze lingered on me for a few more moments with a searing familiarity that although squirm-worthy, I sincerely hoped that I wasn't just imagining in my head.

"It's nice to see you."

"You too. I mean me too… I mean *us*. It's nice *we* seeing you."

I could feel Elisa's head turn to me, but I refused to lower mine in shame. *What was happening to me?*

"Me too," he said with a smile. "I have work to do so I'll see you all later?"

"Yeah," Elisa said. "Come by the store some time."

He didn't understand what she meant.

"James will explain," she said, and waved him goodbye. He nodded and walked away.

I waited a few more seconds for the strength to return to my legs, before letting go of the chair and walking out with them.

"Come to the store sometime?" I said to Elisa, not sure if I was unhappy with her that she'd invited him over, or thankful.

"Oh relax," she said. "You can hide in my dad's office if you don't want to see him."

"What's *that* supposed to mean?"

She laughed softly, enjoying teasing me more than I would have liked. "And what *was* that back there? It's nice *we* seeing you."

"Don't judge me."

"Oh I will," she said. "I am judging. Even I wasn't half as bad when I started dating Matthew."

"Elisa, leave me alone," I grumbled.

She finally did, and turned her attention to Mark.

ॐ

When we reached the store, I immediately headed into the reading area, and laid flat on the floor. I felt drugged as I continued to run the way Nathan had looked at me over and over in my mind, until Elisa came over to sit beside me. Some customers were sitting on the couch so she had to lower her voice when she spoke.

"You alright?" she asked. She had to poke my arm twice before I responded.

"Yeah," I said.

"What're you thinking so hard about?"

"Um, did you notice anything strange in the way he looked at me?"

"Strange?"

"Unusual."

"No, Lennie," she said, amused. "He just looked at you, the same way he looks at everyone."

I frowned at her. "You're an idiot."

She sucked in her breath through her teeth. "In this context, that's debatable. But let's say you did see something- is that good?"

"I don't know."

"Either ways, you can't just lie here and act insane. We still have work to."

"I know," I said and sat up.

I pulled a box towards us and we continued our sorting. Thankfully, the task was able to completely occupy my mind until we headed back home.

Elisa's mom had dinner ready when we got home so I just dug in, helped clean up and then ran upstairs with the books that I'd been allowed to take from the bookstore. It was hard deciding which one to begin with but it didn't matter because at the end of the day, I fell asleep barely thirty minutes into the one I'd eventually picked.

∞

I woke up early the next morning and found Elisa's mom already in the kitchen. I'd gone in there for a drink of water but decided to just stay and help her prepare the biscuits and omelets for breakfast.

She tried to initiate conversations with me, but eventually just gave up when all she received from my end were polite nods and shy smiles. She probably thought I was just reserved, but even though I really liked her, I just wasn't comfortable around her yet. I blamed it on the timing being that it was so early in the morning.

It wasn't long before the house was awake, and I watched with amusement as the kids dragged themselves into the kitchen, and grabbed their breakfast using the plates we had stacked on the table.

I sat at the table in the corner with Elisa's mom. Her dad later came in, already dressed, and headed directly over to her and they shared an intimate look. She then got up to serve him the plate she had specially prepared and kept aside for him.

It was sort of uncomfortable watching them together, but Elisa had no reaction so it might have been a normal occurrence. I excused myself and headed up to the bedroom to get ready for work.

Work ... the very thought of the word felt weird to me, but I looked forward to it.

By noon however, I was thoroughly exhausted. Elisa's dad had given us a list of books he needed delivered to a client, so we had to locate the books and prepare them for delivery.

We were at it all morning and by noon, there was still no hope of being done anytime soon. We continued all through that day as well as the next two so I was completely occupied, except for a few times when James came over to deliver pastries that Elisa's dad had ordered for us, and we stopped to have a chat with him.

I'd felt anxious on the first day when I'd seen him talking to Elisa, but when it became apparent that Nathan wasn't going to ever come along, I stopped hoping and just focused on my work. By the time we were done on the third day, I was back to being unoccupied and once again, wanted to see Nathan.

Going by the cafe was unacceptable now because it would be too obvious, but it seemed like the only way I'd get to see him.

Mark and Elisa had gone out while I was still working so I was left alone. It was just past three in the afternoon, and I was starting to entertain daydreams about Nathan and I when Elisa's dad saved me from myself. There was a request from a customer that had just called so I set out to find the books. I had them stacked in my arms and was heading back to the counter when the glass door to the store was pulled open.

I looked up to see Nathan walk in, and stopped in my tracks. It barely registered when the books left my hand and fell to the floor, but I did come to my senses when he glanced at them and then looked at me with an amused smile on his face.

Embarrassed, I bent down to retrieve them but he was already on it. He quickly gathered them together, and handed them over to me. I muttered a "thank you" and placed them on the counter.

"Hey," he said when I turned back to him.

"Hi," I responded.

Slipping his hands into his jeans pocket, he ran his eyes around the room as he told me what he was in search of. It was some journalism book, so I turned around and led him to the section that held the journalism titles.

I decided to help him search, and was running my eyes through the books stacked on the top shelves when I felt him come up behind me. I didn't want to be weird so I stayed absolutely still, but he was close enough to have caused an eyebrow or two to rise if anyone else had been in the room with us.

"I found one," he said.

"Where?" I asked.

He put his hand on my waist to sort of turn me to the direction that he was referring to, and pointed. I took my time trying to locate it with my eyes, just because I wanted his hand to remain where it was. It caused a sweet burn that seared through my skin.

"I'll get the stool," I eventually said, but he took his hand off my side and went towards it. He was tall enough so he just reached up and pulled it out from the shelf.

"That's one," he said with a sweet smile and gave it to me. I was about to start helping him look for the second when the ding of the front door bell, called me away to the counter. I had just handed over the receipt for the books that I had gathered earlier to the customer who'd wanted them, when Nathan came over with the second book in his hand.

"*Point of Departure*," he said and placed both books on the counter.

"Okay," I said, and proceeded to ring them up. When I told him how much they cost, he brought out his wallet, and the wallet reminded me of the first week we met.

"I still owe you, you know," I said, when he handed the money over to me.

He narrowed his eyes. "How so?"

"The lunches that you got me from that first week. I said I was going to reimburse you but I forgot."

He smiled. "I remember telling you to forget about it."

"And I remember saying that I wouldn't."

"Well, technically you did forget," he said, and took the tote that I'd put them in.

"I'll give it to you next time I see you."

He chuckled.

"Why journalism?" I asked, as I took my time fumbling for change.

He shrugged. "It's always interested me, so I'm doing a bit of research to see what career paths I can take."

"You want to be a journalist?"

"I'm considering it," he said, and his eyes turned watchful- as if he was trying to see what I thought about it without actually asking me. I decided to save him the trouble.

"Well I think you'd be a terrible journalist," I stated, as I handed him his change.

He laughed. "Really? And why is that?"

"Well for one, you're terrible at sharing relevant information, and two, you're too reserved. Wait, is being too reserved a good or bad thing? I feel it's both."

"Well, you're the expert," he mocked.

"I *am*."

"What about you? What do you want to do?" he asked.

"I don't know yet."

"When will you know?"

"When I'm your age."

He smiled. "Fair enough. Where's Elisa?"

"She stepped out a while ago- I'm not sure where."

"Say hi to her for when she returns," he said. "And how's your new job?"

I laughed. "It's not really a job, I'm just helping out."

"Okay, so how's your helping out going?"

"It's good," I responded. "It's really good- I like it."

He narrowed his eyes. "How does your dad feel about you spending midterms here?"

"Oh he doesn't care," I answered with more cheer than was appropriate, and instantly saw his concern.

"How's *your* dad?" I asked to change the subject.

"He's okay now. He left the hospital about a week ago."

"Thank God. That's really good," I said, genuinely happy and relieved for him.

"It is. He's back to being troublesome and bossy again."

"He sounds delightful."

"He is. In a way you remind me of him. Is it weird that I'm comparing you to my dad?"

"It kind of is."

"Well, you'll know what I mean when you meet him."

"I look forward to it."

"Me too," he said, and we laughed quietly at each other.

"Well, I have to run now," he said. "But there's another book I'll need. I don't have time to search for it now so can you help me? I'll be by to pick it up tomorrow."

"Yes, of course," I said, trying to keep the excitement out of my voice, and brought out a pad of sticky notes for him to scribble the title on. I went to search for his book the moment he walked out of the store.

« CHAPTER 19 »

He didn't come the next day.

James came instead with a delivery for Elisa's dad and a request from Nathan to pick up a book from me. At first I was stunned, then as I lowered my head and started to ring up the book for James, my heart started to hurt.

All morning long I had been nervous for when Nathan would come in. So even though Elisa had been trying to get me to help her with the boxes of books that she'd had to sort through all morning, I'd given one excuse after the other and remained at the counter, waiting for the moment he'd show up. But instead, he'd sent *James*.

I didn't matter as much to him, as he did to me. That much was now clear... and I wasn't going to take it anymore. If there was one thing that I'd taken away from my parents' marriage, it was that no one would ever be worth my happiness or the waste of my time.

So as I handed the book over to James, I made up my mind that my silliness all morning was the last of my energy that I was ever going to expend towards him.

"Is he busy?" I couldn't help asking.

"No," James replied, as he received the bag that I'd placed the book in. "We were about to come over together but he changed his mind at the last minute, and went to the park instead."

"Why?"

"I don't know. He had a book with him, so I think he just needed the space to read."

"So he wasn't held up by anything important."

"Nah, I don't think so."

"You know what?" I said. "Do you mind if I just give it to him myself? There's something that I need to talk to him about."

"Okay." he said, but looked concerned as he watched me. It was apparently obvious that I was upset.

I went around the counter, and he handed the bag over to me.

"Are you alright?" he asked, and I gave him a small smile.

"I am. Could you please tell Elisa to take over for me? I'll be back in a few minutes."

"Okay," he said, and left to find Elisa.

The park was about a seven minute walk from the bookstore. And then it took me an additional five minutes to look for him before I eventually found him. He was in a secluded area of the park, and was seated on a bench that was shaded by a huge tree.

He was so engrossed in the book open on his lap that even though I stood there for almost a minute watching him, he never looked up once. The park was bursting with activity so there were enough things to distract someone once in a while, but he never let any of them get to him, just like he was with me.

"Nathan" I called, and walked forward to place his book beside him on the bench. I wanted so badly to hit him with it.

"Hey," he replied as he looked up, surprised to see me. I took a few steps away from him.

"James said you were here, so I thought I'd just bring it to you," I said, and wondered why I was even bothering to explain myself to him.

"Thank you," he replied.

I turned to leave, but had only taken a few steps when I stopped, and turned back to him. I found that he was still watching me. "Why didn't you come to pick it up yourself?" I asked.

He didn't seem surprised at the question at all. He shrugged. "I just thought it'd be better if James helped me instead."

"Why?"

He didn't respond.

"Didn't you want to see me?"

He took off his glasses, and lowered his head as he gently folded them. "Of course I did," he said, and looked back up at me.

"Then why didn't you come?"

"It would have been better for Jam–"

"You've already said that. So don't patronize me, we're not in school right now. Just tell me the truth. And don't worry, it's not going to change anything between us, if that's what you're concerned about. I just want to know."

He continued to stare at me, and after sometime I was convinced that like always, he wasn't going to say anything.

"Nathan, I'm done!" I said to him. I wanted to say more but if I had kept my gaze on him for one more second, he would have seen the tears that filled my eyes the moment I turned around.

"Lenora wait!" he said, but I increased my pace.

I never wanted anything to do with him again. This was all my fault. As if the troubles I'd had to begin with weren't enough, I'd gone on and added him to the mix. Of course he was supposed to disappoint me. He was a guy, and that was what they all did.

Suddenly, I felt his hand take a hold of mine but I jerked it away.

"Leave me alone," I said, and continued walking. But I was forced to stop when he overtook me and came to stand right in front of me. I bumped into him and for some reason, the moment I held unto him so that I could stable myself, the tears rolled down my eyes.

"What is *wrong* with you?" I yelled, refusing to meet his eyes. "Get out of my way." I moved to my left so that I could leave, but he moved with me, effectively blocking me from leaving. I stopped, and let out a deep breath.

"Nathan, move!" I ordered, but he refused.

"Look at me." he pleaded.

"No, I want you to get out of my way. Look, this has absolutely nothing to do with you, so could you please get out of my way before I do something to hurt you."

I heard him sigh, and then he said, "Lenora, I'm in love with you."

I felt the pang, *hit* my chest.

What?

I'd never imagined that those words would ever come out of his mouth, so I'd never thought of what my reaction would be. But in that moment, and as the shock of the words began to wear off, I became angry at him.

"What's that supposed to mean?" I asked. "You're going to throw that in my face because you think it's what I want to hear?"

He took a step back from me, and right then, I realized that I had been wrong. He'd meant every word of what he had just said, and I had thrown it in his face. He moved away from me and started walking back to the bench.

I instantly felt horrible. And as I lifted both of my hands to slowly wipe the tears off my face, I thought of what I was going to do. First of all, I didn't know how to feel because at that moment, a thousand and one emotions were coursing through my body.

On one hand, I was beginning to feel the impact of what he'd just said to me, and on the other hand, it seemed too impossible to believe. I was cold, and I was warm; shocked but still skeptic.

Nathan had just told me that he was in love with me. *Holy Shit*!

I turned around, and started heading back to him. I didn't think I could sit down so when I reached him, I just stood to the side and folded my arms across my chest. He turned his head to look at me.

"I'm sorry," I said, and he shook his head. "It's fine."

We were both quiet for some time. Then I spoke.

"If you… um… just like you said, then why have you been acting insane the past couple of weeks?"

At that he let out a laugh, but it was a strained one.

He looked away from me and straight ahead as he responded. "That's *why* I've been acting insane the past couple of weeks. And also I found out about Beverly bullying you, so I just made the decision to stay away."

I had always suspected that he knew but now that he was saying it out, it made me suddenly nervous and I wasn't sure why. "When did you find out?" I asked. "And how?"

"I confirmed it that morning in the courtyard when I asked if you were alright. You looked so exhausted and upset that I expected you to tell me about it, but when you didn't I had to go find out. Plus Elisa had all her worry for you written across her face."

"*Damn her*!" I said, and he smiled again.

"Anyway, Marilyn was telling me about all of it the day you came over to us in the cafeteria. I apologize for how cold I seemed towards you, but at that moment, I was just so *pissed*."

"That's just the first among many apologies," I said with a laugh, but he knew that I wasn't joking.

"I know." he said softly.

"You could've just told me about it, instead of keeping me in the dark the way you did."

"I know," he repeated.

"So why didn't you?"

I knew then that there was another reason why he had stayed away because suddenly, he seemed even unhappier to be telling me any of this. He sighed.

"I thought I could manage this … thing, between us. But when I kissed you, I realized that I couldn't, and I didn't want to make it worse for you than I already had. So I stayed away."

The pain returned to my heart again, but I resisted the urge to press my hand against my chest. "What do you mean?" I asked, almost not wanting to hear the rest of what he had to say, because I was sure that I wasn't going to like it.

"Lenora we're not ready. At this point in our lives, I don't think that we can make this into what it's supposed to be."

"Nathan, that's bullshit."

"It's not."

"Well what about Elisa and Matthew? They're making it work. Why can't we? "

"That's not what I want with you," he said, his tone somewhat harsh. "No offence to them but their relationship has an expiration date."

Suddenly I needed to sit down, but I couldn't bring myself to move. I unfolded my arms from across my chest. "Nathan…" I warned but he went on.

"I don't expect you to completely understand me, but right now, it's more important to me that you're able to find out who you are, and what you really want.

And you need to do it alone, or not be so invested in someone that you're not able to see properly."

I was stunned. What the hell was he saying?

"You just said you're in love with me," I said. "What does that mean in your book? Because in mine, it means that you're ready to try, and fight."

"Lenora, this is me *fighting*. I don't want to just *try* when there's a very huge chance that we might not work. In fact we *won't* work, because we're still too young and uncertain. Neither of us knows what we want yet, and until we do, I'm not willing to gamble away the one thing that I do know I want."

I snorted in disbelief. "You're just being selfish."

"I am, but I'm not going to apologize for that. Lenora we've seen our parents go from being in love to destroying each other. I don't want that to be us. Falling in love is not a big deal because unless you're able to maintain it, they're just feelings. And they come as easily as they go."

"So why did you bother telling me at all if it doesn't mean anything to you?"

"Because I want you to understand me, and what I want. I want *right now* as much as you do, but do you know what I want more? I want to be able to have a long, insanely crazy, and fulfilling life with you. And if we don't choose the battles that we're going to fight, we'll never have that. If this is not what you want then that's fine. But I'm going to hold out and wait, because right now I'm a mess, and so are you."

"I don't think I can wait," I said, partially honest and also in a bid to threaten him enough to change his mind.

He stood up then, and came to stand in front of me.

"I don't expect you to," he said, as he stared deeply into my eyes. "And I'm not claiming to know why I can feel this way about you today, but still be able to hate you just as much, years, or even months down the line. But until I find out, I'm not going to gamble with you. I'd rather not have tried at all than be with you, and then fail. I won't want to recover from that."

He softly brushed his knuckles against my cheeks, and then went over to the bench to retrieve his books. He came back to me to plant a soft kiss on my forehead, before turning around and walking away.

I felt the loss as I watched him leave, but instead of just the cold, it was accompanied with a strange kind of warmth. It all threatened to put me in tears again but I held myself together, and returned to the store as soon as he was out of sight.

« CHAPTER 20 »

"You're late." Elisa said as she came up behind me. I looked up at her through the mirror and flashed a placating smile.

"I'm almost done," I said, but took a few more seconds before releasing my hair from the curling iron. The curl fell in a glorious wave to join the others and I gently ran my fingers through the mass. Finally satisfied at the look that had taken me less than thirty minutes to achieve, I stood up from the chair and grabbed my sling purse from my bed.

"I'm ready," I said, and we turned around to leave.

"Don't get me wrong, I am happy that you're finally paying extra care to how you look now, but I don't like suffering for it."

"C'mon, I'm sorry," I said, and held her hand. She shot me a wary look.

"This wouldn't happen if you'd just woken up ten minutes earlier."

"I don't think I'm physically or mentally capable of getting up before seven a.m."

She shook her head. "This is the last time, I mean it," she said sternly. I nodded in agreement like I'd done every morning since midterms.

It was Monday again, and the third week after midterms. The light breeze as we headed to the school block gently lifted the soft waves on my head, and dangled strands of hair across my face. The wind grew heavier around us as the sky grew increasingly dark, so we increased our pace to avoid being caught in the impending rain.

Elisa headed to her class while I hurried off to mine, arriving just as Mr. Barron was retrieving his things from his briefcase.

"Miss Baker," he called out in a warning tone. I didn't stop, and hurried to my seat with an apologetic smile on my face. He started handing out our test papers as I settled down, and eventually put mine on my desk.

"Good job, again," he said, and I looked down to see an *A* written in a red marker at the top of the page. I raised my eyes to see him peer down at me from above his glasses, and sent him a tightlipped smile. Hopefully he'd soon start to believe that I wasn't somehow cheating, despite all his eager attempts to prove otherwise.

Through the rest of the periods however, I battled with boredom until eventually, it was time to meet Elisa for lunch in the courtyard.

I took my seat across from her, and placed the test paper on the table next to her tray of food. She sucked in a small breath.

"Again?"

I beamed. "Again. I think Mr. Barron's almost close to believing that I'm actually not cheating now. This is the second test in two weeks."

"But how are you doing it though?" she asked. "You hate Math."

I shrugged and opened my sandwich pack. "Still do. I just learnt that I don't have to love it to know what I'm doing. It requires practice not passion."

"Well, it took you a while to learn that," she teased. I snatched the paper back.

"Funny."

She laughed. "Anyway, this is great ... but does it have anything to do with Nathan?"

"Stop asking me that," I said, and took a bite out of my sandwich.

"Well, I can't help it. You came back that day without a word and now you've turned into *this*. I can't help but wonder."

"I don't want to talk about him."

"I know that," she said. "But I also think you'll want to know that he's back."

I stopped chewing. "He is?"

"Yes," she answered. "I saw him in the cafeteria a few minutes ago."

"Well I didn't," I said, and I frowned at the disappointment that was obvious in my voice. I resumed chewing.

"No worries, he'll find you," she said, but I didn't respond. I didn't need her to know how wrong she was.

"By the way, rehearsals for the arts festival start soon. Well, it's already been going on but the all day sessions begin later this week."

I grunted, uninterested.

"Aren't you participating?" she asked, sounding surprised. I looked up from my meal.

"No, I'm not."

"Why?"

"Because I don't want to- I never do."

"You mean in your three years here you've just stood by?"

"Actually, I've avoided it."

"Well, you shouldn't avoid it this time around. I need someone with me."

I sighed, and told her that I'd think about it just so that she could drop the subject, and my mind could go to other things. Like the boy who'd practically rejected me a few weeks back. He was the first person I'd ever felt that way about, and he'd thrown it back in my face.

That day after I'd left the park, I'd gone back to the house after telling Elisa that I wasn't feeling well and wouldn't be able to stay until the work day ended. I did eventually move past it a few days later.

Then I decided to take some of his advice and create some new dreams of my own. Something I actually had the power to do, which was to make myself better in every aspect that mattered, and that began with my appearance.

Elisa's mom had helped me adjust my uniform just like she'd done Elisas', so now, instead of a pinafore with a waistline that rested on my waist, the bodice had been extended to stop a little below the middle of my hip. So the upper part was fitted to frame what little curves I had managed to develop, while the bottom half was shortened in an array of immaculate pleats that stopped a few inches above my knee.

The added effort in my studies was a decision that followed, solely based on the fact that I deserved to not be insulted anymore, by Nathan or by anyone else.

So I had moved on and was much better than how I was when he had left me, and although I didn't expect him to have any decision-changing epiphanies when he finally got to see me, I did expect a jaw drop, or since I was talking about him here, slightly widened eyes. One thing was for sure, either way and right now, I was fine and content, so the last thing I was going to do was seek him out.

That was my resolve, backed up by the confidence that came with my new self-image. Yet, by the end of school day, I'd hit someone that was standing beside my locker as I jerked it open because I was too busy studying the hallways for any sign of him. I'd also bumped into people because I wasn't paying attention, some of whom accepted my apology while others just made rude remarks or flashed irritated looks at me.

By the end of the day when I'd still not seen him, I returned to my house and tried to completely put him out of my mind. It didn't work, so I went early for dinner, and cajoled Elisa into standing at a corner in front of the dining hall to chat up some boys that she knew. One of them I'd seen around, and as far as I knew he was one of the popular ones in our year and also Matthew's friend.

They started a conversation about midterms but I didn't pitch in or listen; my eyes kept watching the doors so that I could get a glimpse of Nathan when he came in. I tried countless times to convince myself of how ridiculous what I was doing was, but I couldn't get myself to leave. However when two more boys came over to join the conversation, I excused myself, and left.

Just after I sat down at our table, I looked up and behold; Nathan walked in with James.

"Damn it!" I cursed under my breath. I wanted to quickly get up again and go over to pretend to ask Elisa an important question, but I forced myself to stay put.

You're beyond this, I kept repeating to myself, but I couldn't help the disappointment that was now lodged in the pit of my stomach. Elisa came over a few minutes later and took a seat beside me.

"Did you see him?" she asked. I nodded.

"Aren't you going to go over to say hi?"

I shook my head.

Matthew came along then and I was thankful, because it gave me someone else to focus on, and got Elisa to stop asking me questions that I didn't want to provide the answers to.

I paid more attention than was necessary to their chat, slowly eating my dinner and listening to Elisa talk about her plans for the festival. Once in a while my mind did slip up, along with an incredible urge to glance over at his table. However, I was able to control it so when the end of dinner came I was more than ready to leave. But Justin Faulk, the head boy, walked to the front of the hall and demanded everyone's attention.

The hall grew quiet as everyone turned to listen.

"Hello," he started. "As you all know, the festival is coming up very soon so the headmaster has issued a starting date for the rehearsals. It will be on Thursday morning, straight through the weekend and then all of next week."

A deafening roar erupted as everyone expressed their delight at the news. Rehearsals meant that no academic work would be held throughout. I couldn't have cared less.

"So," he continued, "you'll all be meeting with your house heads now, just to be briefed on the various steps to take before then. I think Cartmel should take the first row of tables." He motioned to the first row. "That's Sarah and Craig."

"Lonsdale; second row with Allison and uh … Daniel. Grizedale; third row with Kevin, and Isabel. Bowland can take the back of the second row with Jessica and Mark. Then Pendle; you guys can have the last row. That's Beverly and Jimmy. However, Jimmy is not around for the time being, I think he had some issues at home. So you'll all have to work with just Beverly for now, but if by Thursday he's not back, the housemaster will appoint someone in the interim."

"And please, I encourage everyone to register and participate in something. Your heads have the authority to serve out sanctions otherwise. So, thank you and have fun." he said and he walked away towards his own house, which was Bowland- James's house.

The hall became rowdy at once but soon, there was some semblance of order as everyone found their houses. I saw Nathan move from the Cartmel house's row towards ours, but I lost sight of him in the crowd.

Beverly came up to the side so that everyone could hear her, and with an annoying bright smile on her face, she began.

She gave a briefing of all the various activities that would be available this year, and then set up seniors to represent each of them so that we could register our names.

"Remember," she said in her abnormally high-pitched voice. "We're all required to participate, so make sure to register in at least one of the activities. Anyone found wanting will be on sloth duty for the whole season. Thank you."

I stood up to leave as soon as she left, but Elisa pulled me back down with a frown.

"Where do you think you're going?"

"To my room, I'm exhausted."

"Didn't you just hear the sloth threat?"

I sighed. "Registration doesn't end today. I'll try to make up my mind before Thursday."

"Still, you have to come with me." she said, and she dragged me off to the different lines for the activities that she was interested in. She registered with the fashion, cuisine and dance groups, and then chose to hang around with Matthew while I found my way back to my room.

ৡ

Kate was sitting on my bed when I walked in and although I was startled at first, I quickly recovered and gave her a warm smile. I hadn't really spoken to her since we'd resumed so I was sort of happy to see her there.

"Hey." I greeted, and she smiled back.

"How are you Lennie?" she asked. I took a seat beside her.

"I'm fine. How was your midterms?"

"Midterms were good. I heard you spent yours in London."

"Yes I did, with Elisa."

"And how was it?" she asked.

"It was nice," I replied, wondering why she seemed so courteous. It felt like I was talking to a stranger.

"Well that's good," she said and stood to her feet. It surprised me.

"You're leaving?" I asked and she nodded, the smile gone from her face.

"I just decided to check up on you, it's been a while."

"It has. Well, thanks."

"You're welcome," she said and she forced a smile. I watched her leave, a sense of foreboding remaining in her wake.

I got ready for bed and replaced my journal back underneath my desk. It was only when I was nearly asleep that I wondered what it had been doing on the table in the first place.

෪

"I think Kate read my journal," I told Elisa as we headed to the gym court on Thursday morning. It had skipped my mind for the past two days because I'd been preparing for and had a biology test, but when we'd passed by the dining hall a few minutes earlier and spotted her, it had instantly come to mind.

"Why do you think so?" Elisa asked, and I told her how I'd found it on my table instead of underneath the desk where I always kept it.

"Did you write anything important in it?"

"Well, not really," I answered, so she shrugged it off.

I didn't bother telling her that I had written most of my encounters with Nathan in it. It left my mind altogether as soon as we arrived at the court, and met the pews already occupied by my housemates. Excitement and laughter filled the air as people hung out and waited for the session to begin.

Elisa and I took our seats, and the chaos was soon halted when Beverly walked to the front with a megaphone to her mouth. She spoke an overly loud greeting into it and although it was annoying, the hall was soon quiet.

"We'll begin immediately," she said, "but firstly, I need you all to take this as seriously as possible. No misbehaving will be tolerated. We lost last year to Lonsdale, but this year that's not going to happen. There's a lot of work to do and Jimmy's still not back, but more on that tomorrow."

"First thing you'll have to do this morning is go to the various stations of the activities you signed up for. Just identify the seniors you signed up with so that you'll be able to start your discussions, then set up and fix meeting times. You can alternate if you registered for more than one but please make sure you're duly informed of all that goes on. So, for now that's it until a later briefing. Thanks." she concluded and the whole hall became rowdy again.

Elisa bounded off to find her groups but I stayed far back in the pews, and watched the chaos as everyone tried to find where they needed to be. Somehow, I fell asleep right there and jumped up when the deafening sound of music boomed from the speakers in the court. Annoyed, I stood up and returned to the hall.

I didn't even bother getting out of bed the next morning despite Elisa's rants and threats. She eventually left when I didn't respond, but my joy was short-lived because Beverly burst into my room barely an hour later.

She seemed entirely too eager and I knew I was in for it. She ordered me to the court immediately, but since my plans of undisturbed rest had already blown up, I took my time in getting ready.

She gave me a murderous look when I got to the arena more than an hour later, and found her talking to some seniors from the other houses. She immediately excused herself, and I followed her as she led me to the middle of the court where some of the dancers were seated on the floor. I knew who she tapped on the shoulder before he even turned around.

"Your cousin decided to stay in her room today," she said as Nathan turned around. He had a clipboard in his hand and had been addressing the dancers. I frowned and turned to Beverly.

"What's your problem?" I asked her. "Why are you reporting me to *him*?"

"He's the interim house head till Jimmy gets back," she said. "If you'd been here this morning, you would've heard the announcement."

My eyes widened slightly in surprise, and my mouth would have dropped open if not for the smug look on Beverly's face. So I held myself together.

"Leave her to me." I heard Nathan quietly say, but she refused.

"Absolutely not!" she argued. "I already announced that any culprits would be assigned —"

"I understand that." He interrupted. "But could you just please leave her to me?"

"Fine." She said, looking incredibly upset. Nathan had seemed pissed as he spoke so I couldn't enjoy the annoyed look on her face as she stormed off. I was certain that he was probably irritated with me too, so I kept a straight face and avoided his eyes.

"Why didn't you report here this morning?" he asked.

I met his gaze, and just shrugged.

"Could you go wait for me in the hallway?"

I nodded and walked away, just as he turned around and resumed speaking with the dancers.

I took a seat on the floor to wait, and when he came out a few minutes later, I didn't even bother looking up. I was eager to see what he would do, but he surprised me when he went to the wall opposite me, and slid to the floor.

"What are you doing?" I asked, my tone somewhat hostile.

"I'm waiting for you," he answered in a tired voice.

"Waiting for me to do what?"

"To tell me what you want out of this festival."

"Well I don't want to participate."

"I get that, but I think you should. I probably wouldn't have myself if the housemaster hadn't given me this responsibility, but now that I'm here, I'm happy to be a part of it."

I remained silent.

"I can't punish you and you know that, but I'm asking you to either choose one of the activities to be a part of, or accept the sloth duty. Anything else will make you return to your house and I won't allow that, because it might get you in real trouble."

"I don't need you to protect me."

"I'm not protecting you," he said, and rose to his feet. "Nora, I know you won't accept ultimatums, so I'm giving you options. Please don't make me regret it."

I looked away from him as he pulled the door open, and re-entered the court.

଼ଠ

By the end of the day, I was sure he wanted to kill me. I'd chosen the sloth duty, but ruined every single assignment I was given until I'd been kicked out of all the groups, and the leaders were breathing down his neck.

I dropped a basket of supplies so carelessly on the artists' table that one of their plastic paint bottles overturned, and ruined some of the sketches that they had been working on. Their yells had startled me and at first I had rushed to apologize, but when a girl named Daisy had insulted me, I'd lost my manners.

The dance group dismissed me when I continuously forgot to pay attention to their movements enough to know when to pause and play the music. I also kept mixing up their tracks. I couldn't very well tell them that Nathan was the reason for my distraction, so when they'd questioned my mental ability to handle such a simple task, I'd stood up, and stormed off.

Beverly was leading the singing group but when she caught me staring at Nathan as he addressed the drama group, she sent me to the instrumentalists. I continued to stare from there too but when the racket they made became so unbearably loud, I stood up to leave.

Unfortunately as I was heading down the bleacher steps, I tripped on a wire that disconnected their electronic organ. That immediately stopped all the other instruments, and distracted the entire court. Everyone turned around at the sudden quiet, just in time to see me break my fall with the two bleacher seats beside me, and then struggle to set myself upright.

Nathan responded after that. He immediately ran up to help me, as well as Elisa.

"I'm alright," I said to them, feeling so embarrassed that I couldn't take my eyes off the ground.

"Can you stand?" I heard him ask, and I nodded.

"It's fine, I didn't get injured."

"Come with me," he said, and I got to my feet. My elbows and knees hurt a little bit but of course I wasn't going to say anything.

Elisa put her hands around me and led me down the steps, complaining along the way about how I needed to be more careful. I felt better when by the time I and Elisa crossed the middle of the court, people had gotten over it and returned to their business. Nathan stopped on the way to respond to someone that had come up to him with a request, so I and Elisa headed to the locker room alone to wait. He came in a few minutes later, and asked her to please excuse us.

He came to stand in front of me, resting his back against the lockers and with his arms folded across his chest.

"Stop looking at me like that," I said a few seconds later, when I couldn't stand his stare anymore.

"How do you want me to look at you?" he asked.

"Don't look at me all," I replied. "Just go back to your group."

For some reason, that pulled out a soft laugh from him. It surprised me.

"I thought you were pissed?"

"Oh, I am pissed, and you're *crazy*."

"What did I do? I tried to participate but everyone just kept pissing me off."

"That's not what I heard."

"Well, that's how I felt."

"Of course," he mocked.

"Yes," I asserted.

"So what do you want to do now?" he asked.

I sighed, because I was beginning to sound like a chore, even to myself. "Fine, I'll go stay with Elisa-whatever she's doing."

He shook his head. "No, what do *you* want to do?"

I frowned. "Nothing."

"You can't say *nothing.*"

I glared at him, but it didn't move him for even a second.

"Let's do it this way," he said. "Marilyn has the fashion group, so I'll tell her to slot you in."

"No, I'll go stay with Elisa."

"You're not *going* to stay with Elisa." He said sternly.

"And what right do you have to say that? I can go wherever I want."

"I'm the interim head, and I'm saying you can't. Elisa's group is full."

"No it isn't."

"Well, starting now it is."

I stood to my feet. "You can't do that."

He took a step closer to me. "I just did."

"This is abuse of power, but I'm telling you that I'm going to stay with Elisa, and there's nothing you're going to do about it," I said and started to walk away, but he caught my hand and pulled me back.

"We're not done talking," he said in such an intimidating voice that I had to force myself to remember that this was *Nathan* I was talking to, instead of the interim house head.

I straightened my shoulders and said directly to his face. "We are."

He narrowed his eyes at me. "Are you doing this because you know me?"

"As a matter of fact I am, and even if I didn't, you can't just force me to do what I don't want to do."

He watched me for a few seconds, and then said. "Fine. You can do whatever you want to do."

He turned around and left the room.

« CHAPTER 21 »

I'd felt guilty for causing him all the trouble that I had, so after I left the locker room, I made up my mind to just keep my head down and quietly remain with Elisa. She was occupied with the poetry group, but after almost two hours of listening to them recite poetry in French, I'd found my way out of there, and gone in search of Marilyn myself.

She was happy to receive me when I told her that Nathan had told me to come over, and immediately after lunch, she put me to work.

She asked me if I could draw and when I told her I could, she gave me the draft sketches on the final collection that they would be presenting to re-draw. I took my time with it, and it held my attention until later that evening when it was finally time to end the day. I avoided Nathan as I left with Elisa, and then skipped dinner.

The next day, Elisa came over and I willingly went with her. It was quite strange but I was actually looking forward to what Marilyn's group had in store for the day. We had our breakfast and then headed over to the court to meet Nathan and some other seniors that were waiting to address us.

Beverly was the first to speak, and she started by giving an excessive summary of the songs she had chosen for her group's performance, and how well their try-outs were coming along. Other seniors heading the other groups took their turns in explaining what they had come up with the previous day and when they were finished, Nathan rose and addressed us.

He quickly passed on information concerning updated locations for the cuisine, fashion and marching band groups, and then sent us all to work. I headed straight to the classroom where my fashion group had been relocated to and continued with my sketches.

When I was done with the ones that Marilyn had given me, I moved to the next page on the sketch pad and started one of my own. It was a simple wrap dress, and as I was struggling with how to include the folds, and the length to slant it at, Marilyn came over to peer from behind my back.

I slightly leaned away from the sudden intrusion, until she came around to stand beside me. "That looks really nice," she said with a huge smile. "Do you have interest in fashion?"

I returned the smile. "I'm not sure."

"Well you should be," she said, and gave a small gasp when I flipped the page back to reveal the ones that she had given to me to do. "These are really good. Would you like to handle the rest of the collection?"

"Okay," I said, and I was surprised to find that actually felt excited to do it. "Have they started making them?"

"No, we're going to begin today."

"But, the show's next week ..." I said, not seeing how the entire collection could be made in that time – they had eight pieces to create.

She sighed and said, "I know. Someone's coming over from London today to guide us, and I foresee some sleepless nights. At least they've started on the purses and all the equipment is here."

I looked towards a table to see an instructor surrounded by eager students as he explained something about seams.

"Do you want to join the modeling audition?" she asked. "I think they're about to start."

"No," I shook my head, quite content to continue my sketching.

"Well, okay," she said. "I'll get the collections for you. Brian needs to start them on the computers soon."

She brought them over minutes later, and I proceeded to occupy myself. It was evening when Elisa came to get me and we went for dinner. I joined the people returning to the studios when we were done, while Elisa went to hang out with Matthew.

I continued with my sketching and despite the noise in the room from the machines and people yelling at each other, I was able to completely immerse myself in the task. The place was littered with fabric, and had posed mannequins almost everywhere you turned to in the room.

Everyone had something to do so no one idled away their time. It was a busy space and as I watched the creation going on, I felt contented at being a part of it.

ᏵᏮ

Tuesday came by very quickly and with it, the vigorous preparations for the first phase of the competition that was scheduled to take place the next day. The drama, cuisine and art groups were scheduled to perform so preparations were in overdrive. I was on my sketching seat, and watching the models practice their runway walk when Beverly came to get me. I frowned as soon as I saw her.

"I need you to sort some things out for me." she said.

I asked her why she was coming to me.

"Because you're on sloth duty," she replied, her voice thick with irritation.

I just shook my head and turned away to ignore her.

She jerked my shoulders towards her, making me turn around on the stool. Furious, and completely fed up with her harassment, I got to my feet and faced her.

"Did you just dare to put your hands on me?" I asked. She took a step closer to me.

"Yes I did you brat," she said. "Who the hell do you think you are? I'm a sen–"

"Oh please shut up and go away," I told her.

Somehow I didn't see it coming, but I heard the gasp escape my lips just as the slap landed on my cheek with a blinding smack. My hand went up to my face in shock, and right then, my temper exploded.

Blind with rage, I grabbed the nearest thing that my hand was able to find on the table and swung it at her. It was only when it shattered against her head and knocked her down that I saw what it was – the ceramic pencil holder that had housed my drawing utensils.

I heard the screams around me as she collapsed, and laid lifeless on the floor. I was struck dumb, and could do nothing but stare down at her in a mindless daze. The outside noises slowly began to dim until all I could hear was my own heart thumping inside of my chest. People rushed to her, and out of nowhere I heard Nathan's voice.

I looked up to see him walk in. He saw Beverly's body sprawled on the floor and immediately hurried over to her. After pressing his finger to the underside of her chin, he lifted her into his arms.

"Lenora, come with me," he told me, and it brought me out of my stupor. We hurried out of the room and towards the clinic, and I watched horrified, as he effortlessly carried her limp body. When we arrived, he laid her on the bed and went to get the nurse who came in, and began to check her. It wasn't Laura, the nurse who had treated me, and this one didn't seem alarmed. After a few minutes, she straightened and asked us what happened.

Before I could speak, Nathan told her that Beverly had fallen and hit her head. The nurse turned to examine her head.

She was about to head back to her office when I finally spoke, my voice barely above a whisper. "Is she going to be alright?"

"She's fine," she answered. "She's just knocked out. She'll be awake in a couple of hours but with a painful headache. I'm going to get the doctor."

I shuddered as I released a heavy breath, and then lowered my head. Nathan came to squat in front of me. He raised his hand to my cheek.

"She's going to be fine," he said. I nodded morosely. He then sat down beside me, and held my hand in his. The doctor came in to check on Beverly and a few seconds later, Olivia ran in yelling her name.

A couple of her friends were with her as she ran to Beverly's side, but they calmed down when the doctor told them that Beverly would be fine. She turned tear-filled eyes to me. "You're so evil," she said in a voice so thick with hate that it cut me like a knife. I flinched. "How could you do this?"

Then she turned away, her focus back on her sister, and tears running down her cheeks. I couldn't speak, and didn't want to leave but Nathan managed to drag me with him and out of the clinic.

"I want the key," I said as we walked out into the corridor. To my surprise, he nodded straight away but insisted that he'd come with me. I didn't refuse because quite frankly, I believed that the only thing that was still keeping me standing was his presence beside me. I felt exhausted to my bones at all that had just happened.

When we reached the stream, we sat down on the rock that we'd stayed on the last time we'd been here. Still terrified, I watched the rushing water until I eventually broke down in quiet sobs. Wrapping his arms around me, he led my head to rest on his shoulder and then leaned his head against mine.

He was silent as I cried, allowing me to let out the fear that had gripped me until I eventually ran out of tears. I fell asleep to the soothing motion of his hand as it ran up and down my arm.

₭

We returned when it was almost dark and by then, dinner had already started. Nathan forced me to go to the dining hall and when I saw that it was less crowded than it usually was, I let out a deep sigh of relief. I could feel the gazes on us as we walked in and took our seats but instantly felt better, when Elisa ran over to meet us. Nathan left me with her and stood up to get our meals. I was surprised to see her.

"I heard what happened. Are you okay?"

"Aren't you supposed to be rehearsing your poem for tomorrow?" I asked at the same time, and then shook my head to clear my thoughts.

"I'm fine," I said.

"Have you been with Beverly? I heard she's okay."

"She is?"

"Yes. She's back in the hall now. I thought you were with her."

"No, I was with Nathan."

"Oh," she said, and I could see the questions in her eyes but she chose to postpone them. Nathan returned with two trays in his hands.

"Thanks for taking care of her Alex," Elisa said, and I gave her a dark look. He smiled at her, and then turned to give me a spoon.

I took it and started eating and so did he, while Elisa updated me on the progress in the studio.

"Nathan, when's the kick off tomorrow?" she asked.

"Ten," he replied, "but you're all required to be there by at least nine."

"Okay," she said and then turned to me. "Lenora will you be able to participate tomorrow?"

I frowned at her. "Of course I will- why wouldn't I be?"

She shrugged, and then studied me before saying.

"I'd have expected you to do a bit more damage."

"Elisa …" Nathan warned. She grinned.

"What? She's been a pain in both our sides."

"Don't encourage this, and it wasn't entirely her doing. Beverly hit her first."

Elisa's mouth dropped open. "And you're upset with her for knocking Beverly out?"

"I never said I was upset with her," he said. "I think she did a fine job, but that doesn't mean we should encourage it. It was a terrible risk, and she might still be in trouble for it."

"True," she said and then looked at me. "But why does she look so gloomy? I would've expected she'd be disgustingly smug by now."

Nathan chuckled, and then checked to ensure that I was eating properly. Elisa stayed with us and we listened to her as she spoke, until it was time to leave. By then, I felt considerably lighter but they both insisted that I returned to my room so the incident would quickly die down.

We walked out of the hall together but Elisa went on to give us a little privacy. He pulled me with him away from the reflection of the street lamps, and to a dim area beneath one of the massive trees that flanked the entrance. With a finger on my chin he lifted my face to his.

"Are you better now?" he asked softly, and I nodded. He studied my eyes to make sure and then leaned down to plant a soft kiss on my lips. When Elisa started coughing in the distance, he smiled at her nosiness and pulled me into a soothing hug.

After making me promise to search him out the next day because he'd be too busy to get away himself, he let me go. I nodded, and waved goodbye.

"You're a bloody nuisance Elisa," I called as I turned to leave, and her resounding laughter brought a smile to my face.

ॐ

The next day was a hectic one. The art show was already taking place and there were officials to assess it, but the play was what everyone was more interested in.

It was held in the school's main auditorium over at the Keep, and the hall had been darkened to look like a theatre. I was relaxed in the back with a bag of popcorn, while the officials filled the front. Students occupied all the other seats and we all watched on as the various houses came one after the other, to present their plays.

Elisa had her French poem to recite immediately after the plays so I was looking forward to that. Nathan on the other hand was probably running around trying to organize everyone, so I felt a little lonely sitting all by myself, but still, I managed to have a good time.

The plays soon ended and then the recitals came on, but something strange happened. Lonsdale house didn't have anyone to represent them which was very surprising. So after it ended, I went in search of Elisa. The performers were all backstage so I didn't expect the disconcerting silence that I met when I got there. The house's seniors and some officials were huddled together, speaking quietly in a corner.

I saw Elisa leaning against a table and watching them, so I hurried over to her.

"What's happening?" I asked when I reached her. I could see the worry in her eyes.

"Kate's missing," she explained in a whisper.

I stopped cold. "What?"

"She was supposed to present their recital today, but her roommate said that she's been gone since yesterday. No one knows where she is."

I turned to lean against the table with Elisa, and joined in the gloom that had overtaken the room. Most people kept quiet but the ones who spoke, did so in concerned whispers.

I thought to the last time I had seen her and remembered that it had been last week- on the first day of rehearsals. She had been outside with the rest of her housemates, and the sight of her had made me share my suspicion with Elisa that she had read my journal. I didn't know how to feel about all this, but I sincerely hoped that she was okay wherever she was.

Elisa straightened and forced a smile onto her face. I could tell that she was trying to be positive.

"This is not a big deal," she said in a voice low enough for just me to hear. "They'll find her. I mean she's bound to show up soon. Where could she have gone?"

And so the festival continued throughout the rest of the day. There was still a considerable amount of cheer and excitement because only a few people were aware of Kate's disappearance, but by late evening, it was the talk of the school.

Elisa left with Matthew for dinner but I had to find Nathan to keep my promise. I had only seen him a few times during the day as he worked with his housemaster to conclude the rest of the presentations. I left the hall to our rehearsal court to see only a few people remaining. They were gathering their belongings to head to the dining hall.

I scanned the room several times but I couldn't find him, so I was about to leave when I saw him coming from the locker room with a backpack slung over his shoulder. I stood long enough for him to see me, and when I was sure he had, I walked up to the back of the east pew and sat down to wait.

It was already very dark outside and since only a few lights were on in the court, the area I sat in was dim enough to make it hard for anyone at the bottom to make out our faces. He stopped for a few seconds to talk to some people just before they took their leave, and then headed up to me.

I struggled to find the right position to wait for him in but after twice dropping my legs from the bench in front of me, and straightening my back from my attempts to lean against the wall and seem relaxed, I finally just stood up when he reached me.

He grinned and my heart swelled with excitement. I hid my trembling hands behind my back.

"Hi," he said and to my complete surprise, he pulled me into his arms for a deep hug. Releasing my arms from behind my back, I wrapped them around his waist and savored the sweet warmth that came with him.

"How was your day?" he whispered.

"It was okay. I expect yours was something else huh?"

He leaned away from me to look into my eyes and smiled. "You have no idea."

We took our seats and he brought out a bottle of water from the side of the bag. He offered it to me first and although I wasn't thirsty, I accepted it and took a small sip. He watched me drink from it and then raised it to his own mouth when I handed it back to him. He drank much more than I did, and it made me realize how exhausted he was.

"Let's go for dinner," I said.

He shook his head. "Let's stay here for a while," he said. "I need a break from all the noise."

He combed his fingers through his messy hair and turned to catch me watching him intently.

"Were you okay today?" he asked.

"Everything was fine, but there was the issue with Kate— I'm sure you've heard."

An extra layer of exhaustion appeared on his face as I mentioned it. "I have," he said.

"Do you think she'll show up?"

He pondered the question for a bit and then turned to me. "Honestly, I don't know. I don't think she'd have missed her presentation without informing anyone beforehand if there wasn't something wrong."

"I'm sure she'll turn up soon, and be okay," I said, not willing to consider any other possibility. I tried not to imagine it but I kept on picturing her body on the ground, lifeless, and her brown hair spread out around her head. I shuddered. With a hand on the side of my chin, Nathan gently turned my face to him. "She'll show up soon," he assured me. "And she'll be okay."

I desperately hoped so too. Just then, I remembered as I stared into his eyes, that I'd ignored his birthday during the midterms.

"Happy birthday in arrears by the way," I said, and a full smile spread across his lips. It was infectious.

"You're late."

"Well, you didn't deserve a happy birthday from me at the time."

"I know," he said. "Thank you anyway."

"Maybe next time I'll do better, if you're still not an ass by then."

I didn't say next year because I had no idea where we were going, or how long our newfound truce would last. Everything seemed more or less to be balanced on a thread, where in the next moment it could all tip over and come crashing down. I didn't want to think about any of it so I took a deep breath, and lowered my head to his shoulder. I chose to just appreciate the moment, and hope with all of my heart that Kate would be found soon.

"We'll see." He said, and lifted his hand to pat the side of my head.

✂

Nathan and I spent a few more minutes in the court as he told me about the competitions, and how far the house had gone. Nothing had been officially announced but by the scores he'd received so far, we were in second place, right behind Grizedale and just before Cartmel. The house had still managed to make third place despite Kate's disappearance. Bowland and Lonsdale followed respectively after.

We left the court after that with his hand holding mine in the dark, as we walked towards the dining hall. He let go when we reached it, and we headed to his usual table. There was too much excitement about Kate for anyone to notice us and for us to be bothered even if anyone did, so we just ate quietly with Elisa, Matthew and James.

I got to my room almost an hour later, to find it crowded with Olivia's friends as they threw their opinions around about the million and one things that could have happened to Kate. At first, I was irritated at the noise but when updates on her parents being contacted and also not having any ideas to her whereabouts were shared, I found myself listening intently.

A girl named Holly had thus far been the last to see her. The different houses had been setting up in the auditorium when the news had come to Olivia that her sister had been knocked out. Holly and Kate had been one of the curious people to hurry up to the clinic to confirm the news, but according to her that had been where she'd lost her. One minute she'd been by her side and the next she hadn't. Everyone was baffled.

When I didn't want to hear anymore, I laid on my bed and plugged in my earphones to listen to Lorde's bravado. Pretty soon, the room thinned and then emptied out. I turned on my side and whispered a small prayer for Kate. I prayed that she'd be found, and soon, before any real damage could come to her.

ʕ⊙

The darkness was the scariest part, because in it, she felt like she'd already gone mad. And then the morning brought with itself a cruel sort of hope, that maybe, just maybe all was not lost. But in the depths of her heart she knew- she was absolutely sure that no one would and could ever find her. All except the people that she'd followed here, and she was sure that even if they came back, they'd never know that she was here. Not in this huge, deep abyss ... nothing could find her here.

She was exhausted; oh, how dead she felt. She wished it would all end soon because another night of the torment she would never be able to endure. The hunger and thirst was nothing, but the fear was everything.

It would build with such rapid ferocity and passion that it would almost be as if something was consuming her, and then she would feel every part of her body freeze, as if she was paralyzed. And yes she was. She was completely paralyzed with fear, and she now knew with a bitter humor that the phrase "to be paralyzed with fear" that she'd heard countless times throughout her years, could and had become an utter reality.

She somehow managed to turn so that she could lie on her back. She was way past regret now, and only sought to find what little comfort that she could before the darkness completely took over again. Something had shielded the sky before because now, the stars were out and they shone. She had never realized it before now but they really shone, brightly enough to light anyone's way if they appreciated it enough. But for her there was no way. She'd gone round and round and round … and found no escape. She was completely and utterly lost and the deafening cry of crickets seemed to mock her.

They were so loud, but it was preferable to the rustles she heard every now and then. The strange sounds that seemed so close to her but never produced a face no matter how long she waited- still, and with a stick in hand, ready to at least struggle. There was no doubt that she'd fail, but still, she wanted to at least have tried.

Something clicked inside of her that reminded her that she was still alive, and instantly, she felt the cold. It seeped in from the ground and through her back to fill her chest. From there, it would spread through her entire body until the painful numbness, completely overcame her. Her eyes began to close as she listened to the sounds … the sounds of despair; the sounds of the end.

« CHAPTER 22 »

I shot up from my bed with a loud gasp, and held my chest to calm my racing heart. It was pounding violently, and not until I took deep calming breaths was I able to realize where I was, and remember what I'd seen in my dream.

Morning couldn't come quickly enough for me so as soon as it was bright enough for me to leave, I headed towards the gym knowing that Nathan would already be there. I tried calming myself down enough to think, just so that I could consider this more thoroughly because I was probably wrong. It didn't work.

I ran the rest of the way and then stopped at the door to catch my breath. The few people that stood closest to Nathan turned, but he didn't see me. He was seated and going through a folder of notes. He looked up when he heard my pounding footsteps and I saw his eyes widen in alarm as he took in my urgency. He got up before I had even reached him, and caught me as I all but slammed into him.

"Kate," I whispered with what little breath I could gather. I swallowed. "Kate," I repeated. "She's in the forest."

His eyes slowly narrowed.

"I don't think you locked the door behind you when we went in after Olivia's accident," I said, and instantly, his eyes widened in understanding. He immediately turned to go, but I held his shirt.

"I'll come with you," I pleaded, but he shook his head.

"Stay here." he ordered, and he forced me to the bench. I stood up almost immediately but he was already out of the auditorium before I could tell him to be careful.

&⟩

It felt like forever but by mid-afternoon, the buzz was alive and word was out that Kate had been found. As soon as I heard, I shot to my feet but Elisa pulled me back down.

"I think you should wait." she said and I returned to chewing my nails. The court immediately emptied and for the next hour, I fought against the silence and the torment to leave the court, but I knew that I shouldn't and so did Elisa.

Elisa had arrived soon after Nathan left to see me distraught with worry and fear. After I'd managed to calm down enough to tell her about the forest and Kate's disappearance, she'd patiently waited with me.

"But how did she know about it?" she'd asked, and by then I'd had more than enough time to put the pieces together.

"She read it from my journal." I said, and that stunned her even more.

Nathan walked in exactly four hours and fifteen minutes after he'd first left, to see Elisa and me sitting together, waiting at the back of the court. There was too much excitement about Kate's return so not many people were inside, but the ones that remained turned to watch Nathan as he made his way toward us.

I stood up as he approached, but when he reached me, he held my hand and gently pulled me back down to my seat.

"How's Kate?" I asked, and noticed that he'd changed from the clothes that he'd had on in the morning.

"She followed us that evening since I didn't lock the door," he calmly explained, with his eyes resting somewhere above my shoulders. "But she got lost and couldn't find her way back. Even if she had she wouldn't have been able to get help because by then the door was locked again."

His eyes met mine. "How did you know?" he asked.

"I had a dream about it," I answered, my voice trembling. "She was lying limp on the ground, and then I saw bushes and plants around her... and I heard the stream."

"Will she be alright?" Elisa asked, breaking the tension that was so heavy in the air.

"She was unconscious when I found her, but the doctor examined her and said that she would be okay. She also didn't appear to have broken any bones, so now we'll just have to wait and see." Nathan said.

And that was exactly what we all did.

ॐ

The next few days passed by in a haze, with people talking non-stop about the incident and at the same time intensifying preparations for the festival on Saturday. I hadn't been able to see Kate since she wasn't allowed visitors while she was recovering, but our house parents had eased our fears the previous evening at dinner, with the news that she had woken up and was getting better.

The festival was more than enough to thoroughly occupy everyone's minds, but people were still questioning how Kate had managed to get lost in a forest that had been inaccessible to everyone for more than five decades. The rumor was that since Nathan had been the one to find her, he had also been the one to have initially discovered it, but how that knowledge had been passed to Kate when there was no apparent relationship between the both of them had been the major issue.

Of course the authorities had probably discovered the answers- at least to an extent since no one had yet mentioned a journal or the owner – but we were only given the bare bones of the incident, and informed that Kate was doing well.

Nathan had been removed from his position as the interim head of the Pendle house, and since the afternoon of Kate's return, there had been no sign of him. James had told me that he was in his room and awaiting instructions from the school, because of course someone would have to be held responsible for the entire mess.

When I heard that Kate's parents would be taking her home to get better medical attention, I headed over to the infirmary to try to see her before she left. I expected to have to grovel my way through to be able to see her, but was completely surprised when the nurse immediately let me in as soon as I told her that my name was Lenora.

Kate was on the bed that I'd been on weeks ago. She was dressed in a blue clinic gown and was on her side; her hands hanging limply towards the floor and her brown eyes, behind a pale looking face. She watched me as I approached.

I drew a chair up so that I could sit beside the bed, and was surprised when she rolled onto her back and despite the difficulty, lifted herself up to lean against the wall.

"Hi," I said and though she held my gaze, it took her a few more seconds to say anything.

"I'm sorry," she said, and the apology confused me.

"What?" I said, not quite certain I'd heard her right.

"I'm sorry," she repeated. "I shouldn't have gone after you guys."

"Kate, there's no need to apologize,"

"There is," she said slowly. "And I'm not sure what'll happen, but Nathan removed your name from everything. He told me not to even mention the journal so the authorities think that he stole the key. But they're not sure how and from where since they don't even remember where they'd kept it in the first place."

"How much trouble is he in?"

"I'm not sure," she said. "But I don't think it'll be too bad- the headmaster seems pretty calm about all this."

"I don't think he is," I said. "He's probably just trying to be patient until the festival ends."

"Well, we'll have to wait and see."

"Yes we do," I said, and I gave her hand a gentle squeeze. "How are you?"

She managed a small smile. "Better, my parents will be here tomorrow."

⁊

I left the clinic even more depressed than I'd been when I'd gone in, and that was saying something.

Everything seemed to be in shambles, and I felt as if I was barely hanging on by a thread. Kate was okay, and for that I was grateful, but with Nathan keeping his distance from everyone, and the Headmaster still silent on how this would all end, I was very worried that the worst had still not come.

As I headed down the corridor to return to our rehearsal court, I found myself wishing that I could just collapse and remain unconscious for a while so that everything could pass by without my being a witness to any of it. Then I would wake up content and relieved, because everything would be back to normal.

Instead, I got a better wish. I turned the corner, and was startled to see Nathan walking down the stairs and away from the infirmary. My heart jumped.

"Nathan!" I called out, and sped up so that I could catch up with him. He immediately turned around.

Our gazes met for a moment but for the first time, there was no warmth in his. I stopped at the top of the stairs, and when I saw that he wasn't going to make any effort to speak to me or walk towards me, I took a step forward. But again, something in his gaze stopped me.

"Are you alright?" I asked, but he didn't respond.

"I'm just back from seeing Kate, and she's told me everything. Please tell them about the journal."

"Lenora," he said. "There is nothing to tell."

"But there is," I argued. "I can't let you just take the blame for everything."

"There is no blame for anything," he said. "Everyone made mistakes- let it go."

I hated the way he sounded. "Nathan ..." I said, and took a step towards him, but there was a look in his eyes that didn't encourage me to come any further.

"Nora ..." he said. "Let it go." And he turned to leave.

I watched him walk away, and was stunned because I'd thought that he would come to me. That he would have been happy to see me just as I was to see him.

There were a million and one things that I could have concluded in my mind was the reason for his distance, but I wasn't even sure which to settle on.

I remained there for a long time after he'd left, just watching the spot he'd stood on, and foolishly hoping

-somewhere at the back of my mind- that he would come back and speak to me.

Finally, I just let out a deep, long, shaky breath. I turned around, and returned to the auditorium.

ℂ

When I arrived at the auditorium, I found Elisa very invested in the preparations for the next day. I stood in one of the four entrances and looked around the massive room.

Everyone was busy and hard at work. Tables and chairs were being moved from one end to another, while different groups from various houses were clustered in different areas and discussing their preparations for the next day.

Elisa was by the corner of the stage, where a leafless tree with very crooked branches stood, and was assisting in the hanging up of various sizes of glittering glass balls. I wanted to go over to help her so that I could at least take my mind off Nathan, but as I was heading down the aisle, I changed my mind and slid into one of the middle rows to take a seat.

The auditorium was dark so it hid my presence enough to convince me that I was by myself, and that was just what I needed.

My mind immediately went back to how Nathan had just acted with me. The distance I felt from him reminded me of when I'd first met him, and the difficulty and lack of understanding that had been so colossal between us. I'd never imagined that we could go past that nor did I even think I'd have wanted to, but his care amidst his initial and infuriating arrogance had found a way to soften me to him.

It was the same care that he'd exhibited through the last few months of knowing him, and now, in ensuring that I was completely sheltered from this entire mess with Kate. That selflessness of putting me before him in so many ways was part of the reason why I had completely let him into my heart. I wasn't naïve enough to think that'd he'd remain there forever, but for the first time in so long, I didn't mind if he did. In fact, I wasn't sure how I'd fare if he didn't and it pleased me that apart from Carlie and my mom, that someone else had won a spot there.

I was still yet to find the answer to so many questions, like what had made him continue to help me in the first place, or what had pushed him so much that my welfare practically became his responsibility. There was so much I now wanted to say, so much that I should have said.

I sighed and turned to look at Elisa again. She was now crouched on the floor and sorting through a pile of sparkling shapes that were laid out like jewels on the wooden stage.

I decided I'd tell him as soon as I saw him again. I wanted to explain to him how much he had come to mean to me… and to insist that he allowed me in on this battle so that we could fight it together. He shouldn't be facing this alone as he had all the other times because yet again, I was the major cause of it all.

So I was going to insist that I took the responsibility or at least some of it and even though I knew he'd still refuse. I was going to try and ensure that he did not bear the consequences of this entire disaster on his own.

❧

Later that day, I was in the studio watching the final fitting of the clothes being done on the models, when James came in to see me. I was surprised to see him because his houses' rehearsals were back at the residential grounds.

"Hey," he said, and he drew up a high stool just like mine to sit by me.

"Hi, what are you doing here?" I asked. I was pleased to see him, but was a little taken aback by his hair because his new haircut had gotten rid of his fat ginger curls. "And what did you do to your hair?" I cried. He laughed softly.

"It was getting too long," he said as he raised his hand to touch his head. "Don't worry it'll grow back soon enough."

Only then did I notice that his shirt sleeves were a little damp. "Is it raining outside?" I asked, and turned to glance at the window. I hadn't even realized that it was.

"It is," he replied. "I brought an umbrella with me."

There was a dullness to his voice that I'd never heard before, but I assumed he was just tired since even his eyes seemed a little droopy.

"So, I was just with Nathan," he said, and a pang of fear hit my chest.

I swallowed. "Okay."

"Do you want to step outside with me for a bit?"

With a nod I agreed, and slid off my stool to leave with him. He just kept on walking so I followed, my eyes glued to the linoleum floor. We eventually reached the hallway that led to the courtyard, and only then did he stop. I could see the rain heavily pouring down on everything beyond the glass doors.

"So, the headmaster sent for him," he began, and I listened attentively, although I couldn't get myself to take my eyes off the linoleum floor. "And, he gave him two options. It was either he would be expelled, or he could receive his academic transcript till date and just leave. He requested his transcript and left."

My eyes shot up to his then. "What?"

"His brother came to pick him up about an hour ago. He told me to tell you."

I just stared at James, refusing to believe what he was telling me. It felt like my legs were going to give out.

I could barely hear myself as I spoke. "Why didn't he send for me so that he could tell me himself?"

James shrugged, avoiding my gaze. "I asked him about it but he didn't say anything."

"So ... he's gone?"

He nodded.

Silence ...

"Okay," I eventually said, and I would never know how I did it but I managed to force a smile to my lips.

"Are you okay?" he asked.

"Of course I am." I told him. "Why wouldn't I be?"

James came closer to lightly touch the side of my arm, and then he turned around and went on his way.

I don't know how long I remained there, just standing and staring at the linoleum floor. Eventually, I knew that my legs were going to give out if I didn't find somewhere to sit. So I walked through the sliding doors and into the rain, and I took a seat on one of the picnic benches.

I stared at nothing until the rain stopped briefly. But I couldn't bring myself to leave even when it started again because at that moment, it was the only place that I *could* be.

The rain hid my tears, and it was perfect. I didn't feel them as they rolled down my cheeks...

AUTHOR'S NOTE

I want to sincerely thank you for taking the time out of your busy schedule to read this story. It was borne straight out of my heart, and bears a significant resemblance to a true experience. So whatever you may have felt while going through this book, trust me, it could have been worse.

Falling in love for the first time is indeed a powerful feeling that many get to experience in their lifetime. And since for most it happens at a critical age, it can sometimes seem to take over your entire world. A lot of people recover from it, but some don't. This you will get to see in the sequel to this book – **'The Way to Never.'**

It has been scheduled for a late June release, or at the latest, sometime in early July of 2015. An official release date hasn't been set as of the time of writing this note. For more information you can visit www.oeboroniauthor.com. There you can get in contact with me, and keep updated on all news concerning these books.

I do hope that you will continue on this journey with Lenora and Nathan, and get to see through their eyes, the true meaning of forever.

Omoye Elizabeth Boroni

OTHER BOOKS BY O. E. BORONI
ℬ

1. The Way to Never

When falling out of love, *refuses* to become an option...

Nathan Roque first met Lenora Baker, a beautiful, exasperating, and bitter girl when she was just fifteen years old. He fell so deeply in love with her that he suspected that in his lifetime, nothing else could ever mirror the kind of commitment that she drew out of him. But she is left heartbroken when an unfortunate incident drives them apart.

Thirteen years later, he sets out to reach out to her when he can no longer resist the consuming thoughts of her that have haunted him for so long. However, the same demons that caused him to let go of her in the first place are still holding him back. But when he is thrust into a situation where he has no choice but to become professionally involved with her, a Pandora's Box of angst, resentment, and passion is *unleashed.*

Now they are forced to make the decision on how to proceed. But will it justify the one that they made in the past, or will it mock it?

Now available for sale!